the
other
girl

Also by Sarah Miller

Inside the Mind of Gideon Rayburn

the
other
girl

Sarah Miller

 ST. MARTIN'S GRIFFIN NEW YORK

THE OTHER GIRL. Copyright © 2009 by Sarah Miller. All rights reserved. Printed in the United States of America. For information, address St. Martin's Press, 175 Fifth Avenue, New York, N.Y. 10010.

 Produced by Alloy Entertainment
151 West 26th Street, New York, NY 10001

www.stmartins.com

LIBRARY OF CONGRESS CATALOGING-IN-PUBLICATION DATA

Miller, Sarah, 1969–
    The other girl : a Midvale Academy novel / Sarah Miller.—1st ed.
        p.   cm.
    Summary : At a fancy New England prep school, Molly tries to break up her ex-boyfriend Gideon's new relationship with sexy classmate Pilar after Molly finds herself inside the head of Pilar, hearing her innermost thoughts.
    ISBN: 978-0-312-33415-4
    [1. Exrasensory perception—Fiction. 2. Sex —Fiction. 3. Preparatory schools —Fiction. 4. High schools —Fiction. 5. Schools —Fiction.] I. Title.
    PZ7.M6334420t   2009
    [Fic]—dc22

                                                        2009016676

First Edition: September 2009

10   9   8   7   6   5   4   3   2   1

for prinessa
(rory evans)

acknowledgments

The author wishes to thank Josh Bank, Carina Feldman, Katie Schwartz, Bill Stavru, and Rochell Thomas.

She also thanks all Millers, all L.A. Bears, and Robby.

book
one

chapter
one

There's something about a prep school the week before spring break. The air is cold but full of bright magic. Of course, that magic could just be the sunlight reflecting off all the slush. Love is like this, I think. At least that's how it felt to me with Gideon Rayburn. Yes, he was my first boyfriend and I know it's hard to believe that true love could find me so quickly when the rest of the world waits forever, or in vain. But I swear if anyone felt what I felt for Gideon, and knew how real our connection was, they might understand. Sometimes it felt so strong. Like a wire, or a cable. Then again, there was the possibility that this feeling was like sunlight on slush. A banal thing, temporarily pretty, that was just about to melt away.

Of course, a lot of times when we were having sex or even just fooling around I didn't think about any of this stuff, because I would just stop thinking.

Like this morning.

Gid sat in a pew on the chapel balcony, and I sat wrapped around him. When I came up to breathe, I looked over his shoulder through the octagonal chapel window onto the splendor of the Midvale campus. A tree branch sprouting buds circled in the breeze. Beyond were the neat brick rows of dorms and classroom buildings. Manicured paths sparkled with tiny rivers of runoff, and brownish green grass was coming up in irregular tufts on the quad and beyond, where the playing fields stretched out to low hills. Mist crawled along the tree lines. The unheated chapel air was cold, and when I rested my nose on Gideon's warm shoulder he leaned back, smiled at me, and caressed it with his warm thumb and index finger.

He thought, *I'm not going to tell Molly I love her unless she tells me.*

I waited to hear more.

He thought, *If she kisses my neck, I will tell her.*

One reason that I feel there's something actually tangible between Gid and me is that I just adore him. I adore his wide mouth and his great teeth, and that the color of his eyes and his hair is exactly the same. I love how he is cool enough to act stupid and stupid enough to try to act cool sometimes. I love how, when winter kicked in here and he was shocked by the cold (he's from suburban Virginia, which is cold, but not this cold), he got a fake fur hat with flaps and a chin strap, and that he named it the Hat That Changes Everything, and that he never took it off.

But there was something else besides my love that made me feel literally connected to him.

That is the fact that I am inside his head. I have been in his head now for just over six months. I remember the very first moments of being there. Gid was with his father, Jim Rayburn, a blustering, awkward guy in his midforties, embarrassed and heartbroken over his divorce and trying to make up for it with a lot of nervous laughter, mustache tugging, and a brand-new Chevy Silverado. Gid was on his way to Midvale for the very first time, and I just popped into his head. I had never met him, never even heard of him.

And now I loved him. So it was kind of hard to think that I wasn't supposed to.

Being in Gid's head, by the way . . . it's different from being able to read his mind. I *can* read his mind, but I think of that as something you can turn on and off. I am inside his head every waking minute of our lives. If I'm awake and he's not, I see what he dreams. If we're both asleep and he wakes up, 99 percent of the time, I wake up too. If he's awake and I want to go to sleep, forget it.

When you're inside someone's head, you become an automatic expert at *everything they want.* If Gid was lonely, I was suddenly there. If he wanted to be with his friends, I made myself scarce. If some slut in his class wore a short skirt, I wore one the next day, and shorter, and with cuter kneesocks.

Gid, of course, has never figured out I'm in his head, and I will never ever tell him. First of all, I want him to think I am just amazingly intuitive. And, perhaps more important, he just might consider my being in his head a small invasion of privacy.

I would also never tell anyone else. I am proud Gid is my boyfriend. If people knew I was inside his head, they wouldn't look at me the way that I want them to—*There go Molly and Gid. What a cute couple!* Instead, they'd think, *I know how she got him. She's cheating.*

So here we were, writhing half naked in an empty chapel,

and Gid was caught in the classic romantic dilemma. He wanted to tell me he loved me, but he didn't know if I'd say it back.

But even knowing that, I wasn't going to say it first. I wanted him to say it first. I wanted to be the winner.

Gid thought, *If Molly kisses my neck, I will tell her.*

Poor guy! He thought that he was putting his dilemma in the hands of fate. But what he was actually doing was warning his opponent of his next move.

Of course I kissed his neck. Of course he thought, Wow, there it is, my sign from fate/the universe/whatever. And then, of course, he looked at me, his beautiful brown eyes wide, loving, trusting, and he said, "I love you."

I feigned innocent surprise. "Really?"

"Yes," he said. *Oh God.* "Really." *She better say it back to me.*

I didn't say it back yet. Why not win big? Why not make him sweat a little?

We started to mess around and not think. Gid's head turns off when he is really turned on, unless you count boring stuff like, *I hope my zipper doesn't get stuck,* and *I hate condoms but they're better than no sex.*

We took a break while he looked at me with deerlike tenderness.

"I just can't believe I met someone who understands me so perfectly."

"Well," I said, touching his forehead. "Maybe we just communicate well."

He shook his head. "It's more than that." He had a dreamy look on his face, almost like a girl. "I mean, you knew I wanted to do it in the chapel! And then today, it's my birthday and this is my present? From the first day I got to Midvale, I've wanted to have sex in the chapel."

Yes, I remembered.

I stared back with loving intensity, but I still didn't say I love you. I felt a little guilty. I felt like I was cheating. In truth, the thrill of loving him was only slightly less than the thrill of having an extremely unfair advantage over any other girl whom he might like or who might like him. There would always be someone prettier, someone new, someone who could unwrap a Starburst in her mouth. But there would never be anyone who knew the location of every button on him and exactly when and for how long and how hard to push.

"There's no one like you, Molly," Gideon said. "No one."

I was about to break down and say it when, just across the top corner of the window, a troubling sight came into view.

Pilar Benitez-Jones.

Pilar Benitez-Jones was probably about the most beautiful girl in the world, and as luck would have it, she went to my school. She wasn't just a lot hotter than I was. She was a lot hotter than everyone. And she flirted with Gid. A lot.

She was coming out of the gym—she spent a lot of time there. The gym has big plate-glass windows, and once, during a particularly intense time of jealousy toward her, I am ashamed to admit I stood on a hill outside, watching her work out. She kept going to the mirror and putting her hand on her waist and kind of pushing on it, as if that might make it smaller.

Today, she wore black stretch pants with blazing pink stripes down the side. She had her hair up, and she paused on the path and shook it out with cinematic gusto.

"What is it?" Gid said, and because I didn't want him to turn around and see her, I kissed him again.

I had my eyes closed but I couldn't help but peek: I could see her hips ticking back and forth under her tiny waist like a metronome.

Looking at her filled me with panic, and then a sinking feeling, as if Gid and I were already over.

Then Gid thought, *I want Molly to unhook her bra under her shirt, and then take her shirt off over her head, but like when she already has her bra like, kind of like off, so that her breasts are like already kind of coming out of it . . . like I saw in this movie once, I can't remember the name of it but . . .*

I remembered the movie. I remembered the scene. I knew exactly what Gid meant. Fuck Pilar, who was now gone from my view. She was hot, and she was a big flirt, but whether she really wanted Gid or was just flexing her sizable hotness muscle to see if he reached out to feel it was a matter of debate. But then again, not even worth debating, because she didn't have what I had.

I did the nifty little bra trick Gid was dreaming of, and he watched in awe. He stared at my breasts and the exciting, fancy thing I did with my bra that was so easy but looked so complicated to him, and how had I known that he thought that was so hot! And then he stared at me as if I were God.

We were almost undressed when we heard the sound of footsteps down below.

Like all good prep school students, we dove for cover.

Someone whispered, "What are we going to do?"

"Something good. Something Cockweed will remember for the rest of his pathetic, Cockweed life."

It was Cullen and Nicholas. They were Gid's roommates and closest friends. Generally, they were all right guys. Well. That's an exaggeration. They were both rich and handsome and what they principally suffered from was, quite simply, just too damn much good luck. Cullen was golden and hunky, Nicholas chiseled and tortured. Nicholas was always pissed about something, always dissatisfied. Cullen, on the other hand, was like a golden retriever puppy that chased girls instead of sticks.

They put Gideon through the ringer when he first got here. Every day they made sure that he knew he was dorkier and less sexually experienced, and that he had less cool stuff than they did. But now they were his friends. In fact, because the two of them were such polar opposites—Cullen's canine enthusiasm grated on Nicholas, Nicholas's feline irritability confounded Cullen—at this point they definitely annoyed each other more than Gid annoyed either of them.

Gideon and I watched them through the slats of the balcony railing. The chapel was a narrow, high space with two rows of pews down the front and the balcony hanging over it. We were in plain sight, but you would have to tilt your head back pretty far to see us. Nicholas sank into a pew and sighed elaborately. "Christ," he said, massaging his head.

"Dude. What is your problem?" Cullen bounded down the aisle and did a roundhouse kick, his unlaced Timberlands coming within practiced inches of Nicholas's chin. "This is, like, such an awesome way to spend the morning, and you look like someone peed in your face."

Nicholas glared at Cullen. "Look, just because I don't want to jump out of bed every morning wanting to high-five God for making me me doesn't mean I have a problem."

Cullen grinned. "That is so exactly how I feel! You're a dick, but you get me, and I love that. OK! So. Let's see. Cockweed. If I were Cockweed, what would piss me off? I know! I could take a huge dump in here!"

Nicholas shook his head sullenly. "He'd just clean it up. We don't just want to piss him off . . ."

"Right, right. We want to fuck him up good. Hmm . . . it's too bad, because I really have to take a dump, and it's sort of like win-win—for my butt, and our hatred of Cockweed."

Both of them pursed their lips and stroked their taut abs as they thought about their options. To be accurate, Nicholas was thinking. Cullen was probably just imagining different girls naked and pretending to think.

"Should we just tell them we're here?" Gid whispered.

"I don't know. Up to you!"

Gid stood. "Hey, douche bags!"

Nicholas and Cullen looked up. They didn't seem surprised.

"Did you guys come in here to fuck?" Cullen asked.

"Gross," said Nicholas. Nicholas was weird about girls. He slept with them, but he always seemed to regret it.

"Did you?" Cullen said.

We nodded. Cullen smiled at me admiringly. "Ms. Molly McGarry. Always thought you only let Gideon have that provolone hoagie in bed. Didn't know you were down with the to-go box."

"Hmm," I said. "I guess I am just the kind of girl who doesn't like to share everything with someone who refers to his penis as 'the Monster.'"

"Ha-ha-ha! It's 'The *Old* Monster'!" Cullen corrected me. "As always, the Old Monster salutes you." He backed up so he could see us without craning his neck. "Dude, we came in here to fuck up Cockweed for the trustees' meeting. You know how his lame-ass fake loser job is to set up all this shit? But we can't think of anything to do."

Cockweed—Mr. Cavanaugh—was their housemaster, and he had gone to Midvale in the eighties. Back then, Midvale had a reputation as a top school. This reputation had waned in the last few years, with the economy sucking and all. Basically, if you had the money to pay for this place, they were happy to have you. The school used to kick people out left and right. But times were tough. Tuition was tuition. More and more, the administration turned a blind eye. Drugs and sex were definitely frowned upon and publicly punished, though even then you had to rack up a few offenses to get kicked out. Everything else was sort of, eh, slap on the wrist.

Unless, of course, your parents were broke motherfuckers. Then they were only too happy to show you the door. But first they had to catch you doing bad things.

Enter Cockweed, who was only here because he was friends with the headmaster. He taught a stupid class called Naval History and then, to pad out his basic uselessness, did stuff like set up the chapel and take care of the school's sailboat. But his most important title was Dean of Standards, which meant that he tried to bust people.

And, tuition being tuition, scholarships being their direct opposite, and Cockweed wanting to make himself look useful, he concentrated his "Standards" efforts on the scholarship kids.

Like Gid.

And me.

From day one, Gid had been one of those pot-smoking, sneaking-around students who is ripe for trouble.

I was not—until I met Gid and commenced my schedule of sneaking him into my room every night.

At any rate, even if Cullen and Nicholas got caught flinging their own feces at faculty on the quad, they'd probably just get suspended. Gid and I, on the other hand, needed to watch ourselves.

"Guys," Gid said. "Don't you think we should leave Cockweed alone? I mean, I know you guys are pretty safe, but let's not forget that I'm just poor white trash, living off the kindness of strangers."

"Dude dude dude dude dude!" Cullen said. "We are doing this for you. You're not involved. We are getting Cockweed for you. You don't have to do anything except enjoy. And help us take care of the amazing pot seeds we're bringing back from our trip to the Caribbean."

He put out his hand and Nicholas, grudgingly excited, high-fived him. Gideon smiled at me, sad, also amused, also happy to be included. Probably also pretty psyched to have amazing weed growing right in his room despite the risk. Right now I could smell pot on the boys, even this early in the morning.

"Our intention is clear," Nicholas said. "Cockweed must be fucked with. The question now is just—"

"I have an idea," Cullen shouted, leaping into the air. "Ow. I think I just dislodged my dump over to the other side of my anus. Anyway. I could take a dump *underneath* the rug on the aisle! Cockweed by himself won't see it. But when, like, twenty dudes in four-hundred-dollar shoes come tramping through here . . ."

"Done," Nicholas said. "That is gross and brilliant."

"I am gross and brilliant," Cullen said.

Gid thought, *No, you're just gross.*

Then I said, "No, you are just gross."

Everyone laughed. And Gid thought, *Molly and I are, like, destined.*

Nicholas was smiling at my joke. He wasn't smiling at me, but I'd known him for two years, been dating his best friend for four months, and he hadn't, really, ever. "The plan. I will stand guard. Gid, Molly. You guys get out of here. Cullen, shit and shit good." He saluted us and ran out the front door.

"Sorry," I said. "You didn't get your sex-in-the-chapel dream."

"I got close," he said. "And haven't you heard it's the thought that counts?"

We were walking out and kissing at the same time, two annoying walking kissing people, when there was a tumble of footsteps below and Nicholas ran back in. "Cockweed!" he whispered loudly.

Cullen was already squatting over the rug. "Fuck!" he said, yanking up his pants.

"Up here," Gid said.

Nicholas and Cullen ran up the balcony stairs as fast as they could and crouched down in the pew next to us.

Footsteps grew closer and more menacing. Gid was scared. *Please don't let him catch us,* he thought. We wouldn't get kicked out for this, but we would get written up—students weren't supposed to be in the chapel before 8 A.M., the assumption being anyone who was had to be screwing, partying, or, well, taking dumps. Cockweed was the guy on campus not to get caught by, because he wrote up everything.

And scholarship kids' write-ups had a way of being remembered when other kids' weren't.

I inched up a little and looked over the pew and watched the much-hated Gene Cavanaugh/Cockweed move his hulking body down the church aisle. He stopped to the right of the pulpit, in front of a row of folding chairs stacked at least five deep. He walked over and stood in front of them. "Fuck," he said in a voice raw with helplessness and rage.

I forgot to mention that Cockweed had three bratty kids and a badgering wife and was essentially a broken man.

Cockweed unfolded a chair and then proceeded to make a row in front of the pews. When he finished, he sat down in the last chair. "God damn it to hell," he moaned. Then he put his head in his hands and looked up at the pulpit.

"Hello?" he called out.

We stayed very still.

Cockweed's cell phone rang. "What now, Maureen?" Maureen was his wife. She was tall and rangy with badly dyed red hair. Like Cockweed, she had a patchwork of jobs here, the most important of which was assistant to the school nurse and the least important of which was the fire marshal. "You take him. I can't. No. I don't have time. I have to set up the chairs for the fat cats. Fine. Call me after *The View*."

Gid squeezed my hand. Cullen and I caught eyes and he mouthed the word *awesome*.

Cockweed set up all the chairs. It should have taken him only about three minutes, but it took fifteen, because every time he finished a row, he sat at the end of it and put his head in his hands.

Gid whispered, "When the Cockweed species is alone, it ruminates on failure."

Cockweed's phone rang again. He answered it, "What's up, Dave? No, no, this is a great time." He cleared his throat, stood up, pulled himself up straight, and walked to a wide chapel window that looked out on a parking lot. "I'm just putting the boat away. Yep. She's a beauty. Thirty-two-footer. Yes sir."

This was so great!

"Oh, yeah, life's good. No complaints. Are you kidding? Hot sixteen-year-old girls everywhere. Action? Dave. Come on. Please. You got a campus full of young gorgeous girls. All the guys here are about three feet tall with zits. OK? You do the math! Ha. Action isn't the word for it."

Something about "action isn't the word for it" in reference to Cockweed's life really got me. I inhaled a deep, dusty breath of hymnal. The back of my throat seized up, and I shut my eyes and tried not to cough.

Then Cockweed said, "You know what, Dave? Actually, you better do the math because I am not in the right frame of mind for thinking in the morning, if you know what I mean." Cockweed chuckled conspiratorially, like being a dimwit made him some kind of badass. "But seriously. The truth is that I got so many bitches on my jock here, I can't even see it anymore."

This was pretty funny. And I was mentally patting myself on the back for not laughing at it when Cullen, the dumb ass, started to laugh.

"You fuck," Nicholas and Gid whispered at the same time.

"What the . . . ?" I heard Cockweed pacing the chapel, looking for a good angle. I held my breath, but I knew it was over.

"I see you. Behind the pews. I'm coming up. You are in for it this time."

There was only one stairway out of here and Cockweed was on his way up it. We all stood up.

"Sorry guys." Cullen wiped his eyes calmly, like he'd just gotten off a chairlift. "It was just too good to not laugh. I mean, like, the idea of girls, like, on his crotch? I really am sorry, but we won't get in that much trouble. I mean, it's Midvale."

Nicholas smacked him on the arm. "Dumb ass! For you it's Midvale. But what about our boy here?"

Cullen looked guiltily at Gideon as Cockweed's heavy footsteps came closer. "OK, I'm retarded," he said. "I'll do what I can to turn his Cockorific rage my way."

In the waning seconds before Cockweed got upstairs, Gid thought, The worst thing about getting kicked out of this school would be losing Molly.

I couldn't say anything. But I did look at him, and what my look promised was this: never.

Cockweed stood in the doorway between the stairwell and the balcony for a few seconds, clearly enjoying how his meaty body filled up the space. He smacked his lips. "Let's go, kiddies," he said. "The real party starts now."

We crossed the quad. Nicholas and Cullen walked next to each other, with Gid and me behind them, and Cockweed five paces ahead, wearing an expression of bitter determination. The sun was high in the sky now, warming the grass and the mud-scented air. Airplanes soared—way overhead were the ones from New York going north, and lower, the ones from Boston going west. Our fellow students stepped over puddles, clutching books, bottled water, and bagels to their chests. Some stopped to stare.

We climbed the marble stairs to the administration building. Midvale's motto was carved across the top stair, a Latin saying that, roughly translated, meant "Study Forever." Cockweed turned on us. "You guys are in a lot of trouble." He went inside, letting the heavy green door slam shut.

Nicholas held the door for us. As we passed him he whispered, "Look. It's OK. Even you guys would still have to do more to get booted."

The administration building was the place where Midvale did its best to sell its identity to potential students and donors. It smelled of furniture polish. A center staircase covered with an Oriental runner in rich reds and blues led to a landing garlanded with portraits of men in clerical collars. Office doors were fashioned of carved oak, with brass placards denoting various locations: Dean of Boys, Headmaster, Office of Admissions, Alumni Relations.

Cockweed fancied himself in the tradition of the school's founding fathers, men of learning and breeding, even though he was just a slob. I saw him look at one of the paintings, and I swear he tried to imitate the subject's austere dignity as he stared at us from under the meaty ledge of his brow and said, "You know what? It makes me sick what has happened to this school. When I was here, we were all boys, first of all." He gave me a dark look of blame, I guess just in case I didn't know that I wasn't a boy, and went on, "We had to behave. Or else. Now, this place is like a . . . well, it's just a goddamn free-for-all."

He shook his head in disgust.

"Mr. Cavanaugh?" Cullen spoke up, as promised. "If you liked it so much when it was all boys, I wonder why you were just rhapsodizing to your friend about . . . I believe you used the phrase 'action isn't the word for it'?"

Cockweed snarled at him. He jerked a thumb at the Dean of Boys' office door. "Get in there. Tell Dean Paley your story. And you better make sure it squares with mine."

"Ooh," said Cullen with mock terror. "Dean Paley!" Dean Paley was an old fumbling character in a bow tie who, in the muddy seasons, could be found with his pants legs stuck into the back of his Wellingtons. When his phone rang, he stared at it as if trying to figure out how to make it stop, and always seemed surprised and delighted that picking it up did the trick.

But he was the dean assigned to the boys in our class, and Cockweed, having very little power at all, certainly had no power over that.

Gid's mind was still occupied with worries of eventually getting kicked out and us breaking up forever. I didn't like to see him so upset, but it was cute that he was so upset about me. "Don't worry," I whispered to him. "We just have to keep a low profile for a little while. We're going to be fine."

My dean, Mrs. Gwynne-Vaughan, was upstairs. I touched the back of Gid's hand and turned to head up the staircase. Gid gave me a shy, vulnerable smile. There was something nagging and incomplete at the back of his mind. It took me a moment to figure out what it was.

Cullen and Nicholas were right behind Gideon, waiting to enter the office. "Come on, dude," Cullen said. "Move it!" But Gid's eyes were locked on mine.

"Gideon?" I said. "I love you too."

"Jesus Christ," Cullen and Nicholas said at the same time. Cockweed sneered at us, sweat pooling under the arms of his Midvale polo shirt, his barrel chest heaving with fury. But when Gid and I looked into each other's eyes, and it was as if none of them even existed.

chapter
two

Like all of the administration offices at Midvale, Mrs. Gwynne-Vaughan's office looked like a set from *Masterpiece Theatre*. Polished wood shelves held books, books, and then more books, as if anyone might forget for a second that the person whose office it was knew how to read. Wholly unconcerned with facing any sort of real reprimand, I fought off boredom by chuckling my way through a stack of Midvale's alumni magazines. I paused at a photo of a girl with short blond hair floating in a pool and surrounded by dolphins. The caption read: "I first began to love dolphins, and see their potential for advances in the fight against dementia, in Mr. Casey's animal science class at Midvale," said biologist Jane Anderson, class of '91. Another featured a guy standing in the middle of an old farmhouse, surrounded by piles of rusting junk. He was Richard Dilworth, class of '89, founder of the Museum of Colonial Farm Implements in Turners Falls, Massachusetts, and he said, "I love farm implements, and I want to share my excitement about them with other people."

"Good fucking luck," I said. I so used to be destined to be one of these slobbering enthusiasts, desperate to seek and to serve. *Study Forever.* That was me. Love had shifted everything and I welcomed it. I was happier. I loved Gideon. I was no longer shut up in my room, imagining what I would be one day. I was enjoying life now.

I knew I wasn't supposed to think Gid was everything, but I still did. I know that sounds sick. All I'm saying is, if you don't have someone to love, what is the point of the other stuff? Of course when you have someone to love, you don't have time to do anything else anyway.

Especially when you're inside his head, seeing his every desire and thought, and making yourself available as needed.

Mrs. Gwynne-Vaughan came in the door of her office. She was also my English teacher. She was sixtyish, she kept her hair ash-blond and her tweed skirts snug enough to remind everyone that she was still vaguely hot. She held a travel mug from the Museum of Fine Arts gift shop and a giant Coach satchel overflowing with papers slashed with red ink.

I set down the alumni magazine. "I was just reading about former Midvalians, saving the world, one dolphin and colonial farm implement at a time."

Mrs. Gwynne-Vaughan hung up her bag and jacket on a coat tree and came to sit across from me on a gold brocade sofa. She sat back against the cushions and surveyed me for a long moment.

"Molly, would I be correct in assuming that your reasons for going to the chapel this morning were of a carnal nature?"

I nodded yes.

"Splendid. Well, that conversation is over then. Now for part two. Tell me something, Molly. Do you want to go to a school with other people who are as smart as you are? Do you want to live in a charming room on a beautiful campus where you read Hegel as rain patters gently against your dormer windows? Or do you want to continue to be a little smug and dismissive, and end up struggling over your statistics requirement in a concrete-block dorm filled with puddles of vomit?"

"Is that a trick question?" I asked.

Mrs. Gwynne-Vaughan plucked a stray thread off the armrest and set it in a silver-plated scallop ashtray. She was not amused.

"Part three." She stood up and smoothed her hands over her tweed skirt. She went over to her desk and picked up a stack of papers about two feet high. It was so big that as she walked back to me I saw the skin near the collar of her cashmere twinset turn rosy with exertion.

"What's this?" I said, as she set it down next to me.

"Academic Tête-à-Tête," she said, as if this were something fun.

Academic Tête-à-Tête—Academic Head-to-Head—was a group that went around to other prep schools for scholarly competitions. Several students from each school faced each other while the hosting school's adviser fired off questions about Prussian kings, 1982 Oscar winners, the theory of relativity, the arrival time of the train going from Peoria to Louisville, and so on. There was no buzzer—one student from each school went up alone and sat facing his opponent, so it wasn't just a matter of knowing the answer but having the wherewithal to shout it out before the other loser did, or before you died from the terrible breath he had from pulling an all-nighter for his differential calculus exam. ATAT (as we called it) was so incredibly for dorks that everyone on it made the people I was just reading about in the alumni magazines look cool.

"I don't think so," I said. But what I meant was, no effin way. Not only was Academic Tête-à-Tête a giant nerdfest, they also practiced, like, every night. I had better things to do at night. Like sneak Gid into my room.

I know I used to be a model Midvalian, all buoyed up by the magic of learning and immune to the distractions of vice. But now I just wasn't.

"Molly, why did you come to this school?"

"I came here to get a good education," I said.

"You came here because you wanted to go to Harvard," she said. "And I have some not-so-great news for you. At this point, you would be very lucky to get into . . . I don't know . . . Wisconsin."

She herself had gone to Radcliffe, and from the way she said the word *Wisconsin* you'd think it was a 99¢ store instead of a perfectly decent university.

"Mrs. Gwynne-Vaughan," I said, "I want to go to a really fancy college, the kind of college where all you have to do for the rest of your life is say its name and people pass out at your feet. I really do. But if it means sacrificing everything that makes me happy to do it, well . . ."

Mrs. Gwynne-Vaughan's expression returned to its usual state of calm, administrative concern.

"What makes you happy, Molly?"

I saw Gideon's face when she said this. His handsome, open, brown-eyed face with his sort of square mouth and the smile he broke into when he saw me.

But I just said, "Lots of things make me happy, Mrs. Gwynne-Vaughan."

She turned on me with those china blue eyes that die-hard New Englanders have. I can't say she looked as if she were going to cry because I don't think Mrs. Gwynne-Vaughan did a lot of crying. But she looked upset and frustrated. "Molly," she said, "teaching at this school is . . . well. Let's just say that the level of intellectual engagement is underwhelming. You . . . you and your friend Edie are very smart girls. Of course, Edie is still doing very well. Surely she must have noticed you've been slacking off a bit."

Edie, my best friend and roommate. Roommate for sure. Perhaps erstwhile best friend. We hadn't had a falling-out per se, but she didn't know I was in Gid's head, so there was only so much we could share, seeing as I didn't care about anything else.

"Has Edie not said anything?" Mrs. Gwynne-Vaughan pressed.

I really just wanted to get out of here and get back to Gideon.

I made myself look as contrite and grateful as I could and said, "Mrs. Gwynne-Vaughan, I am totally flattered that you would think of me, and I so totally promise—"

"You so totally promise?" Mrs. Gwynne-Vaughan asked. Her blue eyes were cold. "Ms. McGarry, I'm sure you're aware that 'I promise' is a performative speech act and hardly requires adverbial qualification. But, as long as we're speaking that language, I so totally promise that I am going to make you hear me out on this, and I am going to so totally hope that just a shred of the importance of this makes it into your head."

Even though I was newly willing to make adults displeased with me, the good girl in me still squirmed when it happened. I turn my head away from her, and there, outside the window, stood Gid, hand shielding his eyes, the Hat That Changes Everything on his head but unbuckled under his chin, looking up hopefully. He was waiting for me. He thought, Molly is all I care about sometimes, and my heart flip-flopped, because that was great, but why didn't he think that all that time, like I did with him?

Then I felt that connection, that actual thing between us, like a wire. It was buzzing and warm and I loved it and I loved him, and Mrs. Gwynne-Vaughan and ATAT could, with all due respect, suck it.

I was seriously contemplating just getting up and running out of the room, but Mrs. Gywnne-Vaughan held me with her glance. In truth, she was staring at me, and she didn't look frustrated or annoyed anymore, she just looked kind of obsessed.

"Mrs. Gwynne-Vaughan?" I said. "Are you OK?'

She ignored the question. Maybe she was having one of those senior-moment things, but then the spell seemed to break, and when she spoke, her tone was brisk and businesslike. "Molly, there is a scholarship attached. There is always an ATAT scholarship . . . and I happen to know that if the team wins this year, Ross Volker, who used to be on ATAT, is doubling it. It's worth four years of college tuition. The expensive, fancy, worthwhile kind."

I nodded with mild appreciation, as if she'd just said there was a nice print in the hallway and I should look at it on my way out. Ross Volker was a big computer billionaire. A nerd. I thought about his wormy face, his stupid letters to the alumni magazine about innovation and the importance of always pushing yourself.

That dude was so clearly not getting laid.

"Molly," Mrs. Gwynne-Vaughan said, "did you hear me?"

"You just said that there's an ATAT scholarship. That's great. But how do I even know I would get it?"

"Because I would make sure you did. I know how quick you are. I know how you absorb information. You will be the best one on ATAT, and, frankly, I don't want to be rude, but it's a lot of money, and aren't you . . ."

"On partial scholarship? From Buffalo? White trash, compared to most people here? Yes to all three. But I still don't know that I want to give up every single night of my life to ATAT. I have a lot going on."

She didn't look mad. She just gave me that weird, trancy look again, like she was mystified by my reactions.

"Can I think about it over break?" I said, knowing full well all I was going to think about over break was Gideon. I couldn't help but steal another glance. Anyone who has ever had a cute boy wait for her with an expression of total longing knows it is way better than free college.

"I just don't know why you care," I said. "I mean, I am fine. I am clearly going to go to college."

She looked away. She was going to let me go. I stood up, testing her.

Spying me, Gid jumped up and down. The Hat That Changes Everything flapped like little puppy dog ears. I couldn't wait to just run outside to hug him, and to smell the clean soap scent of his warm neck and shoulder. I cleared my throat of whatever fear was left in it, of the small part of me that still didn't want to defy an adult who was asking me to do something.

"So am I in trouble?" I said. "Do I have to do anything?"

"You will get written up," she said. "The standard information." I wanted her to roll her eyes to let me know that she thought that stuff was bullshit, but she didn't. Instead, she picked up that giant pile of papers she'd taken out and put it on my lap.

"Ow," I said.

"Do you have a camera on your phone, Molly?" she said.

"Yes," I said, confused.

"You're going to take this home with you. It's just a lot of information, for ATAT. And you're going to take a photo of yourself getting on the train with it, which is how I will know you've taken it with you."

I shifted. The thing was giving me a cramp. "Why is it so important to you to see me go to Harvard or whatever instead of Buffalo State, which is, I might add, a very good school?"

"I care because there is nothing in this world more foolish than seeing a smart girl throw her life away for love." I kind of expected her to be smirking at me, but she wasn't. She was totally serious.

"What would you say if I told you I thought that love was life?" I said. "And that this"—I indicated the giant package of paper in my hand—"was just a bunch of words?"

She finally smiled. "I would say that you were sixteen," she said.

She didn't get it.

Whatever. Whenever someone didn't get it, I felt the cord,

that actual connection between Gid and me, even stronger. Right now it tugged me and I ran outside.

I took the stairs two at a time. Gideon was waiting for me. His mind went in a loop, like a crazy polar bear walking in circles at the zoo: *Molly's almost done. I should go. But I want to see her now. She looked hot today. Maybe we can do it in the chapel later? Probably doesn't fit in with the keeping-a-low-profile plan. Cockweed is such a dick. The chapel—will I ever have sex there?*

Then he thought, *Wire, fruit. Wow, it is like wire and fruit. I can't wait to tell that to Cullen and Nicholas. Wow, and what kind of fruit? Coconut? Too obvious.*

Wire and fruit? He couldn't wait to tell what to Cullen and Nicolas about wire and fruit? Why would they care about wire and fruit?

Wire and fruit. Apples? Or more like grapefruits?

"Oh, Geedeon . . . ow a-hare you? You look sad. I mean, you steel look cute. But a leetle sad."

Twenty feet from the door were my boyfriend and Pilar Benitez-Jones. My boyfriend had made a poetic and accurate assessment: her body was so sinewy and so curvy that it looked like it was made out of wire and fruit. Cleavage strained at the limits of a white button-down shirt. Lustrous hair cascaded down her back, and her black pants were snug in all the right places.

Pilar saw me. She greeted me, two rows of gleaming white teeth inside a red, sensuous mouth. "Hi, Molly," she said. The smile deepened to the point of absurdity.

"Hi, Pilar," I said, with a smile that was about a ninetieth of her smile's wattage. I was pleased when she took a step backward, away from Gideon. She teetered attractively on high-heeled suede boots, but the step was still slightly awkward, a clear relinquishing of turf.

I positioned myself next to Gid in the space she had left. Out of habit, his hand found the small of my back. His brain still played with his whole wire and fruit revelation. I had gotten used to these moments. Gid was a guy, after all, and sometimes he checked out other girls. And usually, the other girl he checked out was her.

I smiled at him. "Hey, Gid."

He smiled back. "Hey, Molly." Any other girl would have seen nothing but devotion in the look he gave me. It was pretty good. But his left eye, five or ten degrees off, was on Pilar.

"Oh my God," Pilar said. "What is for that giant pile of papers?"

"Ugh," I said. "Mrs. Gwynne-Vaughan is having some kind of Mr. Chips meltdown and wants me to be on ATAT."

Pilar just said, "Ewww, boring."

I nodded. "Yup." Fuck you, I thought, you're pretty but you're stupid, and you know it.

Gid thought, *Pilar's breasts remind me of a poster I had in fifth grade with these kittens hanging out of a basket.* The Midvale bell sounded: the two-minute warning for the first class.

Pilar said, "Where are you guys going for Espring Break?"

"We're going to Molly's parents' house," Gid said. His hand now rubbed my back. I saw Pilar see it. I saw her eyes narrow just the tiniest bit.

"Ah," Pilar said. "That sounds sooo fun. Where is their house?"

"Buffalo," I said.

"Wow, eesn't it really cold there?" Pilar shivered theatrically.

"Buffalo's average winter temperatures are ten to twelve degrees colder than those in the greater Boston area," I said, sounding like a loser weather nerd on purpose.

Pilar pursed her lips and shook her head. "I don't understand why for when everyone wants to get warm, you go to a place that maybe is colder?" She looked at Gideon. Gideon looked at me.

"It's where my parents live," I explained.

Pilar didn't seem to find this information helpful. "OK," she said, "but don't they have another house?"

It was hard to tell whether she was being mean or just honestly couldn't comprehend—as so many Midvale students could not—how I didn't have another house or know the difference between the Club 55 and the Le Voile Rouge in St. Tropez, or how I could in fact know that two-ply cashmere from Scotland was much softer that the $69 Chinese special at Nordstrom Rack but still buy the cheap one. But I wasn't going to sacrifice any dignity by acting offended. "No, just one house," I said.

Pilar didn't know what to say, and she did something pretty girls do a lot when they don't know what to say. They shrug and go up on their tiptoes.

Gid thought, Kittens hanging out of a basket with really big heads.

"Hi guys." Madison Sprague came sauntering up. We exchanged weak smiles. Madison wasn't my favorite. She was skinny and fashiony and vapid, but not bubbly vapid like Jessica Simpson. Mean, sneery vapid like a not-famous model.

"Hey," she said, in her listless, over-it voice. "What's up?"

"We're just talking about Buffalo," Gid said.

"Ohh," Madison cooed. "Rust Belt chic." She fluffed her hair, which was dark and streaked with dramatic stripes of white. She toyed with one of her hoop earrings. "OK, bye," she said to Pilar and walked away without even looking at me or Gid.

"I'm coming with you," Pilar called after her. "We have a lot to do. Madison and I are going to California, yes?"

"California," I said, "yes."

Gideon gave me a "behave" look. Pilar didn't notice and prattled on.

"We are trying to get a job. Well, an eenternship with a film producer. He went to Midvale and ees very, very cool. He has a lot of projects we can help him with."

Internships. Low-paying or unpaid jobs that got you fancy jobs later. While people like me who had to actually earn that thing called money had to work selling concessions at the little park across from the Albright-Knox, the big art museum in Buffalo. And I wondered what kind of help Madison and Pilar could offer, other than maybe showing someone how to use express checkout on Sephora.com.

Pilar gave Gid a coy look. "You have a good vacation, OK?" She leaned in and kissed him on the cheek. Through Gideon's own slightly quivering nostrils, into his mind, and then, unfortunately, into mine, traveled her heady scent, a mix of smoke, Creed, Crème de la Mer, and Frederick Fekkai Only for Brunettes conditioner. She squeezed her eyes at me. "Bye," she said.

"Take care," I said.

And she wandered off, Gid's hand stayed on my back, and he thought, *Pilar is hot, it's just a fact. It's a fact, and it's not a big deal.*

Then he turned away and abruptly thought, *God, Molly is really cute.*

"What's wrong?" he said. "You don't still feel weird around Pilar do you?"

"Oh," I said. "No. She just bugs me."

"She's really not that bad. I think if you were friends with her you'd see that—"

I interrupted him. "That she was really nice and smart and cool? That's OK. I think I'll just live in ignorance and hatred."

He laughed. I loved it when I made bitchy comments like that and he laughed.

All his attention, all of it, was on me. I could feel it, I could see it. Not one corner of his brain retained even a memory of Pilar.

But it was awful seeing him look at her like that. I could make jokes about it, but it wasn't a joke. Every time I saw her I felt afraid of what she could do to us.

I couldn't help thinking about what Mrs. Gwynne-Vaughan had said about girls throwing their lives away for guys. What if I loved Gideon with everything I had and he ended up dumping me . . . or worse, what if he dumped me for Pilar?

But . . . well. She was out of his head now. I was the one there now. I was the one there most of the time. I knew this. And it was not really all that big a deal, right? Noticing other girls was just what guys did.

"Gid, were you just checking out Pilar?"

Gid looked at me, like, are you crazy? "Molly," he said, "Pilar's pretty, OK? But I don't . . . I don't love Pilar. I love you."

He believed himself so I had to believe him too.

chapter
three

Gideon could never be sure if Pilar Benitez-Jones was really into him, and with all I knew—which was, let's remember, everything he knew plus feminine insight—I couldn't figure it out myself.

Here were the facts: she had flirted with him a lot. They had spent a night in the same bed once, but it was at a party where lots of people were crashing all over the place. OK, his roommates crashed with their penises inside actual girls, but whatever—teenagers, especially drunk ones, often slept in the same bed with friends of the opposite sex without having sex with them.

The biggest moment in their relationship happened over Thanksgiving vacation. Pilar and Gid had ended up in the same bar together in New York. Drinks were consumed. Ultimately, Pilar had invited Gid back to her parents' pied-à-tierre to have sex with him. Gideon was naturally thrilled until Madison tumbled out of the closet with a camcorder. They knew Gid was a virgin, and they were taping his deflowering. If they were going to watch it themselves, maybe Gid would have been flattered. But they were only doing it for the expressed purpose of sending the tape to Madison's ex-boyfriend, Hal, a minor rock star who liked to watch homemade porn of guys losing their virginity.

And this is when Gid came up to see me in Buffalo, and he lost his virginity to me. And I didn't tape it, because I was just that classy.

Pilar and Gideon's little flirtation died down for a while after. Understandably—it's not easy for a relationship to recover from one party's secretly videotaping the other. Every week or two Pilar and Gid had a little chat like they had this morning, and then I would think about it. A lot.

This time, I finally got sick of thinking about them sometime after dinner.

I took out a pile of all the tests and papers I'd gotten back over the past two months. Gid was asleep, dreaming of nothing very invasive. I thought about just how much our relationship had wreaked havoc on my life since the beginning of the school year, when he first entered my head. That was early September. By October I'd fallen in love with him. By December I'd managed to get us to go out. It wasn't easy, with Pilar sort of after him. I had won. And I'd been winning for four months now. And let me tell you, if you graphed my grades around our relationship, you could see a very distinct pattern. When things were going well with him, and I wasn't seeing much thinking-about-Pilar activity, I was in the low A, high B range. When things were weird, I tended to get B minuses. Worst of all were the weeks where everything was super romantic lovey-dovey amazing. Those weeks were Cs.

I looked over at Edie, wishing she'd sense that I wanted to talk. But she was deep in her book. Edie and I had lived together since the second semester of ninth grade, and we had lived with this girl named Marcy Proctor, but she finally left last semester for her own single because we wouldn't let her listen to music while we studied. Our room was sort of a monument to not totally uncool but not particularly cool intellectualness. We'd added more bookshelves to the ones already supplied by Midvale. Between our two beds were framed posters for our favorite movies—mine was *Chinatown* and Edie's was *Anchorman*. If we'd gone to a bigger school with more normal people, we'd probably both be considered pretty. But here, at this quasi country club, I think being smart made us look uglier than we actually were. Though now that I was going out with someone sort of cool, I, and by association Edie, had status-jumped.

Edie was really small. She wore a size extra small and still had to have things taken in and shortened. She had dirty blond hair and bangs. Over enormous green eyes she wore enormous glasses that were that fine line between geek and fashionable. Edie truly didn't give a shit about anything except her mind. Watching her right now, with her brow furrowed over her book and her eyes squinting in concentration, I thought of how I used to be exactly like her, and how that similarity made us become friends.

But now there was tension between us. It used to be so easy to talk to her. Now I was reduced to sighing really loudly, until she finally looked up and said, "Is something wrong?"

Her voice wasn't that warm. It was as unimaginable to me

that we were not superclose anymore as it was that I was holding a lap of mediocre grades, but the evidence was just as concrete.

"I'm not really doing that well in school," I said.

Edie looked back at her book. "Do you care?" she said.

I was hurt by her distance, but I couldn't complain. Not when, two, three, sometimes four nights a week Gid snuck in and she dutifully crept down the hall with a pillow and quilt to sleep in the big closet off the common room.

"I think I care a little bit," I said.

She appeared to be deep in thought. Then she said, "So try harder," and went back to her book.

I really wanted to tell her I was in Gid's mind. Edie wasn't a judgmental person. I really shouldn't be grouping her in with the rest of Midvale, all those people I thought would think less of me if they knew that I was inside Gid's mind, that I had tricked him into loving me. Edie had been my friend long before I even knew Gid existed. But it was a secret I liked to hold close to my heart. If I told anyone, if any one person in the world knew the truth, then it would become real.

I'm not saying I ever tried to pretend this wasn't happening to me. But it was like I had two lives. The one in the world, and the one in Gid's head.

I sensed that a collision would be disastrous.

I tried to think of a way to talk more without mentioning the real issue. "There's something satisfying about bad grades, isn't there, Edie? I mean, they are very clearly a sign that something has gone wrong. They aren't ambiguous."

Again she didn't look up from her book, and I thought I had blown it. But then she smiled. "Yes," she said. "You can't pretend you don't know what's going on," she said. She shook her head at the book. "Dostoyevsky is totally overrated," she said. "It's like, right, the guy's a lunatic. I get it."

I laughed.

"Is Gideon coming tonight? It's OK if he is, I just want to know so I can charge my flashlight."

I hesitated. On nights when I knew he'd been thinking about Pilar or seen her looking particularly hot I generally tried to get him to come over, to remind him of what he already had. But I did have a physics test tomorrow, and if I studied and got an A, that would be a morale booster. Plus, me here with my book, Edie alternately reading and bitching about her novel—it wasn't quite like old times, but maybe it could get back there if I invested a bit. And though it didn't feel as good as being with Gid, it was nice. "No," I said. "No activities tonight. Just studying."

Edie nodded. "I'll just do it anyway," she said. She rummaged in a plastic crate under her bed and plugged a metal flashlight into the charger on the wall.

"OK," I said. "You don't have to."

I was so relieved when she smiled. "It's fine," she said. "I mean, I might as well charge it, right?"

We went back to our books.

It started to rain. It was cozy in that little room, me with my physics, her with her novel, and again Mrs. Gwynne-Vaughan's warning echoed in my ears.

Was I throwing my life away?

Maybe Gid should just come over two nights a week. That was still a lot.

But I shouldn't think about him. I should study.

Which I did until I heard the thump of a lacrosse ball against plaster. It was a familiar sound in Proctor 307—the boys' room, in the biggest, rowdiest boys' dorm, named for Jebediah Proctor, the great-grandfather of our former room-mate, Marcy Proctor. Gideon was awake. The room took shape for him and, an instant later, for me: it was a large, pleasant space under the eves with wooden floors, single beds tucked into its shadows, and a row of desks along one wall. Outside one window was the tree that made Proctor 307 one of the most desirable rooms on campus—it was easy to sneak out of. Decoration was sparse: A Beyoncé poster over Cullen's bed and a framed print of Jean Seberg in *Breathless* hanging on Nicholas's closet. That pretty much said it all.

No posters for Gideon—just the photo of me that he reached for right now and smiled at. At moments like that, I think I loved being in Gid's head, even more than I loved being in his presence.

Then a cell phone was ringing: *Apple bottom jeans and boots with the fur!* Cullen's. "Hey, Pilar! You guys aren't coming over tonight? You have to study? Whatever. That is such bullshit. OK. Later."

Gid thought, *Wire and fruit.* He saw Pilar's breasts. He shook them out of his head. *Whatever.* He pictured my breasts. My breasts were next to Pilar's in his head for a second. He closed his eyes and threw hers away.

Cullen got off the phone with Pilar and started bouncing a lacrosse ball against the wall again. "I'm pissed PBJ and Mads aren't coming over. I like hanging out with them. I feel like they're always about to have a fight and maybe, like, rip each other's clothes off."

Gideon imagined Madison pulling Pilar's shirt in such a way that those breasts were half exposed. *Put your shoes on, dumb ass. Shit. Where are my keys?* He tried to remember where he'd put the keys to the BMW that he had kind of but not really won in a bet about his virginity. "Whatever," he said out loud. He said this about Pilar a lot. Did it mean whatever for her, or did it mean that sometimes you just can't get what you want? His thoughts never got worse than this. I kept waiting, but they just didn't. He always whatevered himself before he thought something I really couldn't bear.

Nicholas was using a Bunsen burner to make green tea out of distilled water. He was obsessed with health, fitness, and aging in a way that was amusingly female. "Madison and Pilar are nuts," he said. "Did you know they're, like, going to work together this summer? I mean, how much time can two people spend together?"

"We spend a lot of time together," Cullen said, feeling Nicholas's butt.

Nicholas just shook his head. He thought the best way to deal with Cullen's idiocy was to ignore it, and he was probably right. "We should go soon," he said. "I will be really pissed if they're out of it."

Cullen snorted. "Cullen, honestly, can you imagine the WMDT having a late-afternoon run on superglue?"

Vectors would have to wait. I couldn't study with them going to the WMDT—World's Most Depressing Target—for superglue. For something. What?

Gid picked up a blue T-shirt printed with red letters that said SKI DEER VALLEY—BAKED. Underneath the writing was a drawing of a pot leaf with a face, wearing skis, flying over a mogul. His keys were underneath the shirt. "What a surprise," he said, throwing the T-shirt to Cullen.

Cullen took the opportunity to change, and ran his large

hands appreciatively over his muscular chest. "You're a slob," Gideon said.

Cullen pointed at Nicholas. "At least I'm not gay."

Nicholas sniffed. "I don't need to deflower poor unsuspecting Midvale freshmen to prove I am heterosexual," he said.

"No," Cullen said, "you just have to not be gay. And that's freshwomen to you. OK. Fresh pussy!"

Gideon laughed out loud. "You are so fucking ridiculously stupid," he said to Cullen.

"You're right," Nicholas nodded at Gid. "When you're right you're right."

"Oh yeah," Cullen said. "And when you're a giant pole smoker with a picture of a dude on your closet, you're a giant pole smoker with a picture of a dude on your closet. Look. If I'm so stupid, how come I'm the one who thought of the most amazing plan in the world to make Cockweed look like a douche bag and totally get back at him?"

"Jean Seberg," Nicholas said haughtily, "is considered one of the most beautiful women in history."

They all went into the hall and Gideon locked the door. Two freshman boys were sitting on the ground doing trig problems together. Star struck, they looked up at Gideon, Cullen, and Nicholas.

Cullen walked up to one of them. "What's up, Ethan? Joe?"

"It's Etan," the kid said.

"It's Giles," said the other.

"Whatever, you're both gay," said Cullen. "OK. Someone with no tits and a shaved head is . . . fill in the blank."

"A dude?" Etan bit his thumbnail.

"Yeah," Giles nodded. "A dude."

A few minutes later Cullen, Gid, and Nicholas were on the road that went from Midvale to the highway. It was a picturesque, tree-canopied, curving road lined with distantly spaced old houses. Very few cars passed them, but those that did were of a classy, expensive European sort, all with windows sealed up to keep in the climate-controlled air and the pure, dignified sounds of Mahler and NPR. Gideon drove five miles over the speed limit, whistling. It was quiet for a while, and then Cullen sing-songed, "I love you too, Gideon."

I wondered when that was going to come up.

Nicholas snorted. "Yeah, I can't believe you're still going to lame-ass Oswego with the g.f." This is what Nicholas and Cullen call me behind my back. It evokes perfectly the worst things they feel about me and our relationship. They like me, I guess, but nowhere near as much as they'd like Gid to be free to pursue idiocy with them.

"It's not Syracuse, it's Buffalo," Gid said. "Oswego is in the Finger Lakes region and—"

"Did you just say the Finger Lakes?" Cullen said. "Because that just reminds me of all the girls you're not going to finger in St. John."

Gid said, with a patience cultivated from months of being in love in the presence of two heartless bastards said, "I have a girlfriend."

As they continued down the road there was a lonely stretch of marshland, followed by a subdivision.

"Oh Christ," Nicholas said. "Do you know that not only are you going to miss out on the best snorkeling ever—"

"And hot, sandy beave!" Cullen piped up.

"But that one day," Nicholas continued, "you're going to live in one of those giant beige mansions with a highway sound barrier in your backyard. With Molly."

This made me feel better. I can get to thinking that these two fuckheads know Gid better than I do. But we would never live in a subdivision.

"You're going to look back at all this and think . . . I don't know . . ." Nicholas stroked his ribs.

"I do! I know what you're going to think," Cullen shouted. "You're going to think, I missed out on a lot of snatch."

They pulled into the Target parking lot. They attracted a lot of attention, three clean-cut handsome sixteen-year-olds getting out of a large BMW. Housewives in dingy sweats with bad dye jobs glared at them as they closed minivan doors around their sniffling offspring. Boys their age with mustaches and baseball hats tracked them out of the corner of their eyes as they trudged to their after-school jobs. *I really don't ever want to get kicked out of Midvale. I got written up today. I get written up twice more and I think I am fucked. I don't want to be the guy sucking down that last Marlboro Light before the four-to-eleven shift at Applebee's.*

They traipsed through the store. Passing the Intimates section, Gid caught sight of a pair of silky pink underwear, and when he let his finger brush them—Cullen and Nicholas were safely ahead—he shivered and asked himself, *Am I really this simpleminded?*

They came out of Target with three bottles of superglue.

Gid drove home. The guys fell asleep, and he listened to Radiohead and thought about the way the fluorescent light in the store left a little twinkle of light on the sheen of the underwear's silken fabric. A twinkle of promise.

Back at school, they parked the BMW on the street, on the road above the chapel.

Minutes later, inside the darkened chapel, they squeezed tiny drops of superglue onto the chair joints. This prank was very them. Clever and stupid all at once. They worked quickly, silently, and with solemn dedication, as if they were carrying out a mission for the French Resistance.

"Be careful not to get it on your skin," Nicholas whispered. "It will give you lymphoma."

"Lymphoma, huh? Another entry from the Book of Medical Facts by Nicholas," Cullen said.

When he first got to Midvale, Gideon had been totally accepting and reverent of every piece of holistic health bullshit that came out of Nicholas's mouth, and every lame-ass piece of Cullen's chick advice. But now he saw them more clearly. They were funny, they were fun, they were his friends. But even if he was really as stupid as they tried to tell him he was, they were stupid too. "OK, guys," Gid said. "This is good enough. Let's go."

"We gotta get all of them. We want Cockweed to be chiseling superglue off these for years," Cullen said.

"Guys?" Gid whispered. "Keep your voices down. There are no leaves on the trees now. Sound travels."

"Jesus," Cullen said. "Listen to fucking Hiawatha here, tellum talk story. All right. Our work is done."

Gid watched the confident, happy faces of his roommates as they made their way back to Proctor. He hated Cockweed just as much as they did, and his whole body buzzed with the pleasure of illicit fun. He pulled the Hat That Changes Everything down over his ears. Nicholas and Cullen, who'd grown up skiing the Rockies and the Alps, weren't even wearing hats.

Don't forget, Gid told himself, *you're lucky, but you'll never be as lucky as these guys. Watch yourself.*

Gideon would never have told me all that, not in so many words. I knew next time I saw him he'd be feeling a little vulnerable, and I would of course treat him with extra tenderness.

And the next time we had sex I'd be wearing silky pink underwear.

Back in his room, Gid lay on his bed. He sent me a text message.

Want me to come over?

I did want him to come over, but I had to study. And besides, since Pilar and Madison weren't going to sneak into Proctor to party tonight. I texted back, *Wait for Buffalo.*

No girl has ever been sorry about making a guy wait for sex. Gid was sweet. He wasn't totally like other guys. But he wasn't totally unlike them either. Now that I had turned him down, he would be supernice until we did it.

OK, going to study now too, CU tomorrow. Ur so hot.

I wrote, *UR 2.*

I went back to vectors. Edie was still reading. I wanted to say, "I'm glad we're hanging out tonight," but naked expressions of sentimentality didn't go over well with Edie. So I just said, "Maybe later we can watch *Lost* or something. I need to catch up before the new season."

She didn't smile, but she did nod and say, "OK."

An hour passed, and I was deep into a line of figures and symbols and other nerd stuff when suddenly I heard Cullen shout, "Suck it!"

"What the fuck?" Gid said. "God. You scared the crap out of me."

"Madison and Pilar *are* coming over. And get this. Pilar said she wants to see you before she leaves."

Cullen ran around the room doing war whoops.

I got a sick feeling as I waited to see what Gid thought about all this.

Wire. Fruit. A brief image of Pilar getting out of a pool in a white bikini, coming toward him, slipping her hands under the straps. Me, in a sundress. Why did I get the sundress? Me again. Pilar was slipping away. But: *I guess it would be fun to hang out with Pilar.*

"Dude, did you hear me? Pilar totally wants to, like, take your balls and put them so far down her throat."

I texted Gid as fast as I have ever texted anyone in my life.

> *Come over.*
>
> I thought u were wrkin.

I was going to get a B on this test if I stopped now. I tried to access some part of myself where I cared, but I couldn't find it fast enough before I wrote:

> *Done w work!*
>
> CU soon.

"I'm going over to Molly's." He thought, *I am relieved. I don't want to deal with Pilar.*

Did that mean, I don't want to deal with Pilar because she is a pain, or I don't want to deal with Pilar because . . . Oh, Jesus. I was driving myself nuts.

Gid was brushing his teeth. His roommates were telling him he was a pussy. It was business as usual. The white bikini was gone. He was thinking of me.

I knew I should just leave him to temptation. If he stayed and nothing happened between them, and all he did was think she had nice boobs and a nice ass and gorgeous hair and then she went her merry way and it was over . . . but since I could, why shouldn't I just get him out of there? This is what I told myself every time I used my being inside Gid's head in this way: why shouldn't I?

"Edie," I began. "Gideon . . ."

But she was already grabbing her blanket, pillow, book, and flashlight. "Good thing I charged this," she said as she went out the door.

That made me feel bad.

More than ever I wanted to tell her I was in Gid's head. That I just couldn't help myself, not just because I was in love, but because I had the very special power to ensure, almost beyond a shadow of a doubt, that I would never lose him. Surely she would understand. Well, after I convinced her I wasn't crazy she would understand.

I got up and went to the door. Edie was already halfway down the hall, so very small from this perspective, a corner of her blanket trailing behind her. I wanted to call after her. But Gid was on his way and, for better or worse, that was all I really cared about.

chapter
four

The moment the door was shut behind us, I began to kiss Gideon up and down his neck and run my hands over his chest. "You are so sexy," I murmured into warm skin. "You are adorable and special and the best!"

"Whoa," he said, slipping his hands under my shirt, "what did I do to deserve such—"

But I covered his mouth with my hand and unbuttoned his shirt.

"Wow," he said, when I took off my pants. He gave me that same look of adoring wonder he'd given me when I'd taken off my bra in the chapel. "I love that underwear."

It was always good, but this time it was even better than usual.

After, we lay there in my little bed, me packed against the wall and Gid on his side propped up on an elbow. We were cozy. We were happy. Pilar Benitez-Jones was probably sitting on Gid's bed right now, annoyed that he wasn't there, unable to believe he could pass up the opportunity to flirt with her when he could be having sex with me. Or this is what I liked to think she was thinking.

I looked into Gid's eyes. He was thinking about Buffalo, about walking through the train station holding hands, about standing in some hideous form of precipitation between rain and snow, waiting for my parents to come get us.

"I was really nervous telling you I loved you this morning," he said.

"I know. I mean . . . I can imagine that," I said.

"I . . . I probably shouldn't tell you this, but . . ." He trailed off.

I pushed myself up on one elbow. "What?" I said.

"It's not me . . . it's Cullen and Nicholas. They like you. It really doesn't have anything to do with you. It's just . . . they put a lot of pressure on me to, like, be with other girls."

I blinked a few times. "Do you want to be with other girls?"

"No!" he said emphatically. He hugged me and pinned me down. His face was right over mine. "It's just that the guys bug me. I don't even know why I am telling you. It's not that I want to do what they say anymore. It's just more like . . . how annoying it is." He lay back down. "I mean, you must have people in your life telling you not to be so serious about anyone, you're so young, etc."

"I know what you mean," I said. "But I mean, they don't know how we feel about each other. They're not us."

I thought of Mrs. Gwynne-Vaughan and my enormous pile of ATAT information and the scholarship.

"No, they're not us," Gideon said, turning his face toward me and shifting his body closer. His eyes were inches from mine. "They aren't even like us. I mean, I guess . . . maybe . . . some people just meet the person they're supposed to meet when they're young, right?"

Ever since the first moment I got inside Gideon's head, I had been dying to hear him think this. I hadn't even dreamed of hearing him say it.

"Maybe we're each other's true love," Gid said, swallowing. His face was soft and vulnerable. "Maybe we feel this way because we're just meant to be together forever."

We were intertwined again, making out. I had never felt so close to him before. All the anxiety about my grades, about Pilar, about Edie and the question of whether our friendship would survive my relationship with Gid fell away, and there was nothing in the world except the two of us in this bed, kissing.

It was like this for a while. Then a thought of Gid's intruded: *My leg is falling asleep.* I moved. *My arm is cramped.* I shifted to set it free. *I hope I can do this again,* he thought. I tried to help in this area as well. I think I was helping a lot. Gid's mind whirred around images of various body parts. I recognized mine in there, and he thought, *This is working.*

We kept kissing and everything seemed to be going just fine when, all of a sudden, I saw what had made his mind stop shuffling images and the image he'd rested on that had made him stop worrying that he was too tired to do it one more time. There was a body in his mind, but those weren't my breasts, my legs. I saw hair—longer than mine, similar in shade but darker, bigger, long looping curls that snaked around the curves. The pieces came together, and suddenly I saw the whole thing. It was wearing a white bikini.

I don't know how long it took me to claw my way out of

the tangle of his arms and legs, but when I did, I jumped up as if Gideon was fire. He fell on the floor, his limbs splayed out around him. "What?" he shouted, dazed, shocked, angry all at once. He grabbed at the blankets hanging off the edge of the bed.

"Molly," Gid cowered behind a sheet corner. "What the hell's going on?"

"I just felt really claustrophobic," I said.

"Claustrophobic? Molly, it's not like we haven't done that before."

I just looked at the floor, my face limp with sadness and defeat. I was miserable and I was going to be miserable for the rest of my life.

"What?" Gid said, and he came over and put his arms on my shoulders. I shook them off.

I gathered up my clothes—my cute T-shirt, my cute pajama pants, my silky pink underwear—and went to dress in the closet. I didn't want him to see me naked. I had to get him out of here. I had about two minutes left before I would start to cry, and if I started crying, I might start talking. And I didn't want Gid to know how I felt or what I knew.

"I know it sounds really sudden," I said. "I just have been thinking lately . . . and sometimes I just don't see this going anywhere."

That was true. Sometimes, when I thought about the fact I was in his head, I thought about something like this happening, and it had just happened.

Being in and out of Gid's mind, and watching him think about other girls was bad, but it was bearable. But I never, ever thought I would find myself in bed with a guy and know for a fact that he was thinking about someone else.

I could hear Gid getting dressed behind me. *Get dressed slow,* he was thinking, *make it look like you're doing what she wants but try to stay until she calms down.* "What happened?" he kept saying. "What happened?"

He didn't know. He had forgotten about thinking about Pilar.

I don't know if that made it better or worse. I zipped up my pants with an air of finality.

"Molly," Gid said again, "can't we talk about this? Are you really telling me that this is over, just like that?"

"Yes," I said. "That's what I'm telling you." My boyfriend had thought of Pilar Benitez-Jones in a white bikini while he was in bed with me. Even if he didn't remember it, I would. And if it happened once, it would happen again. I wasn't willing to take that chance. I remembered what Mrs. Gwynne-Vaughan had said: "There's nothing in this world more foolish than seeing a smart girl throw her life away for love." I had thought she just didn't get it. But maybe the one who didn't get it was me.

chapter
five

Friday a taxi came to pick me up and take me to the train station alone.

The driver wore a beret and was blasting very cheery music with lots of drums and chanting. "Miss," he said as he took my luggage from me, "are you all right?" He had a nice French accent.

"Oh yes," I said. Since Gid and I broke up I had been functioning, going to classes, taking exams, but I didn't talk much and I moved as if in pain, like an old person. "I'm just a little tired."

"You are too young to be tired," he said as he put my luggage in the trunk. He snapped it shut. After what seemed like forty or so minutes I had managed to ease my body into the backseat. We were about to leave when Edie came running down the Emerson steps holding the giant ATAT folder. "This says DO NOT FORGET TO TAKE HOME," she called out. "So I didn't want you to forget to take it home."

It was raining out. Edie was in slippers, holding a small blue umbrella. "Thanks," I said.

Her eyes were wide with concern. "Molly," she said, "are you OK?"

I had told her Wednesday morning that Gideon and I had broken up. We had spent the past two days in silence. I wanted to tell her what was going on, but it wouldn't make any sense unless I told her everything.

Everything not being an option, I told the oldest lie in the world: "I'm fine."

I added, "I don't think anyone's ever died of a broken heart."

Edie closed her sweater against the wet cold. "Well, yes, certainly, but I was just wondering if . . ."

"Well, don't wonder," I snapped. "I mean, what the hell am I supposed to do? Can I sit in a cab and get out of it and then sit on a train and get out of that and walk across a station? Yes. I think I can manage."

Edie backed away. I knew I was being a bitch, but whatever. I hate it when people ask you if you're OK. It's such a meaningless question. Obviously on some level you are, because there's not an arrow through your head, and on some level you're not, because you wish there were.

I shut the door and then remembered something. "Hang on," I said to the cabbie.

We'd gone about twelve feet. He stopped and I rolled down the window and called out to Edie. She came shuffling over.

I handed her my phone out the window.

"Take a picture of me," I said. I held up the ATAT folder. "Get this in, and the taxi." She snapped the picture.

"I'm going to do you a big favor and not make you explain what that's for," she said, handing me back my phone.

"I appreciate that," I said.

"Yeah," she said. "I thought you might." I watched her pick her way through the puddles as she walked away.

I e-mailed the photo to Mrs. Gwynne-Vaughan, as promised. "I know this isn't from the train station," I wrote. "Extenuating circumstances."

Those being that the person who was supposed to take that photo would not be around to take it.

We made the left out of the Midvale campus onto the road. I sat back and listened to the music and tried to absorb the absurd notion that somewhere, someone had once been happy enough to have written this song.

Meanwhile, Gid was packing his stuff to go to St. John. He willed every step, mechanically placed items in his Fairfax Pee-Wee Hockey duffle: two white T-shirts, two red, two black, bathing suit, jeans, shirt with buttons. There were no words in his head, just a dull ache of pain and loneliness. He sat down on his bed and put his head in his hands. How I wanted to call him. I looked at his number in my speed dial. But as soon as I placed my finger over his name, the image of Pilar in that white bathing suit came into my mind.

I knew that I could never look the way Pilar looked in a white bathing suit.

That was just a fact.

But what about everything else that I was? Did it really, for Gideon, not add up to Pilar in a white bathing suit?

I'd handed him my heart on a silver platter, and he'd accepted it with one hand while keeping the fingers on his other hand crossed behind his back. If he hadn't loved me at all, I could have forgiven him. But he did love me, just not enough not to think of a hot girl in a white bathing suit while we had sex, and that was . . . well, first of all, it was gross. And it left me with two choices. Hate myself, or hate him.

I erased his number. Since I would never forget it, it was just a symbolic gesture. But it was a step. One small step away.

chapter
six

When my parents pulled up to the Buffalo train station in their snow-caked 1993 Volvo station wagon and saw me standing there by myself, my father reached for the radio dial and I saw my mother's mouth form the words "Where's her boyfriend?" Even my brother, who was five and in a car seat, was alarmed. "Mom, why is Molly alone?" he said as I got in the car. He looked at me suspiciously. "You said you had a boyfriend," he said. "You lied."

I'd recently read an article that claimed sarcasm makes young children feel unsafe and confused. That seemed like a satisfactory alternative to physical punishment. "Sorry to disappoint you," I said. "But I killed him." Indeed, his cherubic little face whitened with terror. Mission accomplished.

I snapped on my seat belt in the backseat. "We broke up," I said.

My mother looked really sad. She's one of those mothers who

gets really sad when you're sad, which is nice at times, but at other times can make you think twice about being sad. She reached out and caressed my face, which just made me feel like crying.

My father watched me in the rearview mirror, and then his eyes shifted over to my mother. He was concerned about me, but he was probably mostly worried his wife was going to freak out if I freaked out.

I needed to say something. Something that would make them think I was all right but would also make them leave me alone.

"I direct you to the adage 'Time heals all wounds,' and ask for understanding and privacy. No questions, please, at this time."

My parents kind of smiled at each other, relieved that I was the same old Molly.

I wasn't the same old Molly and didn't know if I ever would be, but at least I still knew how to act like I was.

My brother looked at my mother. She shook her head, and he busied himself with making his Mantax doll run up and down the window frame, making Mantax noises. That and the rain pattering on the roof were the only sounds during the short drive to my house.

Our house is old and white with green shutters and a big porch in front, a small yard on the side and a big yard in back. It's decorated with leftover furniture from my grandparents' houses, some antiques, some stuff that's just sort of plain and functional. It's a cozy, unpretentious house, with a lot of hooked rugs and Afghans and lamps. It's a nice place to sleep, so when we got there, I went immediately upstairs to my single four-poster bed, which was my mom's when she was a girl, and that's what I did.

•   •   •

I woke up just before noon. A third of the day, already gone. Good. The tree branches were still bare and grayish brown here. Out my window fell a steadily accumulating snow, which had already fallen on Boston, where Gid lay in a fetal position on top of a hideous hotel bedspread. From his window he saw white rooftops, antennas, and a sign reading DAYS INN SAUGUS LOGAN AIRPORT—NO VACANCY. Nicholas sat in a flowered upholstered chair by the window, reading *The New York Times* on his iPhone. The sound of a running shower came from the open bathroom door.

"Wow," Nicholas said. "The entire Eastern Seaboard is snowed in."

The shower went off and Cullen emerged from a cloud of steam, wrapped in a towel. He rubbed his hands together with relish. "And half of them are prep school hottinas and hottettas stranded right here!" Cullen grabbed a handful of ice cubes from a black plastic bucket, dropped them into a glass, and dumped in about a cup of Cutty Sark. Cullen had a real fake ID, with his picture and everything, that said he was thirty-four. He drank from the glass like he was drinking water, and then asked, "How's the patient?"

"He's improving," Nicholas said. "I got him to stop thinking about just jumping in a cab and taking a train to Buffalo."

You didn't get me to stop thinking about it, Gid thought. I just don't want to stand up.

It was annoying to me that Gideon was so miserable I'd broken up with him when he was so obviously not completely in love with me.

Gid turned away from the window, closed his eyes, and continued his systematic inventory of our last moments together to discover the cause of our breakup. He couldn't make any sense of it. He just knew he wasn't happy.

Gid rolled onto his stomach. He whispered, "I will be OK." He then rolled back onto his side because the bedspread smelled.

Good for him. I was glad he was miserable. I was glad he missed me, even though I had no idea why, and he was obviously more interested in Pilar Benitez-Jones in a white bikini than reality with me. I was glad the bedspread in his room smelled like sweat and sag paneer, and I hoped he'd be there for his whole vacation, because that's what guys who picture other girls naked while having sex with their girlfriends deserved.

Suddenly, I felt hungry enough for toast.

I didn't expect to find anyone around, but when I entered the kitchen, there was my father sitting at the green Formica kitchen table, staring through frilly orange-sherbet-colored curtains at snow that was now falling in cotton-ball-sized clumps. He was doing bills: in front of him was a blue vinyl ledger book and in his hand was a black felt-tip marker. I thought about sneaking back upstairs. But our house was old and creaky and sneak-proof, and the second I set foot on the kitchen floor, my dad snapped to attention. He looked guilty, like I'd caught him at something.

I learned long ago that your parents do not need to know how you really feel.

"You have ink on your face," I said, keeping it light.

"Oh?" He dipped a napkin into a glass of water and rubbed

where I was pointing. "I'm afraid that's the least of my problems."

Generally I didn't like it when my parents were upset. Their best trait was their stability, and when things were awry with them, I had the sensation that the world was about to go hurtling into space. But I was so glad he hadn't asked me about me that I sat down.

"What's wrong, Dad?" I said.

He winced a little. I knew he didn't want to bother me, but I also could see that he needed to talk. "The stock where I put most of your money for college funds is . . . well, let's just use the word *underperforming.*"

I thought about my concrete-block dorm and the statistics requirement that Mrs. Gwynne-Vaughan had warned me about. My parents would be devastated if I didn't go to a really fancy college. It was their whole plan for me. I was their special weird little genius. "It's OK," I said, "I mean, I'm sure that everything will get better in the next few years."

My dad looked sad. "It's not really OK," he said. "Your sister is already in college, and we're not going to make her go somewhere cheaper. And I think that she might use up a lot of what we already have."

My dad got up and sat back down again. He reminded me of a dog you'd just yelled at.

"I just keep looking at the numbers, expecting them to look different," he said. "But numbers have a way of always looking the same." He rubbed his temples. His hairline was receding, his crow's-feet deepening. I felt a surge of something primal. I was young, and my aging father needed my protection. Or at least that's my excuse for the really big lie I told.

"I'm probably getting this really big scholarship," I said. "Like, really big."

I thought of that colossal pile of ATAT facts and figures in my room and felt a little sick to my stomach. But my father's face lit up.

"Really? What is it?"

Further description would have shed light on the highly fabricated nature of my claim. "It's pretty complicated . . ." I said. He looked upset again, so I added, "But it's pretty much a done deal. But it's weird. I mean, you know how all that nutty skull-and-bones prep school stuff is."

This was complete bullshit, but my father nodded seriously. I was taking advantage of the fact that he knew nothing about prep school or the fancy world he worked so hard to have me live in.

"Jeez, Molly," he said. "I don't want to pressure you, but that sure would be amazing." He shook his head, as if he were waking himself up from a bad dream. "Can I tell your mother?"

"Hmm." I tried to think fast. My mother was a stress case, and I knew it would make life a lot easier for my dad to ease her mind about this. "Let's just keep it our little secret. That way, we can really celebrate when I get the letter."

"You're such a good kid," my dad said.

I nodded and hoped he couldn't see my face turning red. "I'm going to go upstairs," I said. I no longer wanted toast. "I have a lot of studying to do."

"Of course," my dad said.

I was halfway up the stairs when his voice stopped me.

"Molly?" he said.

"Yeah?" I turned around.

Not only was my dad smiling, but he almost looked young.

"Thanks for reminding me that I never have to worry about you."

The ATAT folder sat on my desk in my room, looming like an enemy tower.

It hadn't even occurred to me how my single-minded interest in Gideon might affect other people. Here my parents were making all these sacrifices to give me a better life, and I was the worse teen cliché ever . . . a stupid boy chaser.

I spread out the ATAT stuff on my bed. It was all divided into categories: history, science, math, literature, geography. This was all divided into subcategories: European history, American history, algebra, geometry, et cetera.

It was a vast, intimidating field of information, and it did remind me that, even though my head was having a lot of trouble focusing on anything but one boy lying on a bed in an airport hotel, there was, nonetheless, an entire world beyond him, beyond me.

I could try to join that world, if only for a second.

I picked up a list of facts about English kings: Jameses, Johns, Georges, Williams. I studied the sketches of their faces and reminded myself: these were all people who had been born, lived, and died without ever knowing Gideon Rayburn. Amazing.

Molly, Gid thought, far away in that snow-covered hotel. Molly Molly Molly.

I thought of my father, looking at me with all that fatherly trust. And I just pushed Gid as far as I could to the back of my head and started to do something I hadn't done in a long time. Work.

I drew a crude map of Europe. Gid rolled over and I tried to ignore the feeling of his cheek on the cheap pillow. I made a list of all the English rulers from 1066 to 1848. I memorized the years of their births and deaths and the names of their wives and murderers. Gid picked out something to wear, and I tried not to notice if he was thinking about looking good and instead drew lines between the countries of their enemies in red, and their allies in blue. I didn't feel cured, but entire seconds, then minutes passed when I was actually thinking of something else.

By the time I had taken out a pink highlighter to signify any two countries joined by a royal marriage, I was actually moved by the idea that I could be strong. Sure, I was miserable and heartbroken. Yes, my head was utterly occupied with the comings, goings, and thoughts of another human being with whom I was obsessed, but I was going to smart my way out of it. No matter how much Gid beckoned, I was going to learn every single fucking fact and date and equation in this pile of data. I was going to face every single encyclopedic mind at every prep school from Baltimore to Burlington, and I was going to crush them for the glory of Midvale. I was going to snatch my family from the jaws of financial despair, and my parents would drive me to Harvard in the brand-new Prius I got them after I had not only gotten a full scholarship to college but also invented a light bulb that heats houses in winter and cools them in summer.

And then Gideon's phone rang.

He had a piece-of-shit Nokia hand-me-down from his dad, and the crappy LCD screen said PILAR.

Gid's heart skipped a beat, and mine was right behind it.

It was one thing for Gid to think about Pilar. It was quite another for her to call him.

"Hi," Gideon said. I didn't like his tone. He sounded like he was thinking about being happy.

"Oh Geedeon," Pilar said. I heard her take a deep inhale on a cigarette. She exhaled dramatically and said, "I heard you and Molly broke up. I am so essorry! Are you OK?"

Gid said, "I don't know."

I'd like to say that that was the moment where intellect and responsibility triumphed over girlish longing. If only I could convince myself that what I felt for Gid was just girlish longing. I put down my very important secure-you-and-your-family's-future documents and turned my full attention to the criminally pretty, extremely curvaceous, somewhat mysterious, and almost certainly sexually licentious heiress and her never fully serious but nonetheless never-ending half-pursuit of my recent ex-boyfriend.

"Oh Geedeon," Pilar said. "Ees there anything I can do for you? You know, we are also here. At the Days Inn. Our flight for LA doesn't leave until the very early morning. I just wanted to make sure you were OK, not lonely!"

Gid hit mute. Then he hit it again. "Can you hang on a sec?" he said.

Cullen was standing right there, rubbing his hands together in anticipation.

"Pilar's here," Gid said. "She's in the hotel. She wants to know if I'm lonely. She's on mute."

"Ha!" Nicholas said, not looking up from his iPhone. "She knows you're with us."

"Which means she wants to know if your penis is lonely."

Gid scowled. Cullen actually reached out and shook him. Then he grabbed Gid's phone, "Pilar? It's Cullie. Yeah. We're having a party. In like, I don't know, an hour. Yes, you're invited, you hot bitch. You and Mads, who is a slut for not calling me. Ha-ha-ha. You're hilarious."

Cullen hung up. He looked at Gid.

"Hi," he said.

"Hi," Gid said warily. He knew he was about to get some Uncle Cullie wisdom . . . which was, of course, a contradiction in terms.

"Has Uncle Cullie ever told you his Alamo story?" Cullen asked Gid.

"I don't believe he has." Gideon sighed. "Is Pilar the Alamo?"

"Just listen. I went to San Antonio once to visit my cousin. And my mother told me I had to go see the Alamo. And I was wasted the whole time, and I forgot. And I was in this bar on my last night, all shitfaced, and it occurs to me I haven't seen the Alamo, and my mother, who is from Texas, is going to kill me. And I am just about to panic but then I have to puke, right? So I go outside to puke, and the Alamo is right there. I saw it. And I didn't even have to try."

"What is the point of this?"

"You are worried about not seeing the Alamo. You're worried that you're fucked. That your life is over. But I'm telling you, you have to let the Alamo come to you. And it's coming."

"I'm going to take a shower," Gid muttered.

He was acting all uninterested, but he was also wondering where his razor was.

"Going to get all pretty," Cullen said.

"Don't get all excited," Gid said. "I'm just taking a shower." He went into the bathroom.

Gid hadn't taken a shower in a few days.

"I think we all know what it means when a guy takes a shower," Nicholas said, which is exactly what I was thinking.

chapter
seven

I had been in Gid's head once before when he and Pilar spent a whole party hanging out together. It was a house party on Cape Cod, at this girl Fiona Winchester's house. Fiona was one of Cullen's little playthings for a while. At any rate, Gideon and Pilar had snuggled in a big chair and then slept in the same bed in a beautiful room overlooking the ocean. Nothing had happened, unless you count Gid getting blue balls.

We weren't even going out then. In fact, officially, we hardly even knew each other, and still it traumatized me so much I don't think I ate for a week afterward.

I didn't even want to think about how disturbing it would be to see them together now that I loved him. Now that we had slept together.

I'd seen him chat with Pilar. But not alone. In the dark. With drinks.

God, I wished I could get out of Gid's head.

But it just had to be impossible. Of course, I hadn't ever tried. I had been so busy trying to make being inside his head work for me that it had never occurred to me.

I obviously didn't have the faintest idea of how to do it myself.

I Googled "inside someone's mind." Some bullshit stuff came up, like, women's magazine shit about how to read his mind. Ha. Those people didn't know how good they had it in their ignorance. A guy named Linus Anderson in San Rafael, California, had written an article called "Inhabiting Consciousness," but it had phrases in it like *cognitive mechanisms* and *morphogenetic field,* and all this math and stuff in it and graphs of brain activity. I was just about to look for something else when I read something I actually understood: "Shared consciousness is really not as rare as people think. This is especially true as our minds get more powerful, and as more and more people accept the notion that energy and thought are capable of dynamic movement."

This was a quote from a Dr. Stanley Whitmeyer, who had written a pamphlet called, simply, "Shared Consciousness."

Now I Googled him. He identified himself as an independent scholar, and there was an e-mail address and an instant message handle on Google. I wrote to it.

> My name is Molly McGarry. I'm 16, and you have to help
> me get out of my boyfriend's mind.

A few seconds later this message popped up on my screen.

> *Tell me what kind of stuff is happening to you.*

I typed feverishly.

Uh. Well, I hear everything that's inside Gid's—that's his
name—head. I don't know what else to tell you. I know
what he's thinking. I hear everything from, i hate aspara-
gus i think . . . and that girl's hot. Well. I mean, what if I
didn't have a girlfriend . . . I would think she was hot but
wait. I can think she's hot. I just am not supposed to, like,
hit on her.

I get it.

You do?

Yes. It is not common but it does happen.

OK. What is it?

If I knew that, I'd be very rich.

LOLIICL. That's LOL if I could laugh.

LOLFR. LOL for real.

Can you help me?

*The power of thought when it connects to love is
always very strong.*

OK. But what does that have to do with me?

*I don't know exactly what this stuff is. But it is basi-
cally just an advanced form of empathy.*

OK.

You are in his head for some reason.

Other than to drive myself crazy?

*The less sarcasm you can display about this the
better. Sarcasm is just a defense mechanism. If you want
to get out of his head, you need to think about why you
want to get out.*

Well, I am trying to get this scholarship. It's dependent on my team winning a championship on this quiz team thing . . . It's like *Jeopardy,* but with teams, and I can't concentrate with this girl in my head . . .

Forget about that. That's intellectual. It's not emotional. Why do you want to get out?

Because I can't study.

That's an effect. What's the cause? Ask yourself, Why can't you study?

Because I can't concentrate.

And why can't you concentrate?

Jesus. Because i am sad.

There was no response and I wondered if I had gotten it.

Can you say more?

Because I love him, and it hurts. And now that I'm not going out with him anymore, it's like, what am I doing here? I just want to be in my own mind. There's absolutely no use to being in Gid's mind anymore.

OK. Now we're getting somewhere. Tell your mind that. Tell your mind that at the precise moment you really think you can't stand it anymore.

To tell you the truth, Dr. Whitmeyer, every moment seems pretty excruciating.

One thing i've learned . . . There's always a more excruciating moment. You'll know it when you see it. Nova is on. Goodbye.

Dr. Whitmeyer?

But he was gone.

That was pretty weird. I would have thought it was weirder, but since I'd been in someone's mind for six months, my definition of weird had definitely expanded.

I tried doing more searches, but all I came up with was that Dr. Whitmeyer was an independent scholar who'd written a pamphlet called "Shared Consciousness," in 1979.

It was out of print. Big surprise.

Two hours later thirty marooned teenagers stuffed themselves into the boys' hotel room, and proceeded to get completely shitfaced. Pilar and Madison arrived just as that second-drink euphoria was kicking in, or maybe they were the cause of it, but suddenly the music got louder, the chatter sped up, and the flashing lights of snowplows in the parking lot gave the grim room a disco feel.

Gid stared at Pilar and watched everyone else in the room staring at her. *Something about that face. Why can't you look away from beauty like that? Why can't anyone in this room? She's coming over to me. The girl everyone is looking at is walking over to me. Some people look awestruck, some people look mad. God, she is so beautiful it makes people mad. That's insane.*

She leaned in to hug him. *The girl everyone was looking at just hugged me.*

Pilar wore jeans and a sparkly T-shirt. Against the window, snow falling in the darkness, she was part of the glittering winter world. Gideon had drunk a glass of Cutty Sark, and a layer of chemical giddiness lay over his despair like a silk sheet as the two of them sat apart from everyone, on the floor between the second bed and the window.

"I love esnow," Pilar said, and Gid saw her beauty as he

had never seen it before. It really was so cute how she said "es-now." It was gorgeousness mixed with the naïveté of not quite getting things right. That's what made her so special.

I was so grossed out. I mean, she was a hot girl and English was her second language. It wasn't fucking science. And she hadn't invented the accent.

He reached under the nightstand. "Have you seen my hat?" He slapped it on his head. "I call it the Hat That Changes Everything!"

He'd said that because he knew I thought it was cute. He was even thinking to himself, Gid, this is a lame trick. But Pilar laughed and clapped her hands. She liked it too! As she threw her head back the light caught the glint of her lip gloss—and Gid thought of the way that the light in Target had shone on those pink panties, and then he thought of me, and then he took a bigger gulp of Cutty Sark.

Gid let his brain sink into icy alcohol bliss and thought, *Molly.* Pilar shifted on the floor, and her knee pressed into his thigh. *Alamo.*

It was bad, but it wasn't worse than last time. I had no idea if Dr. Whitmeyer was a lunatic or not, but I did kind of like what he'd said. It was worth a try. I concentrated on the main reason I wanted to get out of Gid's head—it was just painful noise, not serving any purpose.

Nicholas was walking around wearing a snorkel with the tube part of it stuck inside a bong. Five girls danced on the desk to some Brazilian lounge music. Madison was there, sitting on the bed with the pretentious guy who'd come, promising to stay only if everyone would listen to his iPod, and no one was sober enough to argue. Madison's heavily lined eyes drooped with intoxication and boredom. One of the dancing girls tripped over the docking station and fell into Madison's lap. "Watch it," Madison snapped. "Hey, Pilar, let's get out of here soon. I think we can get that 5 A.M."

"Let's just take the later one," Pilar said. "I'm having a good time." She looked up through her lashes at Gideon.

Cullen was suddenly at Gid's side. He had folded the desk blotter into a tiny three-cornered hat. "Ahoy," he said. "Are you getting ready to board this vessel?" He cocked his head in the direction of Pilar.

Gid shook his head and squared off his body so that their conversation was more private. "I'm not ready for—"

"Hold up, hold up," Cullen said, kneeling down next to him. "You do realize that fate has stranded you in a hotel room with Pilar Benitez-Jones?"

"There are, like, eighty other people here," Gid said.

"She has her own room," Cullen said.

"How do you know that?"

"She made a point of telling me."

"Well, maybe she likes *you*."

"You are hopeless," Cullen said. "I mean, the Alamo has shown up right at your door. All you have to do is walk over to the sidewalk and puke. And you're fucking up." He shook his head. "Wait," he said, "I have an amazing idea! Nicholas! Take that magic snorkel out of your mouth and give me a hand."

Suddenly he and Nicholas were pushing everyone off the beds. Madison stood up, glowering, holding her cigarette out in front of her like it was a dog she was walking. "What the hell? I am not playing Twister, OK? I have my period."

"We're not playing Twister," Cullen said. "We're playing spin the bottle."

It took some time to assemble the circle. There was some question about the carpet's being bunched up in once place so that the bottle might never make it to one side of the circle. "Maybe that side of the circle is just ugly," someone shouted, and twenty rich teenagers laughed out loud at the absurd notion that any of them could be considered ugly.

"This is a perfect game for you," Gid said to Nicholas. "You get some contact with girls without having to talk to them before or afterward."

"Ehh," Nicholas said. "I prefer higher emotional stakes."

Pilar made a face at him. "You are esso immature," she said.

Nicholas said, "You may be right," and sat down. Gideon sat down next to Nicholas, and Pilar sat down a few feet away.

"Madison, you first," Cullen said.

"What? Why me?"

"Because you need to make out with someone under thirty." Nicholas handed her the empty Cutty Sark bottle.

Madison tried to look annoyed, but you could see she liked having her tastes spoken of publicly. She spun.

She got Gideon and did not attempt to conceal her distaste. "Uhhh," she said, supersizing her eye roll and advancing toward the center of the circle on her knees as Gid did the same. *Wow*, he thought as they kissed, *there was a day when I would have thought this was such a big deal, but now, I just feel like I'm going to the store.* He went back to his place and thought about how far he'd come that he could find a girl as hot as Madison so bitchy that he didn't want to kiss her.

"Dude," Nicholas muttered.

"Sorry," Gid said, taking up the bottle. He closed his eyes. As Gid spun, he thought, *Alamo.*

It landed between Pilar and the girl next to her, a girl who, although she didn't look like me up close, from far away looked like me a lot. We were the same height and weight, with the same hair—a pretty but unspectacular brown-haired look.

Pilar and the other girl both stared at the bottle. It really was directly in between them. Pilar looked brazenly at Gideon.

Gideon looked everywhere else. Cullen had appeared, shirtless, now, still in his hat. He began to chant. "Dealer's choice, dealer's choice!" and everyone reacted to his incredible charisma and joined in.

Gideon wasn't going to argue for Pilar. Besides, wasn't he just supposed to go again, weren't those the rules of a spin-the-bottle tie anyway, a do-over?

But Pilar spoke up. "Eet's pointed more toward *me*," she said. "I mean, you maybe can't see it from that angle, but eet is." She smiled provocatively at the other girl. "Want to fight me for it?"

This is really happening, Gideon thought. *This is really happening, and maybe Molly dumped me for a reason. Maybe I am about to get out of the car and puke right now, and I don't even know it. In a good way.*

The girl made a be-my-guest gesture, and Pilar strutted right up to Gideon Rayburn. *She has amazing posture*, he thought. It was like her breasts were floating on top of her body.

He put his hands on Pilar's shoulders and let one hand fall a little bit down her arm. Their eyes met. In hers, he swore he saw something like lust and devotion. *I might be so wrong*, he thought, *but I might as well kiss her as if I were right.*

I could have been in Buffalo right now, Gid thought. *What do I think about this? Am I sad? Am I happy? Do I just think life's weird?*

He covered her mouth with his.

I felt her mouth close around his, and I felt the hungry way his tightened in response. There was a flash of panic that his mouth wouldn't move, followed by a rush of determination. He thought about a line he had read in both good and bad books: he took her. He almost laughed that he was thinking of that line, but as he thought it, the determination surged more, so he thought it again. Why not? *He took her.* His hands were moving. They were now on her neck, in her hair, on her face. He felt her swoon. *We* felt her swoon. It really was a thing you could feel. Her hips gave way, she felt heavier and lighter at the same time. Her softness was insane, but she was kissing him back *hard.*

He kept kissing her and she kept kissing him. Some people kiss and it's nothing, and Gideon and Pilar weren't nothing. Gideon and Pilar weren't necessarily Gid and me, but we didn't exist anymore, anyway.

I thought about what makes two people kiss well, and I wondered if he liked kissing her more than he liked kissing me, and I wondered also why he wasn't thinking about that. People were clapping. I wished they would stop because the noise was prohibiting Gid from thinking about what I wanted to know. Instead, he was thinking, *Do I like kissing Pilar, or do I like having everyone see me kiss the hottest girl at the party? Well, the hottest girl in the world, maybe.* He didn't pull away from her exactly, but he moved his mouth and, aware he was drunk, aware this was stupid, whispered into her mouth in feverish, sleep-talking tones, "The hottest girl in the world."

A voice—Cullen's—shouted "The Alamo!"

Was Pilar the hottest girl in the world?

I thought maybe the party had gone suddenly quiet. For a second I was afraid something terrible had happened, like a drunk person had fallen out a window and everyone was just staring at a corpse and Gid was too numb to think or something, but even when he was too numb to think, I could see what he was seeing. But right now I couldn't see him seeing anything. There was nothing left of Gid. Just the quiet. Just my head.

Was he *gone*?

Gideon had slipped out of my head. I just sat there on my bed. I closed my eyes and tried to concentrate.

He couldn't just all of a sudden disappear.

But seeing as he had just whispered the words *the hottest girl in the world* against the lips of another girl, why didn't I want him to disappear?

I had a panicked feeling, like I'd lost my wallet with thousands of dollars in it, or like I was driving with no brakes. *How was I supposed to know what he was doing now?* What if he was heading off to sleep with Pilar? I had to know. What had I done?

I lay awake. I waited for him to come back. I worried about what I would see when he did.

He didn't come back.

He was gone for good.

This was the most terrible silence. When I was thinking about wanting to get out of his head, I was just thinking about not being in pain.

I forgot about this whole *alone* thing.

I wanted to sleep, to escape, but what if he came back quietly and I missed him?

I don't know how long I lay there awake, longing to see Gid, longing to hear him, no matter what he was doing, just to know. The harder I found myself concentrating, the more sure I was he was gone.

book
two

chapter
eight

I had kind of been hoping to sleep into the next day, but as luck would have it, I woke up at the tail end of afternoon— exactly the time of day when the upstate New York winter dishes out its most heaping helpings of annihilating despair. I lay in bed for a while, wondering how I was supposed to handle being this sad. It was hard to take it all in at once: Gid and I were over. He had kissed Pilar, and he had liked it. Not only had he liked it, he had whispered that she was the most beautiful girl in the world while he had kissed her. I had tried to get him out of my head, and it had worked.

And I missed him.

In my bedside table I found a Spice Girls pencil and a notepad from the Buffalo Marriott. I wrote on a piece of paper: Gideon Rayburn is a fucking dick. I wrote, Gideon Rayburn just wants someone perfect so he can prove to himself he's cool, because he is a loser and he knows it!

I could hate him. I could get myself there.

Predictably, it started to rain. Buffalo, like love, couldn't stay beautiful long. In just a few minutes, the winter wonderland would be a sodden mess.

I heard a sound like water dripping into a bucket. Even with the covers over my head, the sound grew louder and louder. It was definitely water. It wasn't rain. It was water trickling into more water, but with soothing regularity. It was the sound of a fountain. I sat up.

I knew my family did not have a fountain. Buffalo wasn't exactly an in-home fountain kind of town.

I lay back down and shut my eyes. The fountain sound persisted.

Probably I had gone a little crazy.

Then I heard a voice: *I know Madeeson likes these shoes, and she could only pretend she doesn't like them because she knows eef I could get them how awesome I will look in them.*

It was Pilar Benitez-Jones's voice. The musical tone. The use of the conditional when the past tense would have been more appropriate. The accent that was pretty much gone except for the occasional inability to produce a soft "I" sound.

If I wear these shoes tonight, that guy will for definitely geeve me that job.

There was no question it was her.

Great. I was back inside of Gid's head, but he was shopping with Pilar Benitez-Jones.

I imagined their cozy morning conversation. She had tucked her perfectly shaped chin into her creamy shoulder, and said, "Come shopping with me."

Gid's eyes blazed with desire as he stared at her. "Oh, yes," he said. "I never went shopping with Molly once, because I hate it, but I love you so much I will go."

I had wanted to be back in his head. I guess I deserved whatever I got. Gideon had decided not to go to St. John with his buddies and had gone to LA with Pilar? I had never been to LA, but I just knew they were there because I saw blond people in loose, casual, expensive clothes toying with their sunglasses, and this is what I had always pictured people did in LA. Outside, satiny palm fronds waved across a blue sky.

I had worried about them kissing, and when I woke up thirteen hours later, they were going out?

Gideon and Pilar were on a romantic vacation in Los Angeles, and I was going to have to watch all of it through Gid's eyes.

"I really don't like those shoes, Pilar." This was Madison Sprague's voice: lockjaw edged with sneering impatience. "They definitely have this thing about them where they want to be sexy, but they're just, like, not."

How was it that Pilar had just talked shit about Madison to Gid with Madison right there? She wasn't whispering to him, either.

This didn't make any sense. Gid shopping with Madison and Pilar. Unbelievable. He didn't even like to listen to me and Edie talk on the phone. "It makes me feel like I'm going to turn into a girl," he would complain. But now Gid wasn't complaining, even to himself. Was he having fun with them? I didn't see how. The place was boy hell: racks of belts, glass cases full of jewelry, wall units stuffed with expensive folded jeans, girls tittering to each other, "Oh sweetie! That is so cute on you!" and "I swear to God, he is going to *die* when he sees you in that." I did locate the source of the fountain sound: a concrete wall streaming water into a square concrete tub decorated with tiles reading HOPE, HAPPINESS AND ADVENTURE. Santogold pulsed out of invisible speakers.

Pilar's voice again: *With the right shoes and the right way I put my hair, I will be the eentern to Elias Ganz. Not Madison. And she is trying to stop this from happening, but it weel.*

So apparently every time Madison walked away, Pilar said something nasty about her to Gideon. I had always tried to keep my bitchiness to a minimum around Gideon, thinking it was kind of a turnoff, but apparently Pilar was too good-looking to worry about that sort of thing.

Someone answered a phone: "Fred Segal." I think I had heard of this place, or read about it, or something. It was like a department store but mini, and superfancy.

Pilar was looking down at the shoe now, pivoting it back and forth, back and forth so she could take in every angle. It was a white patent leather T-strap with a high heel. I heard: *Madison is so clearly just jealous of me. I mean, she has a nice body and everything, but when you do the equation, with my face, mine is better, and really, her body is only, like, better for clothes, and that isn't in the equation anyway.*

What was the equation? And why wasn't Gid like, equation, what? Are you insane?

Pilar went on: *This shoe makes me look reech, and that's good.*

I had a terrible revelation: that endlessly pivoting shoe. I wasn't looking across at that shoe. I was looking right down at it, *as if it were on my foot.* And Pilar wasn't saying these things out loud. She was just thinking them.

Pilar looked up from the shoes and stared at herself in the

mirror. I watched her admire the line of her eyebrows, the shine of her hair, the smallness of her waist, and the perfectly articulated swell of everything around it. Behind her, she could see Madison, dressed in super low cut jeans, a white tank top with no bra, and an Hermès belt—her signature look—poking idly though a jewelry display. *Madison is so thin.* Pilar now studied her stomach, frowning. *My stomach is not perfect. It is not right. My stomach will be perfect, and then everything will be perfect, because with a perfect stomach maybe I am the prettiest girl in the entire—well, Kobe Bryant's wife might be prettier than me. And maybe Catherine Zeta-Jones, but only in Zorro, and maybe Beyoncé, except my cousin saw her in person once, and . . .*

Pilar stared at herself for so long. I stared at Pilar staring at herself. But I was staring at the mirror. I was seeing Pilar as if I were looking out from her eyes.

Two girls—one tall and brunette, the other black with a blond afro—walked past.

Forty percent, Pilar thought, looking at the brunette, and then, looking at the black girl, she thought, *25 percent.* I didn't know what she meant, but that wasn't the point. The point was that I now knew that she wasn't talking out loud. She was talking to herself, and I could hear her.

I was now inside the mind of Pilar Benitez-Jones.

chapter
nine

I instant-messaged Dr. Stanley Whitmeyer.

> Out of boyfriends head now in horrible girl's head. That
> boyfriend likes. And is nightmare pretty. She's so pretty
> people look at her like they want her dead.
>   Hello? Hello?

Nothing.

I didn't know how I had gotten into her head. I didn't know how I'd gotten into Gid's. Not only was this not the plan, this was the opposite of the plan. What had I been thinking about that had landed me in here? I tried to remember the last moments of being in Gid's head. The more I thought about it, the more confused I got. And the more I thought about it, the more I realized how hard it was to think while being in Pilar Benitez-Jones's head because she did a lot of thinking herself.

I should say instead that she had a lot of thoughts. I don't know if thoughts can always be called thinking. *Look natural. Don't look like you care what Madison's doing. Is supima a natural or synthetic fiber? Oh, I just dropped that thing I was looking at on the floor. Oh well, that salesgirl will get it. That's her job. She likes to pick things up or she wouldn't work here.*

Indeed, momentarily a salesgirl slipped past her to return the garment to its gray silk padded hanger.

Pilar's eyes ticked over the girl's face, body, and outfit and a number popped into her head: *40 percent.*

What was she doing?

Pilar and Madison drifted into another section of the boutique. It wasn't as busy, it was more spare and, with no music playing, it seemed to whisper, things like *Fashion is important* and *No fatties.* It was the dress boutique. The place people bought shit to go out in. I would have thought Pilar would be in her element here, but she was pissed. Pissed and nervous. She watched Madison out of the corner of her eye.

She better not get a dress here. We have a plan of outfits, and eef she changes it, she is such a . . . Madison was examining something aqua blue and sheer, and Pilar watched her intently, finally sighing with relief. *Thank God, it's just a camisole. She ees just looking for clothes for general. Not for tonight.*

Madison studied the item with great seriousness until something about it seemed to disappoint her. She scowled and tossed it over a rack. Another salesgirl appeared to clean up her mess. This one had a black pixie cut and wore a long green vintage slip with lace-up Victorian boots. Pilar openly stared at her, and now I was able to follow her mind through its whole process. *The face is an eight, the body, well, I can't see it that well, let's just geeve it an eight, but style is a ten. Great vintage Celine boots. Beautiful red glass earrings.* Pilar multiplied the face number, eight, by three; the body number, eight, by two; and the style number, ten, remained on its own. She added these numbers together, divided by three, and came up with the number sixteen and two thirds, which she rounded up to seventeen.

It was this number that led Pilar to the decision that this girl was 78 percent as hot as she was.

Gid was always saying there was more to Pilar than meets the eye, but I had always suspected she mostly occupied herself with checking out other girls and thinking how much hotter she was than they were.

I had never imagined she had an actual formula for this. And I couldn't help but wonder, what number would she assign to me?

Pilar continued to walk around the dress boutique with that slow, contemplative walk most people use in museums. Other than her and Madison, there were four of five other young women shopping, all in varying uniforms of tight jeans, tight T-shirts, and high heels, all keeping a respectful distance from one another so as not to interfere with this holy business of shopping. I don't think I am exaggerating when I say that every single one of them looked at Pilar in awe. The same questions seemed to linger in all of their eyes: what is it like to be her? With a girl that beautiful around, why do I ever bother?

Pilar soaked up their attention like a sponge.

I saw them looking at my hair, wondering how I get it to curl like this. Eemagine how sad they would be eef they knew it was natural. And that one girl who would stare at my chest like she wanted to punch me because mine are real and so high up and hers probably feel like a doll's. I am going to look amazing tonight.

OK, like a *crazy* sponge.

But Pilar's self-satisfaction seemed to dissolve when she looked at Madison. *I am going to look amazing tonight eef Madison doesn't look better than I do. I know he said that he might hire both of us, but I theenk I heard something about the economy not being so good. If he just would hire one of us, it would have to be me.*

Now I got it. Pilar and Madison were meeting their potential employer tonight, outfits had been chosen, and on the basis of these outfits, Pilar was sure she was going to be his first, if not only, choice. But if Madison changed her outfit, Madison could be the favorite.

Twisted logic, but I could follow it.

Automatically I picked up the phone to try Dr. Whitmeyer again. But then I put it down. For the first time since Gid had broken up with me, I smiled. I had always thought of Pilar and Madison as a united front, two wealthy, stylish goddesses allied against the world of bargain-bin mortals. But there was trouble in paradise.

Maybe I would watch for just a little longer.

Pilar pretended to examine the hem on a dress knit so loose it looked like a spiderweb. She said casually, "I'm a leetle hungry. Are you?"

Madison turned away from a rack of dresses made out of tiny tiles. "Yeah," she said.

Oh please, let's go. Let's go back to the hotel and thees will be over and I can sleep a nap . . .

But Madison said, "Let's smoke a cigarette and then look around some more."

Pilar's heart sank. *What can I do to get her out of here?*

They walked down a Lucite staircase, through a set of glass doors, and onto a brick walkway lined with pink and white flowers. Pilar lit a cigarette. "I'm already getting lines around my mouth," she said. *Maybe eef I can convince Madison I'm not that much prettier than her she won't feel the need to get another dress.*

Madison nodded and ashed.

"OK," Pilar said. "So after this do you want to get going?"

Madison took a deep inhale and watched two women in matching orange leggings, one in a cowboy hat and the other in a headscarf, get out of a Lexus SUV.

"Madison?" Pilar said tentatively.

"I heard you!" Madison snapped. She lit her own cigarette and shook her match out, ignoring Pilar. "You're the one who took, like, a million hours in Miss Sixty."

I don't understand how I can be prettier than Madison but sort of scared of her. She should be scared of me. I absolutely have to make sure she gets out of thees store not buying a better outfit than mine for tonight. But I can't let her know I am doing that. Madison might have a flat stomach, but she so does not understand the importance of matching an outfit to a décor, and her outfit does not match the décor and at this point, two hours before, she isn't going to find the perfect thing. I am so getting thees job.

The store's heavy glass door opened and Amber, the girl who had been helping Pilar with her shoes, stuck her head out. "So!" she exclaimed to Madison. "I have a bunch of dresses for you to try on. Just like you said, casual evening, like, day dresses that just happen to go to night. I think some of them are really amazing!"

Oh no. The whole time we were looking through the dresses, she already had thees planned. Why is that salesgirl giving me that giant smile, like we're best friends? All she did was talk to me about a pair of shoes. And what is Madison's problem about Miss Sixty?

Amber clapped her hands excitedly. "You must be so excited to see your friend in all these amazing dresses. I mean, does she have the figure for it or what?"

Is this girl trying to torture me, or is she just stupid? "Oh, yes," Pilar said. "I just can't wait."

She followed them toward the dressing room. Amber and Madison were several paces ahead of her, and Pilar stared at their tiny butts with envy. *They're like tiddlywinks. I can't believe Madison doesn't even like eating.* A slideshow of delicious food items paraded through Pilar's head: pizza, burritos, cake.

Amber led Pilar to a bizarrely shaped chair, made out of metal and woven pieces of orange elastic. "This is an original from artist Raul Amudsen," she said to Pilar.

"Wow," Pilar said. *Who the fuck cares?* She sank into the chair and looked at the back of the dressing room door, where the dresses Amber had selected were hanging. *Those are all exactly the kind of thing I can't wear. They are for human hangers.*

Amber was still desperate to please. "Can I get you anything?"

Pilar was hungry. "Water," she said. "With a cucumber slice."

There was a knocking sound. I thought it was Amber knocking on the door of Madison's dressing room, but it was someone knocking on my door.

"Come in." My voice came out totally cheerful. Wow. I was actually not in a terrible mood. I was kind of having fun.

Mom gave me a sort of shy smile, the kind of smile you give to someone depressed to be upbeat, but not annoyingly so. "Hi," she said.

I tried to figure out from her face if my father had told her my giant lie about getting a scholarship for winning a championship I had not yet won for an organization I had not yet agreed to join.

"Do you want something from Jim's?"

Jim's Steak-Out has the best hamburgers in Buffalo. My mother is pretty healthy, but she eats them when she's really stressed out. So now I knew my father hadn't told her. He might have even encouraged her to get food from there tonight as a sign to me that my mother didn't know.

I said I wanted a double with bacon.

She looked relieved that I was hungry.

"It seems like you're doing better," she said.

"Oh . . . ," I said. "I was just looking at something really funny." Obviously I was talking about Madison and Pilar's competitive shopping trip, but my mother thought I meant one of my books.

"Glad to see you're better." My mother left and I went back to Pilar.

I want my stomach to be flat like Madison's. I know that eef it was then I maybe could not feel so upset that Madison was supposed to wear that Yves Saint Laurent vintage tunic. It was so supposed to clash with the décor, and it didn't show off her collarbone, which is just stupid when you're that thin. I just need to get her out of here. The problem is, I don't know how.

A louvered door swung open, and Madison emerged in an unflattering dress with weird ruffles on it. "Ick," she said. "I look like Tweety Bird." She kind of did. She frowned. "Where the fuck is that chick with my Coke?" Madison said, going back into the dressing room.

"Hmm," Pilar said. "I don't know. That looks nice."

Madison leveled an evil glare at her. "It so doesn't look nice. What is your problem?"

Ok, thees was worst lie ever. I can't believe she is drinking Coke when she knows my metabolism is not good for Coke. Pilar sipped her water dutifully and without pleasure, and then let its lone slice of cucumber float onto her tongue. She crunched the cucumber up and swallowed it. *Fuck. Eating cucumbers reminds me of pickles, and that reminds me of Reubens and Cuban sandwiches. I am hungry. What can I eat? Nothing. I hate it when my stomach hangs over the top of my pants. I will eat tomorrow, I guess.*

Amber trotted back in. "Anyone need anything in here? How are you liking those dresses?"

"I looked like Ryan Seacrest's gay mom in the first one," Madison said coldly. "Where's my Coke?"

"Sorry," she said. "I'm sorry . . . I . . ." But Madison swung the louvered door closed. Amber looked as if she was about to cry. Then she saw Pilar watching her. Amber pasted on her smile. "How are *you* doing?" she asked Pilar. "I love that top. I totally just wish I had boobs."

Pilar smiled as she realized, *Madison is so jealous of me. I have boobs and she doesn't. That's it. That's exactly how I am going to get out of here.* She checked the dressing room doors to make sure they went all the way to the floor, so that you could take your underwear off but no one would know.

"There is something you could do for me," Pilar said, indicating that she and Amber should move out of the dressing room area. "Bikinis," Pilar said quietly when they got outside. "Bring me some bikinis." *Madison hates it when I try on bikinis. She gets so jealous of my boobs. That's why she's trying to get back at me right now. Because I tried on all those bikinis at Miss Sixty and she was, like, trying them on too at first and barely filling them out so she stopped. I will now try on bikinis and she will get so jealous of my big boobs, then, she will stop trying on dresses and she will wear that Yves Saint Laurent tunic that is not right for that bar, and I will get the job.*

Amber prattled on. "Don't you love summer! Cute tanks, boy shorts! And it is so fun to just think about going to the beach, right, when you're trying on awesome, supercute bikinis!"

"Shhh," Pilar said.

"Supercute bikinis," Amber whispered.

"Right," Pilar whispered. "The kind with the push-up thing."

"But what about her Coke?"

"Fuck her Coke!" Pilar whispered. "Bring the bikinis first. . . . Oh, but act like . . . you just thought they would look good on me. Like I didn't ask for them or anything, OK?"

Amazingly, Amber nodded. "Got it." Pilar was clearly not the first person to make such a request to her. I got the feeling a lot of shit like this went down at Fred Segal.

But it wasn't as good was what was about to go down, because I don't think a lot of shoppers here had people inside their head.

I wanted to get out of Pilar's head. But as long as I was there, I might as well have a good time. And make sure she had a bad one.

I wasn't going to do anything terrible. Just something to make me feel just a tiny little bit better about the fact that she'd made out with my boyfriend and didn't even care.

chapter
ten

I actually stood on a pile of my brother's Golden Books to make myself a little taller. It was effective. I dialed and cleared my throat.

"Fred Segal. Carolyn speaking."

"Hello," I had said in a smooth, adult voice. "This is, uh, Ann-Sylvie at Miss Sixty."

"Hi, Ann-Sylvie! What a cool name!"

"I grew up in Montreal," I said.

"Oh my God, so did my ex-boyfriend!"

"We had a customer in here earlier, and she . . . well. She was trying on bathing suits . . . and she and her friend were talking about how they were going to Fred Segal's afterwards. I wanted to make sure she doesn't wreak the same havoc on your inventory that she did on ours."

I fully expected her to hang up on me. I mean, it was ridiculous. But in fact, Carolyn gasped, "Thank you so much for telling me. You guys are always so good about alerting us to this sort of thing."

"You're welcome," I said, dumbfounded, and was about to hang up, when Carolyn said, "Hello? Hello? What does she look like?"

I told her about Pilar's long shiny hair and pretty eyes and perfect skin. I said, "I mean, you can't miss her because she is probably, I have to admit, the most beautiful girl in the store." I think Pilar would have liked my description.

"'The bathing suit inventory at Fred Segal's is not at your disposal.'" Madison cracked up every time she said it. "It was so good."

Pilar was indignant and humiliated. I'd expected that. But the added bonus was that they were in the limo now, on the way to the bar, and Pilar, having taken four showers at the hotel, was still afraid she had some terrible, impossible-to-locate odor. How else would the woman at Miss Sixty know . . . Oh, it was all too terrible to think about!

Pilar crossed her arms and looked at the passing landscape, the klieg lights charging through the dark sky, the shining fenders, the self-satisfied smiles of people in convertibles, and the parade of bare legs and beautiful shoes. *I have never been so humiliated, ever. Everyone tries on bathing suits without underwear. How does she catch me? How?*

And then there was the little matter of Madison's dress, which Madison had emerged wearing at the exact moment when trembling Amber came in to inform Pilar that "the bathing suit inventory at Fred Segal's is not at your disposal."

The dress Madison had finally found was a perfect dress.

First of all, it was white, and Pilar considered white to be a color that had been created especially for her. She owned white. It had a high halter neck, which (a) showed off Madison's sublime collarbone and (b) was a look Pilar desperately wanted to be able to pull of, but, having rather large breasts, could not. It was short and inventive, with little cut-out triangles all over that showed glimpses of skin, but not so inventive that you saw the dress and missed the svelte object of envy underneath. It was the best dress Pilar had ever seen. She stood there, reeling in horrified embarrassment at the memory of trying on bikini after bikini at Miss Sixty, with each try-on breaking the California state law that prohibits people from trying on bathing suits without underwear.

Now, sitting in the limo, shamed, jealous, unhappy in her high-waisted black pants and low-cut sweater, she burned with a desire to be vindicated. *Elias Ganz better pick me. He weell see how incredibly beautiful I am, and he weell pick me.*

Poor Pilar. Crazy Pilar. Lucky me for thinking up such a nasty trick. I had just meant to have some fun. The fact that she was so totally unraveled for tonight was just an added bonus.

I IMDb'd this Elias Ganz character. He hadn't done anything big yet, but he had a couple projects coming out, one called *Tricky Sticky Ricky* and another called *Salon Rorschach*. A quote attributed to him in *The Hollywood Reporter* online read, "Bottom line: filmmaking is the best way I've found to communicate with the world. Look, if I were a Bushman, I'd just get really good at clicking my tongue."

Which was just a roundabout way of saying, "I'm a total douche."

Pilar entered the bar, causing the same kind of stir she'd

caused walking into that hotel room back in Boston. Women's eyes widened over their glasses of wine, men's jaws went slack. Adrenaline and sudden confidence coursed through Pilar's body. *This is where I am meant to be, at exactly this moment. This is the center of the universe, and I am at the center of that center, wearing an awesome outfit.*

She sounded so obnoxious, but seriously, she wasn't wrong. The sheer amount of energy directed at her was undeniable. I couldn't ignore it. How could she?

I spotted Elias the instant she did. He had wavy dark red hair that he wore combed back, and a strong chin. He was seated in a buttery leather chair with a view of the room, a long, dark space whose neutral surfaces looked creamy and expensive under flickering candles. Behind him a long swimming pool surrounded with spindly, prehistoric-looking plants rippled and gave off a bright turquoise glow. A red lamp over his head cast a flattering shadow. He pushed his hair off his forehead and looked up. When he saw Pilar, he smiled, ever so slightly. It was a predatory smile, and Pilar liked it.

She was aware of him, and everyone in the room, watching her as she walked across the room, muttering to herself, *Stomach in, butt out, stomach in, butt out.*

Pilar hung back as Elias kissed Madison's cheek and leaned into her, with two left fingers on her flank. "Madison," he said, "amazing dress."

Pilar stiffened. But then he turned to look at her. There was no mistaking what was in his eyes, unbridled lust. Pilar was used to grown men looking at her like this. *All right. Here we go, Madison.*

There was a couch perpendicular to Elias's chair, and Pilar lunged for the place next to him. "Such a pretty garden, planted around the pool like that," she murmured to Madison, as if that were her reason for sitting in this spot. Madison drew one leg over the other and leaned back elegantly. *I'm slouching,* Pilar thought, and snapped upright. *I have to remember not to drink too much. OK. I can do that. I got this.*

A waitress in a white shirt, gold lamé skirt, and heels appeared at his side. Pilar sized her up immediately—70 percent.

"Connie, would you be so kind as to bring a bottle of the Perrier-Jouët?" Elias said. "Three glasses for now."

Connie smilingly obliged and was gone.

"So," Elias said, leaning back grandly in his leather chair and running a hand through his thick, mogulesque head of hair. "I had an insane day of work."

"I can imagine," Madison said. "I know your job is non-stop."

"After I have a long day I always like to get a foot rub," Pilar said.

Elias smiled with one side of his face. He eyed his feet and eyed Pilar's lap. She patted her thigh. They laughed.

"So why was your day hard?" Madison said quickly. "What are you working on right now?

Madison would never have the idea of giving him a foot rub.

His iPhone buzzed. "Excuse me," Elias said. "Tina! Ha! Fuck you."

Madison turned to Pilar. "Dude. Don't act like such a slut. I can't believe you're worried about what I would tell him and you're telling him you're going to give him a foot rub."

"What?" Pilar said innocently. *I am going to get somewhere with thees Elias guy. I can feel it.*

Elias hung up. The bottle arrived. "You're busy, angel. I got it." Connie sauntered off. "Where was I? Oh right," Elias said, popping, then pouring. "I really am dying to know . . . you know, I'm from here, so I don't know what it's like not to know this place, and I want to know, what do two East Coast girls do when they come to LA?"

"Shopping," Pilar said, drinking fast.

"Going to museums," Madison said, taking a sip.

"We went to one museum for maybe half an hour," Pilar said. "I don't really like the museums."

"No?" Elias crossed his legs and inched up a little in his chair. Pilar saw his heavy eyes turn down just a little and she knew he was trying to get a look at her chest, so she inched over a bit as well to help him out. "Why's that?"

"You can't buy anything in them."

"Are you serious?" he said. "Is she serious?" he asked Madison.

Before Madison could answer, Pilar laughed. "I'm a hundred percent serious." She turned to Madison. "You hate museums too."

Pilar had thought he might find it cute, her ribbing her friend, and she seemed to have been right when he laughed.

"I don't hate museums," Madison said. "I loved the Lucian Freuds yesterday."

"Oh yes," Elias said, "Lucian Freud is very good."

He doesn't care, Pilar thought.

The iPhone buzzed and Elias rolled his eyes at it. "Excuse me," he said, and ducked out of the room.

"Pilar," Madison said, as soon as Elias was out of earshot. "Why are you making him think you're not into school or, like, art?"

Madison ees just trying to screw me up. "He said grades weren't important," Pilar said. "And, like, aren't we in competition for this job, so, like, eef you don't like how I'm acting, well, I guess that's good for you."

"Well, he could give it to both of us," Madison said. "If you decide to come across as, like, sort of, like, kind of smart."

"People make movies here, not libraries," Pilar scoffed, and helped herself to more champagne.

Then Connie was at her side. "Hey, someone at the bar wanted to send you a shot."

"Me?" Pilar said.

"You better not drink that," Madison warned.

But Pilar poured it down. She had just thought about what happened with the bathing suits, and it freaked her out. The shot went down and the thought went away.

Elias came back and sat down. "So, tell me about Midvale! How is my old alma mater?"

"Ugh," Pilar said. "What do you want to know?"

"How are your classes?"

Pilar laughed. "They'd be a lot better if I could bring a sleeping bag and a bottle of wine."

Elias broke into a smile again, and as he shifted his position, his leg rested lightly against hers.

Madison sat up and crossed her hands in her lap. "We saw all the Éric Rohmer pictures the week before break, and I thought they were pretty good. But I really just love Tarkovsky," she said.

Pilar drizzled the last of the champagne into her glass and said, "Tarwhatsky?"

"You two are hilarious," he said.

Pilar knew he just meant her.

Madison and Elias chatted on about movies. *I can tell he ees totally bored,* she thought. *And, like, he keeps looking away from her while she's talking and looking at me.* At one point Elias whispered into Madison's ear, looking right at Pilar. Madison looked back at Pilar. *She looks pissed. He must be asking her about me.*

An hour passed. Elias's friends showed up, Terry Hall and James Aslan, indie film bad boys and best friends, famous enough so that even I knew them. They made sort of artsy violent movies with Asian girls running around nude and lots of people getting killed. Terry and James were always together, drinking and touching their stubble, pretending they didn't want to be lovers.

The men all bear-hugged one another while Madison inched over to Pilar. "Pilar," she hissed. "Watch it."

"I'm not drunk," Pilar said. Two more shots had been sent over. She couldn't tell who had sent them, and she didn't care. She felt good.

"Take it easy," Madison hissed. "And next time, check that camel toe at the door, okay?"

The guys sat down on the couch, Terry on the other side of Pilar, then Madison, and James on the end. *James Madison,* Pilar thought, *wasn't that a person?* James was blond and surfer-y, Terry was dark-haired and mutely serious. He just stared at Pilar. "Jesus," James said. "You're really hot. Your breasts are like cupcakes."

"Uh, dude," Terry said.

Pilar moved her head around until she caught Elias's eyes. "Help," she said.

Madison and Elias were still talking about movies. "I really enjoy Louis Malle," Elias was saying.

"Oh, he is wonderful," Madison said. "*Murmur of the Heart* is one of my favorites."

Terry and James ordered drinks and kept staring at Pilar. "How old are you?" James said.

"You like *Murmur of the Heart*?" Elias said. "I'm impressed."

"Help," whimpered Pilar.

"You look like you're doing just fine," Elias said. And Pilar was pleased to see the wolfish look in his eyes again. Sure, he was talking to Madison, but he hadn't looked at her like that, not once.

"Oh," Pilar said, arranging one of the gold sofa pillows under her head and resting on it, her cleavage now well displayed, her hips slightly off the couch. "I guess I am."

Now Elias and Terry and James were all staring at her. Their attention hit her like a beam of light that began in her shoes and went all the way to her scalp.

Madison made a cut-it-out gesture. *She ees so jealous of all my attention.* "So," Madison said, changing the subject, "tell me about what you're working on right now."

Oh my God. Look at her trying to get attention. It is, like, so sad. But to her surprise, James and Terry pried their eyes from her cupcake breasts, sat up straight, and began to speak to Madison in level tones. "We're working on a picture about hope," James said.

Terry nodded and touched his beard. "It's a little more serious than what we've been accustomed to."

Pilar took the opportunity to lean over into Elias's lap. "Hi," she said.

"Hello," he said. His eyes were heavy.

She braced herself against his thigh. "Your hand is on my thigh," he said.

She smirked. "If I take it off, will you give me the eenternship?"

"No, but if you leave it there, I will." Elias put his hand over hers, holding her where she was. "Do you really want to spend the summer in LA?"

"Yes," she said. "I do."

"You know it gets really hot here." Elias lowered his eyes and stared with unabashed interest down the front of her shirt.

Pilar couldn't help but giggle. "I don't mind heat," she said.

"Yeah, somehow I got that sense."

Pilar giggled again but went to sit up.

"Hey," Elias said, his hand stiffening over hers. "I thought we were making a deal here."

"Oh," Pilar said. "I . . ."

At this point Connie arrived with another shot. "This is for you, again," she said to Pilar.

"Oh, my," Pilar said. She didn't sit up. She was still sort of bent over onto Elias's lap. He held the shot. "May I help you?"

"OK," Pilar said.

Madison stood up, clutching her box of Export A Ultra Lights.

"Pilar," she said, "let's go outside for a second."

Madison has just got to be so jealous of me at this point. I mean, I feel bad for her. I mean, Elias just practically gave me the job.

"Open your mouth," Elias said.

Pilar opened her mouth. She felt James's and Terry's attention turn back to her. *They are, like, famous. When they look at me, I feel like I am on TV.* Elias, with a half smile, took the shot and poured most of it into her mouth. When it was almost gone he coughed theatrically, jostling his hand, and the remaining drops landed on her lips.

"Like sweet summer dew," Elias said, and Terry and James,

enraptured, nodded. Pilar licked her lips, thinking, *I want to feel like I am on TV forever.*

"Pilar. We are going outside," Madison said.

"I don't want to," Pilar said. "It's cold out. Besides," she said, "I want to get a tiny hamburger. Isn't this the place with the tiny hamburgers?"

"I'll give you a tiny hamburger," Elias said.

Pilar giggled. *It ees going to be so fun working for him this summer, hanging out with his friends. Why ees Madison alone out there smoking? Shit. I should probably go talk to her.* She tried to stand up, but Elias grabbed her wrist. "Where are you going?" he said. He pulled her back down so she was sitting next to him.

"I'm just going to talk to Madison."

"So," he said. "Why don't you come upstairs with me?"

"Upstairs?" Pilar said. "Why?"

"Why?" Elias said, spreading his bulk into the edges of the leather seat. "So I can see you naked, that's why. Not that I can't kind of see you naked already." He reached down and touched her ankle.

Pilar stopped him. "I don't think so," she said.

"You don't think so?" he repeated, angry.

Terry and James upended their drinks into their gaping mouths and made a mad dash for the bar. Elias let go of her hand. He moved forward on the sofa and, suddenly all business, gave his Prada trousers a tug at the knee. Pilar leaned toward him. "Elias?" she said.

"Mmm," he said.

"I just think we would be weird eef we had sex and then we were working together, no?"

He laughed and poured his drink down his throat. He

pushed back his hair and rubbed his thumb and forefinger on his nose. He looked at Pilar. "You're very pretty," he said. "But you already know that."

"I don't know eef I know that," Pilar said. "I sometimes feel . . ."

"I don't see this," Elias said. He downed the rest of his drink and gave her a look. Then he nodded. "I can't have someone like you working for me."

"Someone like me?" Pilar suddenly felt very dizzy. "What . . . what am I like?"

"Well," Elias said. "At this point, you are either someone who wants this job, or you are someone who doesn't."

At first Pilar didn't quite know what he meant. Or she knew, and she didn't want to believe she knew. But then she looked at Elias's face and saw his tongue suggestively wet the middle of his lip.

"I . . . I guess I don't want the job," she said.

Pilar was still asleep when my parents drove me to the train station the next morning.

"You know you don't have to leave," my mother said, turning around to face me in the backseat. "You could miss a day of school if you're still not feeling up to it."

I grabbed onto the Volvo's sturdy rectangular headrest and pulled myself up closer to her. "I have to get back. I have a lot of studying to do."

My father kept winking at me in the rearview mirror. He was so excited about my scholarship. I hesitated. If I didn't get out of Pilar's head, it was going to be very hard to study for ATAT. Impossible, maybe. I had texted Dr. Stanley Whitmeyer, but he hadn't answered. And truthfully, I didn't know if I wanted to get out today anyway. Pilar hadn't thought about Gid at all while she'd been in Los Angeles, but I wanted to see what happened when she did see him. I could get out as soon as I saw Pilar and Gid together, just to make sure there was nothing going on with them.

"The thing is," I said. "I don't know if Dad told you this, but I am getting this big scholarship. And it's going to be a lot of work. So I mean . . ."

Seconds later I had my mother's arms around my neck, and the Volvo headrest pressed up against my face. "Oh, my baby!" my mother said. "I'm so proud of you."

I inhaled flame-retardant Swedish vinyl and tried to think if there was some way to downplay my achievement.

But when my mother pulled away, the tears shining in her eyes let me know there was no turning back. "I don't even know why your father and I worry about you," my mother said. "You always take care of everything!"

chapter
eleven

My train ride was overnight, so I got back to Midvale in the
morning. It was an absolutely beautiful New England day, the
air was crisp and clean, the sky a pale blue deepening under a
slowly warming sun, and chickadees and robins bounced and
twittered in the tree branches.

Pilar was in the business-class section of a plane bound for
Boston, asleep, dreaming of Spanish singer Mala Rodríguez.
She'd seen her in a magazine article before she'd drifted off.
She'd stared at the photos of Mala for a long time, trying to ignore Madison, who, next to her, was sighing loudly and impor-
tantly over the script Elias Ganz had messengered to the airport
gate. Pilar was dreaming that she and Mala were shopping for
a present for Elias, and in the dream, Pilar was confused as to
why she should get him something, but also hoping that he
would really like it, and like her.

I did ATAT crap the entire time on the train. How could I not, after my mother's tearful vote of confidence in me?

The dorm was dead quiet. People would be streaming in all day, but I was one of the first. As soon as I opened the door of my room, the smell of Gideon Rayburn hit me like a gale force wind: his soap, his detergent, the slight toasty smell of his skin.

I left the door ajar and was cranking open the windows and just about to burst into tears—just a quick, cleansing burst of tears, from which I was going to emerge strong and refreshed—when I turned around and saw that Edie had come in. She wore a yellow cashmere sweater and a jean skirt and clogs, and carried a cute orange leather pocketbook.

She didn't look like a little girl. She looked like . . . well, not quite a hottie, but like the librarian who takes off her glasses to reveal her smoldering beauty. Even though she was still technically in glasses.

It took me a second longer than usual to respond because I had to think: what would I say right now if I were feeling normal? "Wow. You look . . . uh . . . pretty."

Was she wearing eyeliner?

"Thanks," Edie said. "Why are you opening the windows?"

It was still fairly cold outside.

"Because it smells like Gideon in here."

Edie sniffed, and when she lifted her head, I saw that she was not only wearing eyeliner, but mascara. "You're right," she said.

We unpacked in silence. I noticed that she took a new pair of black high-heeled boots out of her bag. Edie was a methodical person. She never did anything without a reason.

I so wished that we were the kind of friends right now where I could just ask her.

But I didn't want to be questioned, so I didn't question her.

When she got to her school stuff, and she took a giant pile of papers out of her knapsack. I could tell right away it was the ATAT stuff.

"Oh my God," I said. "That's the same crap you brought out to the car for me. When I left. You're doing ATAT too?"

Edie nodded. "I thought you weren't doing it. Mrs. Gwynne-Vaughan told me she didn't think you were going to do it."

I shook my head. "Oh no," I said. "I'm doing it for sure. I decided it probably won't be that bad."

Edie nodded. I could tell she didn't believe me. "I need the scholarship," I said. "I mean, I really need it."

It was nice to be able to confide something, even if it wasn't the big thing. Edie nodded understandingly. Her father was a dentist, so she wasn't annoyingly rich, but she didn't need the scholarship.

"Why are you doing ATAT?" I said.

Edie got a funny look on her face. "I don't know. I just want a challenge, I guess. Did you tell Mrs. Gywnne-Vaughan you changed your mind? She's going to be psyched."

I shook my head. "It's weird that she is so into this. I mean, who cares?"

"I know," Edie said. "She actually called me. In Seattle, over break. She told me she really wanted me to do it, and also, did I think you would. I told her I didn't know what you were going to do, that you hadn't mentioned it, but then I remember I'd given you that pile of stuff and I told her you took it home with you, and she was kind of psyched. It was weird how psyched she was."

"Hmm," I said. "Well, some people, when they get older they get obsessed with weird things. Maybe she just doesn't have anything else to do."

"Yeah," Edie said, "could be. Anyway. I kind of forgot to think about how weird she was being, because after I said I would do it, she started telling me all the shit we have to do when we get back . . ."

I felt a wave of exhaustion. "Don't tell me we have practice tonight."

Edie winced.

"Oh, Jesus. What do we have to do?"

"You don't have to do it," Edie said. "I do. I mean, me and Dan Dooras and Sergei Romanov . . . we have to convince Devon Shine, Mickey Eisenberg, and Nicholas Westerbeck to join ATAT."

What? This couldn't be right. Other than Cullen, those three were the guys at Midvale absolutely least likely to agree to joining something like ATAT. "Impossible," I said. "She's got to think of other people."

"Mrs. Gwynne-Vaughan said there are no other people. I mean, she knows the students really well. She says with this team, we have a chance of winning. But without even one of these people, she says there's no way. She says these seven people are basically the only really smart people in the whole school."

I opened my mouth and then shut it. Mrs. Gwynne-Vaughan was probably right about that. Sergei was just a crazy math and science genius. A rumor had circulated that Midvale paid *him* to go here. He actually did his own research—it was on lobsters but apparently it had ramifications for humans. Mickey Eisenberg knew the outcome and highlights of every single sporting match in history. Dan had a photographic memory and a creepy obsession with military history. Nicholas, Edie, and I just read constantly and, if I do say so myself, just kind of knew everything about everything. But Devon? Devon was one of Gid's friends. He was fat and lazy. If he was indeed intelligent, I'd never seen him apply it to anything other than video games, pot cultivation, and the crafting of cruel insults. "I didn't know Devon was smart."

"He's actually my suggestion," Edie said. "Remember he's from Seattle? I was in gifted and talented with him in elementary school. He has a 180 IQ. The same as John Stewart Mill."

Edie wasn't trying to be funny, but for some reason this really killed me. Devon was a pig who just happened to be an off-the-charts genius. I started to giggle and couldn't stop. Edie started to laugh too. "Picture Devon as one of those distinguished alumni on the wall in the Admin Hall," I said.

"Oh yeah," Edie agreed, "with a pipe in one hand, a joystick in the other, and a joint in his mouth."

But then reality hit me. I needed to win the scholarship. We needed to get those people on the team. And if a freak like Sergei and a loser like Dan, not to mention Edie—a girl—asked Mickey, Devon, and Nicholas to do anything, the answer was going to be three big fat no's.

"You have to let me help you," I said.

I saw Edie giving this some thought. I wasn't always the most reliable person lately.

"I . . . I know Nicholas really well," I said. My face burned with my secret. Edie's eyes flitted over my face.

"I . . . I think I know how we can get him to do it," I said. "But we have to get everyone else first."

"OK," Edie said, "Dan and Sergei are coming over to Emerson at two to talk strategy. So . . ."

And now, of course, Pilar's plane was landing, she was waking up. As soon as she turned on her cell phone, she had a text message from Gid.

We landed. U guys on time? Want a ride back?

Pilar turned to Madison. The plane was taxiing, and Madison had her eyes closed.

"Do we want to get a ride back from the boys?" she asked.

"Oh, God," Madison said. "I'm already nauseated from this, and now I'm going to have to watch you flirt with Gideon the whole time. Double nauseating."

"I'm not into him," Pilar said. "I mean, he is Gideon Rayburn."

Madison ignored this. "I'm happy to take the free ride. Write back to your boyfriend."

"I don't flirt with him," Pilar said.

"Whatever," Madison said. "Then you use him like a flirtation cat toy. He's like your little suede mousie."

"Wow," I said out loud. "That is so true."

"What?" Edie said. "That the boys are coming over at two?"

I had forgotten I was standing here, in my room. Edie looked at me expectantly, but I couldn't focus, because Pilar texted back:

We'll see you in baggage claim.

I thought I had a few more hours before Gid and Pilar would even see each other. And now they were going to be in a car—and I would bet money they'd be sitting next to each other—for a whole horrible hour. But I would have a good idea of what to expect. And then once I got a hold of Dr. Whitmeyer, I'd get Pilar out of my head.

"Molly?" Edie's voice was annoyed, impatient. "Do you want to help me or not?"

"Yes," I said, grabbing a jacket, hat, and gloves. "I'm . . . I'm going to go for a walk, and I will be back at two. We're going to figure this out."

I ran down the hall. Poor Edie. I thought we'd come together a little bit in the last few minutes. I'd ruined it. Pilar had ruined it. Why couldn't she just leave my boyfriend alone once and for all?

The woods were cold and dead quiet. There were trails that snaked through a large swath of woods between the campus and the train tracks, and I walked around and around as I watched the first postkiss interaction between Pilar and Gid unfold.

Here's something I hadn't expected.

Pilar didn't even know my name.

So I like Gid and I flirt with him a little. What's the harm? He likes it. He isn't even going out with—what's her name? Monica? Mandy? Molly!—anymore. I hate baggage claim. Eet's so ugly in here. Why are the ceilings so low? We just got off a plane. Would it kill them to give us a nice high ceiling? And it's cold in here. At least a lot of people are looking at me. Everyone. The men, the women. The women look mad at me. It makes me feel bad and good at the same time. I have to just ignore everyone, be my own person. Her Louis Vuitton bag was coming up over the crest and dropping down to the baggage claim conveyor belt. Pilar ran around the other side of the belt to get it, but it was gone.

"My bag, my bag," she cried, giving looks of desperate appeal to any man in the baggage claim area who was not standing with another woman. Four or five stepped forward eagerly, ready to offer their services. "Someone took it," Pilar wailed.

She felt something heavy butting against the back of her leg. She turned around to see Gideon standing there, the weight of his duffle burdening one shoulder, her big Vuitton valise straining against his forearm.

"Hi," Gid said. I was prepared for thinking he looked good, better than he might have looked if we weren't broken up, and the fear turned out to be a reasonable one. He was tan and very slim. He had to have put himself on some sort of Nicholas-driven self-improvement kick. He'd gotten a haircut. He'd had something weird going on with his hair where it was cut superstraight across the back and looked like a cat's hair looks against its collar, but that had been mended.

Gid said, "Do you remember the first time we met? I carried your bag."

Pilar touched her big silver hoop earrings. She watched as all her eager-beaver helpers slunk away. "I don't know eef I remember," she said.

I could tell Gid felt awkward, the way he kept moving from one foot to the other. "It's OK," he said. He added, "You're so tan."

"Thanks," Pilar said. *He does look good. Better than usual. But I am not going to flirt with him. I am not going to give Madison the satisfaction.*

"I saw a shark," Gideon said.

"I have seen many sharks," said Pilar. *There is something*

about his face that I wish I could change. I don't know what it is. If it changed I might flirt with him for real and not like Madison said.

"This was a big shark. And it swam right by me."

"You know," Pilar said, "sometimes a shark could be magnified by the water and it ees not as big as it looks."

Gid scowled at her, and he looked cute when he scowled, because he was having fun. "Pilar," he said. "Seriously. You can be as cool as you want. If you swam by a shark, I swear to God, you would shit yourself."

Pilar burst out laughing and, at the same time, thought to herself, *I like the way he looks right now. If he looked that way all the time, I could like him.*

Madison had been lagging behind, buying eye cream at the duty-free. Now she walked by as Pilar giggled. She whispered, "How's your little toy velvet mousie?" Pilar stopped laughing abruptly, clamping her hand over her mouth.

"Oh, Geedeon," she said, laying her hand on his arm. "Well. Madison says I flirt with you, but I don't so much, really, do I?"

This question was, of course, the very definition of what Madison was talking about.

"I don't know. Keep doing what you're doing and I'll let you know."

Hmm. OK, he looks kind of cute right now.

Cullen sat on a SuperShuttle waiting bench, Madison astride him, smoking a cigarette. They were cousins, and used this relationship to shock people with inappropriate sexual behavior. Pilar could hear snatches of her conversation: Elias, totally amazing, so creative, such an amazing experience.

Nicholas pulled up in the car, and they all lined up at the trunk to put their stuff in. Madison's bag was tiny, and Cullen and Gid didn't have much, but between Nicholas's scuba stuff and Pilar's bag, the trunk wouldn't close. "It's Pilar's bag," Madison said. "I told you not to bring such a giant bag."

Nicholas got out of the car and studied the problem. "We need something strong to tie it all down," he said.

"What about my dick?" Cullen suggested.

"I think a bungee cord will do—plus, it's wider." Nicholas found one under the spare tire and managed to pull the trunk at least semi-closed. "All right," he said. "Let's roll."

They all folded themselves into the car, Madison and Nicholas up front, Gid and Cullen and Pilar in back. Gid was in the middle. The car smelled of leather and marijuana. It was raining out and warm, and the car didn't fit five people all that well. Nicolas put on BBC America. It was a program about fish farming in Southeast Asia. "Give me a break, like you like this shit," Cullen said.

"He does like it," Gideon said.

"He's just trying to pretend to be intellectual," Cullen said. "I'm sure all he thinks about is pussy. That's all anyone thinks about." He looked at Gid. "Am I right?"

Gid reddened and said, "No. I think about other stuff."

"Ha. There's an answer from someone who definitely only thinks about pussy."

Pilar adjusted herself as if she were trying to get more room, but when she found herself a little too far away from Gideon, she shifted just a tiny bit into him. *Madison can't see me, and it feels kind of nice.*

"Everyone needs to stop breathing so much," Nicholas muttered, cranking up the defrost.

"Dude, I am sorry, but I need all the oxygen I can get," Cullen said. "I've had my face buried in sandy muff all week."

Everyone groaned.

"Why are you esso deesgusting?" Pilar asked.

Madison turned around and gave Pilar an amused look. "Hmm," she said. "You think he's 'deesgusting'?"

Madison turned back around. Cullen had a joint going, and Madison took a puff on it and cracked the window to blow out the smoke.

"What's that supposed to mean?" Pilar said. Pilar tried to see Madison's face, but they were going through a dark patch of highway. Then they drew near an exit, and Madison's face was suddenly illuminated, and what Pilar saw on it was cruel delight.

Madison took another puff on the joint. "Nothing," she said.

Cullen sat up in his seat. "Well, well, well, ladies," he said, rubbing his hands together in eager anticipation of a fight. "Let's not end this conversation before it gets started."

Madison was suddenly prim and reserved. "I think this is a private conversation between me and Pilar," she said.

"You're the one who started it," Pilar said. "So let's hear it." She sounded confident, but she was terrified.

Madison put down her book. "All right," she said. "Yeah, I know Elias hit on you. But you totally present yourself to everyone that way, so . . ."

"What way?" Pilar demanded.

"Please," Madison said. "Let's think about that night. You get there. You sit right next to him, you are all over him, and—"

"But, I was just trying to . . ." Pilar was truly confused. "I was just trying to get the job. I was just being flirtatious."

"There's a fine line between flirtatious and ho-bag." Madison said. "And you were solidly in ho-bag territory. OK, *ho-bag* is a strong word. All I'm saying is, if you act like a dumb hottie, that's what you're going to get treated like."

Everything went silent in the car.

I thought Pilar was going to throw up. *Yell at her,* she told herself. *Tell Madison to fuck off. But maybe everyone does think I am a dumb hottie.*

Madison continued. "You're like Paris Hilton, except no one knows who you are."

"Hey," Gid said, turning to Pilar. "Weren't you on a gossip page once called *People Are Talking About?*"

Madison said sneeringly, "She was just standing *next* to people people were talking about. No one was talking about *her.*"

Pilar blinked back tears. *Not in front of her.* She managed to keep from crying, but after a few minutes, she couldn't help it. She sniffled.

"Holy shit," Cullen said. "This is kind of harsh."

"Well, what the fuck did you think was going to happen?" Gideon said. "You started it."

It was quiet now. Nicholas turned the radio back on. Cullen tugged Madison's hair and soon was trying to grab her boobs, and she was giggling and trying to act like she was stopping him. "Are you OK?" Gid said to Pilar.

She swallowed really hard. *Even now, as I talk to him, I'm thinking about how dark and liquid and pretty my eyes look. There's something wrong with that. There's got to be something wrong with thinking about what you look like all the time, and always trying to get someone to respond to it.*

She whispered, "Later."

"OK," Gid said. He inched away from her, and she didn't inch back.

All things considered, it couldn't have gone any better. Pilar fell asleep and had a dream about walking in a forest of quilted summer sandals, and I ran off to attend to that pesky little thing called my life.

chapter
twelve

I burst into the Emerson common room at five minutes after two. It was a drafty, rectangular room with dumpy plaid furniture, scratched-up tables, and long windows covered with dusty velvet drapes. Ansel Adams prints proved someone had pretended to decorate.

Sergei and Dan were sitting on opposite ends of the couch, each looking sour in his own special way. Sergei was black-haired, medium height, and so thin that in some desperate refugee moment, back in the Ukraine, his parents had surely contemplated folding him up and putting him in a suitcase. I think he wore his mother's hand-me-down jeans, and I wondered why no one had explained to him yet that, now that he lived in the United States, he couldn't wear such ugly pants.

Dan had a pasty face and lifeless medium brown hair. He was always wearing a black fleece pullover, and the shoulders were white with dandruff. Negativity and bitterness poured from him like lava from a volcano. The absolute only reason I could think of why his parents would send him to a snotty prep school was that they hated him.

Edie sat in a chair near the fireplace. "You're late," she said.

I wasn't very late. I knew that she meant that I was just late in general. That I hadn't been around, that I didn't seem very trustworthy, unless you were perhaps relying on the fact that I would, without explanation, just take off again.

"I'm very, very sorry," I said. "But I swear I am not going anywhere until we get this done." And I really wasn't. It didn't seem like Pilar and Gideon were going to hook up today, if ever, so best to get down to business. "OK," I said, rubbing my hands together with enthusiasm. "What have we got here?"

"We've got nothing," Edie said. "They keep saying, 'Let's just ask them.' I keep saying that isn't going to work, and the three of us can't think of anything."

"You should just let us do it," Sergei growled. "Dan and I are the smartest kids in the whole school. And we were the only people left from the remaining ATAT team. They'll do it if we ask them."

Dan looked at Sergei and they both nodded confidently. Edie and I looked at each other. I know we were both thinking the same thing. That Devon, Mickey, and Nicholas barely even knew who Sergei and Dan were, and if they tried to talk to them, getting laughed at was about the best they could hope for.

"I think you're definitely right that we shouldn't all go at once," I said. "But I think that, really, Edie and I should talk to all of them."

A greasy strip of Sergei's dark hair fell across his forehead. Dan scratched his head and a fresh shower of dandruff fell from his shoulder onto the couch as he leaned to whisper in Sergei's ear. "Can we have a minute?" Sergei said.

"Sure," I said. I waited. I realized they were waiting for us to go into the hall.

"You want the minute, you go," Edie said before I could.

They pouted but they left.

"Whoa," I said to Edie. "That was pretty ballsy. I don't know what to make of you with the—"

Edie crossed her arms over her chest. "Molly, what's going on with you?"

As innocently as I could I said, "What do you mean?"

She shook her head. "One minute you're in a terrible mood, and now, you're, like, all giddy."

I guess I was giddy. I was just glad Pilar didn't really seem to like Gid. She was in her room now, doing sit-ups.

"I don't know, Edie," I said. I was stalling. "There's really nothing wrong with me. I—"

"Look, Molly," Edie said. Her new clothes seemed to come with a slightly more forceful personality. "I'm not saying that you have to move out or that we can't do ATAT. But I just want you to know that, at this point, we're not really friends."

I started to protest but she held up her hand. "I'm not mad at you. But it's just that if you can't tell me what's been going on with you, basically for the last six months, well, I can't really be your friend. I can't pretend everything between us is normal."

I felt stupid for all those times we'd shared a tiny moment, like about Devon this morning, and I'd actually believed we could go back to being close. God, I wanted to just tell her. But

I couldn't. Maybe before, about Gid. But this Pilar shit was crazy. She wouldn't believe me, and then, not only would we not be friends anymore, she would think I was nuts.

What was I going to say? Fine? We're not friends, starting now? "I hope you change your mind," I said. Edie looked annoyed, and realizing that wasn't the point, I rushed to correct myself. "I mean, I hope things change between us, and . . ." I didn't want to say I'm sorry, because it would make it seem as if I had rejected her and she was merely responding to that. "This isn't how it's going to be forever," I said.

It was vague, but it was the only thing I could say that felt kind of true, and I was pleased when she didn't frown. She didn't smile either.

I think we were both relieved when Dan and Sergei came back into the room, walking side by side. They were grimfaced, trying to look tough. "We'll do it your way," Dan said.

"But you better be right," Sergei added.

They stood there a few more seconds. And then they left. We watched them walk across the quad together, talking excitedly.

"So. Mickey first? Then Devon?" I asked. "And then, for the grand finale, Nicholas?"

"OK," Edie agreed. "This is going to be a challenge."

"No," I said, "climbing the Matterhorn is a challenge. This is going to be a nightmare. And one that . . . one that I would like to begin alone."

Edie looked at me apprehensively.

"Let me get Mickey by myself. We can both talk to Devon and Nicholas," I said.

Now she looked at me with suspicion. "Are you doing something . . . like . . . weird?" she said.

"Trust me," I said.

It was the wrong thing to say, since she had just told me she fundamentally didn't trust me.

"Trust me for now," I said.

Mickey was the campus drug dealer. Well, along with Gid and Cullen and Nicholas, who grew pot occasionally, he was. He was really short and arrogant. He was smart and he knew it. He wasn't mean, but there was something about his total self-satisfaction that made him seem mean.

But for a drug dealer he didn't drive a very hard bargain.

"Absolutely," he said. "I see PBJ muff and I will not only join, I will never even complain, not once."

In exchange for joining ATAT, I'd promised he could see Pilar Benitez-Jones, naked. I'd expected him to ask me how many times, but apparently once was enough, because within minutes, we were out the door. "We have to hurry," I said. We were in the common room of Gid's dorm, Proctor.

"I don't even need a coat," Mickey said. "Let's go." As soon as we were out the door, a window on the second floor of Proctor opened and someone shouted, "Eisenberg! You midget douche!"

Mickey didn't break stride. He turned around and walked backward shouting, "Oh, yeah, you know what, if you were me right now, you would absolutely shit yourself." Turning to me, he said, "I can't believe how hot Pilar is. It's like, you can't decide whether to look at her face or her body. You just can't de-cide!" He let out a delighted laugh and looked at me admir-ingly. "Did your boobs get bigger?"

"I think I just lost weight," I said. "They just look bigger by comparison. I can't believe you could wrest your eyes away from my face to look at them."

He laughed hard, as if this were very funny. Then he said, "Well, you're getting that tits-on-a-stick look, and it's nothing to sneeze at," he said. Then he whistled. "But that Pilar Benitez-Jones, I mean, you're a pretty girl, but she is, like, I mean, just thinking about her makes me want to like, shoot . . ."

Mickey shut his mouth when he saw my withering stare. "Mickey, I am plenty aware that Pilar far outshines my tepid girlish charms. That's why I'm bribing you with this. Now shut up."

It was dark now, and we tiptoed up the Emerson fire escape. Mickey whispered, "Oh boy, oh boy, oh boy." We were timing it perfectly. Pilar had just finished working out, and when we got to the top landing, Pilar was just removing the first of her smooth, muscled golden legs from her cotton and spandex pants. "You have to lean over that railing," I said. "Her window is right there. I'll wait for you here."

I sat down on the bottom stair of the landing. Our room, and pretty much every room at Midvale, looked like some forgotten corner of Staples, but Pilar's room had been *decorated*. It wasn't like she was just some idiot rich girl who had a pink room. Her room was kind of tasteful, and amazing. It was painted a deep blue and had a four-poster vintage iron bed, and a small love seat tucked into the window. One thing it did not have was curtains. In a few seconds I heard Mickey whispering, "Holy shit. Look at her boobs. Oh my God. I have jerk-off material for months, even if she stops here. What's the fucking deal with her not taking off her underwear! Shit. Oh my God. Turn around. Turn around, turn around. Oh my God. I saw it. I saw it."

The whole thing lasted about ten seconds. Mickey came and sat next to me. His face shone in the moonlight. "I saw Pilar Benitez-Jones's beaver," he said. "You know what's weird though?"

"Let me guess. She is so hot you couldn't even properly stare at it."

Mickey looked amazed that I understood this. "That's exactly right," he said. "God. I could die now, and I would be happy."

I pulled him up. We had to get out of there. "You can't die now. You have to do ATAT."

Mickey smiled. "I told you, I see what I want, you don't hear a peep from me. I am your loyal servant. How did you know she'd be naked? I mean, as I said, it's not the first time I've looked in that window."

"I can read her mind," I said spookily.

I knew Mickey wouldn't believe me, but he liked that idea. "Freaky lesbian witch stuff," he said. "Hot."

"If I show you her naked one more time," I said, "like, maybe next week, will you do one more thing for me?"

"To see her naked again," he said. "I would have my rectum removed."

"Are you serious?" I said.

"One hundred percent," Mickey said. "Do you know that she is the only girl in the school every single guy thinks is hot? Most girls encourage at least some lively debate. But mention Pilar, and everyone just sort of starts to get, well, kind of upset."

"Thanks, you can stop there, Mickey. Anyway. I want Devon to be on ATAT. And I'm going to text you in a little while. And when I do, you call him and tell him that as long as he's on ATAT, he gets free Ecstasy. Deal?"

"Deal." Mickey ran back to his dorm for his hotly anticipated alone time with his hand and memories of Pilar's spec-
tacular nudity. I made my way toward my room. It was dark,
and we had to go get Devon, and get him to say he'd be on
ATAT before dinner, or else my plan wasn't going to work
with Nicholas. Pilar was quiet enough for me to tune her out,
and she wasn't thinking about Gid, but I listened to her anyway.

*I remember back when I was a little girl and I was smart. I was
smarter than Madison. Way smarter. And then I got pretty and I
didn't care anymore. And now I forgot how to care. And I care. I can't
believe I didn't get that job. I'm such an eediot.*

Poor Pilar. I never thought I'd say that. Yes, I was jealous of
her. But I also felt increasingly that it must be hard to be Pilar.
How were you supposed to not be a dumb hottie if everyone
thought you were so hot? Maybe she *was* actually really smart,
but she just didn't bother trying because no one cared.

Shit. I'd promised Mickey he could see her naked again.
Well, I'd show him tomorrow. Then I would get out of her
head.

*I must be still smart. If I weren't smart, I wouldn't be able to
dress so well. That's a kind of smart, right?*

She grabbed a pad and pen on her nightstand. Her pad
was from the New York Sherry-Netherland, not the Buffalo
Marriott. She wrote: *Every day: Meditate five minutes on how to
have a smarter mind.*

*Wait. My pants feel kind of tight. Wait. How am I going to do this
eef I feel fat? I mean, every time I feel my stomach, I have to think
about it and how it ees fat. I want to be smart, but I can't be smart
until my mind can think about something other than my stomach.*

I should probably get a flat stomach first. But I can't meditate on just that. It's, like, too shallow. And since I am not going to see Madison that much since she is mad at me, I need to always see someone else whose stomach makes me jealous.

Pilar opened up her laptop, went on iTunes, and downloaded a Mala Rodríguez video. She watched it, her eyes riveted to Mala's stomach.

Then she ripped up the note on the Sherry-Netherland stationery and on a new one wrote: *First my stomach, then my mind. Five minutes watching video to motivate flat stomach. When stomach is flat, switch to meditating just about my mind.*

Then her phone rang.

It was Gideon.

"Hey," he said. "I just called to tell you that Madison Sprague is a bitch. You shouldn't worry about what she said today."

"I know," Pilar said. "But seriously . . . I am going to undergo a self-transformation."

"OK," Gid said amiably. "Starting when?"

Pilar thought about what Madison had said earlier, about how she flirted with Gideon for practice on other people. She squeezed her eyes shut against the shame. This was true! She couldn't deny she had been pressed up against Gideon the whole trip, just for the attention. Just because she knew he liked her. But then she had backed away. And even though she liked his calling her now, liked having someone call, she really had to think about herself.

Pilar said, "Starting now. Good night."

She hung up in the middle of his good night.

It was a good night indeed.

• • •

Edie was sitting on her bed reading *Angels & Insects* when I came back. "I got Mickey," I said.

She put a bookmark in her book. "How?" she said.

"I just asked him. He said no at first, but I told him there would be hot girls there, and . . ." My voice trailed off.

I saw her trying to decide whether she was going to tell me she didn't believe me. She finally sighed and stood up. "Do you want me to go with you to talk to Devon?" she asked.

"Yes, absolutely," I said. "Please, I could use the help."

She gave me another look to let me know she knew I was just being patronizing, that I didn't need her help at all. But she came with me anyway.

I was pretty sure we would find Devon in the Proctor rec room, playing video poker with his best friend, Liam, and I was right. Devon wasn't so bad. A fat guy who wears barrettes couldn't be altogether hateful. But I disliked his best friend, Liam Wu, intensely. He was good-looking and soulless, the embodiment of everything about Midvale, and in fact life in general, that sucked.

"We should get another hobby," Liam said as one game ended and they began another.

"We should. Problem is, there's not that much you can do stoned that makes you feel smart," said Devon.

"Hmm," Liam said. "Good point."

"You see?" Devon said. "That wasn't a good point at all. But it seems like one, because we're stoned, and we're playing video poker."

When the game ended I cleared my throat and Liam

whipped around. "Whoa," he said, jumping up. "How long have you guys been there?

"Long enough to hear you guys acting like retards," I said. "Devon, we're here to see you." Liam scowled at me and reset the game to play alone.

Devon got up off the couch, hiking up his pants. Devon was a good thirty pounds overweight, wore barrettes to keep his greasy red hair out of his sort of bulging eyes, and he had a faint odor that wasn't totally pleasant. That said, he was a self-proclaimed pussy magnet. His eyes lit up when he got a load of Edie and her new look.

"Well, hello," he said. His pants were crooked, and he straightened them out. A tight blue T-shirt was riding up the hunk of fat that hung over his waistband. He had once told Gideon—Gideon didn't know I knew this—that wearing tight clothes was all part of his game. "Chicks respect the balls it takes for me to think I am hot," he had explained to Gid. "Without the fat, I would just be your average douche . . . like . . . well, like you."

"Go ahead," I whispered to Edie.

"So, what we're looking for, uh," she began. I could tell she was flustered from Devon's attention. His green eyes skipped between her chest and her face. "We're looking for someone to be on ATAT because—"

"Who else is on it?" he said.

"Molly, me, and Mickey Eisenberg. And people you don't know." That was Sergei and Dan.

"Really?" Devon said. He leaned against the back of the couch, clearly flattered.

"Get your fat ass off my neck," Liam growled.

Devon moved a little bit to the left. "So," he said. "You're on it too, right?

"Right," Edie said.

"Do you think I'm smart?" He gave her a penetrating stare.

Edie looked scared. "Uh, it's not me who chooses. It's Mrs. Gwynne-Vaughan."

"So you don't think I'm smart? Remember when we were in elementary school together?" He shifted on the couch again, and once again his butt came close to Liam's head. Liam turned around and punched him.

"Ow," Devon said. He shook his head at me and Edie. "Do you believe he just punched me in the anus?"

"Yes," Edie said. "I do. Uh . . . not about believing that he punched you in the anus part. But yes, I believe you're smart."

Devon stared at her a long time. "Admit it, when you saw my name on the list you were, like, oh, that kid I went to elementary school with? Who used to eat his boogers? He's not smart," he said.

"I don't think you're not smart," Edie insisted. "I didn't think anything. I don't remember you eating your . . . your . . ."

Edie was flustered.

Devon's phone beeped. "Pardon me for a moment, will you?" he said to Edie, as if he were actually polite. He checked his phone. "Shit. Mickey Eisenberg said he'd give me free Ecstasy all semester if I do ATAT with him." He smiled. "Fuck off," he said aloud as he typed the same into his phone. "Send," he said, winking at Edie.

We all waited a sec. The phone beeped again.

"Free everything," Devon read out loud. "Awesome. So. What is this? Like, a match every weekend?"

Edie nodded. "And lots of practices."

I thought that might make Devon change his mind. "Whatever," he said. "Clearly, I'm going to be so high, it's not going to matter."

"So you're going to do it?" Edie said.

"Yeah," he said. "Why not?" Then he whispered, "Watch this." He jumped up into the air, landed on Liam's lap, and let out a thunderous fart. Liam struggled to get out from under him, but his friend outweighed him by a good fifty pounds, and he was reduced to futile squealing and flailing limbs. "You love it!" Devon shouted. "You love it!" He called after us. "Hey! Hey! I was going to do it anyway, but don't tell Eisenberg. I want him to think he's doing something useful with his drugs!"

We opened the door of Proctor, and I found myself face to face with Gideon, Cullen, and Nicholas. Cullen and Nicholas tucked their heads to the ground and just kept walking, but Gideon and I locked eyes immediately. It was terrible to look at his face. When I didn't see him I could kind of pretend he didn't exist. But to look at his face, his beautiful face, and feel all that terrible, useless want. After an awkward second, Edie proceeded out the door, Gid and I just stood there, staring at each other, until finally he said, "Hi, how . . . how was Buffalo?"

I said it was fine. God, it was weird not being able to tell what he was thinking. Was that sheepish look on his face because he wanted to run away, or because he was afraid I would, or . . .

"Did you have a good time?"

"What kind of a question is that?"

That just popped out of my mouth.

Gid looked confused. "Molly, if I did something wrong, I mean, can't we talk about it?"

"Something wrong," I repeated. "You didn't do something wrong. But there was something wrong with us."

Gid stepped inside and into the corner. When he saw that we were alone, he said, "What? What was it? Tell me, and I'll fix it."

He looked so sincere, and sad. But I shook my head. "You can't fix it. It's too bad, but you can't."

"But . . . but," Gid sputtered. "Why can't you just tell me?"

This was a good question, but I had an answer. "If you can't fix it, what's the point?"

I left the dorm. I knew he was looking at me as I walked away, because the door never shut. He must have just been standing in it, watching me walk back to my dorm. It took all my will to not turn around, and I realized that, to get over him, that's all I had to do. I just had to keep not turning around. I would try to see him as little as possible, and if I thought of him, I would tell myself to think of something else.

He would have to go away eventually.

Unfortunately, my whole avoid-Gid plan would have to go into effect after the next morning because my ATAT/Nicholas plan inadvertently involved him.

"Explain this to me again," Edie said. She was even dressed kind of sexy for bed. She used to wear just sweats and old, long T-shirts, but she'd bought a few of those little sleeping outfits, little tanks and little shorts.

"Hey," I teased. "Did you read one of those women's magazine article about how wearing sexy clothes at night makes you feel cute during the day?"

Edie looked kind of serious. "Molly, I don't want to be a bitch, but I kind of meant what I said."

I felt really stupid.

"Let's restrict this conversation to ATAT, OK?"

What could I say to that? Luckily she started the conversation again.

"So. Nicholas. You want us to just show up and work out tomorrow? At the track?"

I nodded. It was sort of a half-baked idea, but time was of the essence, and I didn't know another place I was sure to run into him.

"And we don't tell him about ATAT, but you think you know how to make him ask us about it? And even when he does, we don't tell him we want him to be on it?"

"That's right," I said.

Edie put her book down and turned out her light. "Well. You've gotten everyone so far, so I guess we'll go with your plan."

She didn't say good night.

I sat in bed that night, half studying, half waiting for Pilar to go to sleep. She had put on black silk pajamas, and she'd even found a pair of reading glasses that she wasn't going to wear out of the room, but would help her, she thought, feel like a serious person. She sat on her brocade sofa with a blue angora blanket around her bare ankles and read the novel they were reading in English, *Tess of the D'Urbervilles*. She got up to see what page they were supposed to be on: 125. She was on page five. *I'm hungry. I guess I will watch the video again.* She did and she felt better. She read five more pages and fell asleep, thinking of her new life as a serious person with glasses, a person who read before bed and woke up feeling thin, too. Her last thought: soon I will be perfect.

I thought, soon I will stop lying awake thinking about Gideon. It was my last thought too, but it went on a lot longer than hers.

chapter
thirteen

I got up really early and went to the bathroom and sat in the big window overlooking the campus. It was a cloudy day, and a layer of mist hung ghostly and white over the quad as I wrote Dr. Whitmeyer another text message.

> **Hello? Help!**
>> *So you're in this young woman's head. How extraordinary!*

"No!" I shouted. Enthusiasm was not what I wanted right now.

> **Tell me how to get out!!**
>> *You can't control this.*

This was alarming.

I have to get out. I have to.

A long silence. Then:

> *Remember to think about why. Why do you want to get out of that girl's head?*
>
> Because she's annoying. All she does is think about how pretty she is and then think it's bad to think she looks pretty and then, when she's not doing that, she thinks up ways to make herself prettier. It's like, get a life.
>
> *You should be thinking about what you have in common.*
>
> What? We have nothing in common.

Pilar was awake now and getting ready to work out. So what else was new? But she put on two bras. Two bras?

I hope I am alone at the track. I don't want anyone to see that I run like a duck. No one needs to know that.

Pilar was going running.

> Dr. Whitmeyer, I have to go. The girl . . . Well, it's an emergency.
>
> *Just keep trying to think about how you really feel.*

As if I could forget.

I ran back to the room. "We can't go," I said. "We can go tomorrow." I didn't want to be in the same place at the same time with both of them. But what if Pilar was running tomorrow too?

Edie was in workout clothes and tying a sweatshirt around her waist. "We're late," she said. "We have to go," she said. "Otherwise we're never going to get to talk to him. I mean, you are right. Every other part of the day, he's with Cullen and Liam and Devon and Gid. At least right now he's only with Gideon. Which, I guess sucks for you, but . . ."

"It's not that it sucks," I said. I was totally lying. "I just don't want Nicholas to think that I'm, like, insanely stalking Gid."

"Who cares what he—" But then Edie just shook her head impatiently. "I'll just go by myself," she said, leaving the room.

Our old roommate, Marcy Proctor, came out of her room in a towel as I was chasing after Edie, and I almost knocked her down. "Hey, Molly," she said. "How are you doing?" She had that fake-sympathy look that always means someone wants gossip.

"Fine, Marcy, how are you!" I said, not bothering to stop or slow down. I caught up with Edie on the stairs.

I stepped in front of her on the landing. She looked at me without any emotion. "I'm sorry," I said.

She made a noise of impatience. "Molly, I am sick of Gid. 'I have to see Gid. No, I won't see him. I have to see him. I can't see him.' If you are so freaked out, just go out with him again. You're the one who broke up with him!"

Two girls in junior squad lacrosse uniforms stepped around us, their eyes wide with their contained giggles. I waited until they scampered down the stairs. "It's complicated," I said.

"I'm sure it is," Edie said, "for a ten-year-old."

"Edie—" I hated the pleading tone in my voice, but I couldn't get rid of it. "If I could just explain to you what . . . I know you're mad, and—"

"Thank God you can't," she said. "I'm not mad. I am bored. This friendship bores me."

I wanted to burst into tears. But let's face it, nothing would be more boring than that.

"Let's just go," I said. "Let's just go down to the field and follow the plan."

Edie rolled her eyes at me.

"Give me a second," I said. Heading back to the room, I made a plan to recoup my dignity. We'd get this ATAT recruitment out of the way. I would get out of Pilar's head, and I would silently and with great fortitude white-knuckle my way through the months it took me to forget Gid. I would get my scholarship and this would be over. Somewhere along the way, I might develop a tolerable personality again, and Edie might regain her interest in being friends with me. This was all, of course, dependent on my not killing myself.

I had two jump ropes underneath my bed that I'd swiped the night before from the gym Cullen's dad had built with money earned by making diet cheesecake out of, essentially, air, olestra, and Splenda.

"We're just going to stand out in the middle of the track and jump rope and hope Nicholas talks to us?" Edie said.

"That's the plan," I said.

I was not looking forward to watching Gideon watch me, knowing he thought I was a crazy stalker.

It was a depressing morning. On a nice day, a prep school can charm you. The brick buildings look pretty against the blue sky, and the institutional neatness of it all seems reassuring. But today, the sky was gray, everything else was brown or yellow, and Midvale just looked like a jail. The train whistle sounded, lonely and stark, cutting through the screaming of a thousand crows. An icy wind blew in from the mountains, and the air smelled of pine needles and, as always, the cheap bread that went moldy so fast in the cafeteria. Edie and I crested a small hill, and down on the flat below, Gideon and Nicholas, in unison, moving with ease, and Pilar, clunky but determined, ran around the track. Running wasn't the most flattering activity for her. *Everyone now knows I run like a duck. Oh well. I guess that ees just the breaks of trying to have a flat stomach.*

I can't believe Dr. Whitmeyer wanted to know what I had in common with her.

As we came down the hill Gid saw me. His leg missed a beat, then another one. Nicholas's eyes flashed at me, and I could see the blue in them from this far away, and then his head shifted back to Gideon. He said something to him, and Gid looked away from me, then he looked back.

Edie and I began to jump rope in the middle of the field. I had selected this precisely because we would trip a lot and have to stop. I hadn't anticipated looking like such a fool.

"This is so stupid," I said to Édie. "Sorry."

"I just hope it works," Edie said. She didn't say, "It's OK," or "It's not stupid."

We jumped a few times, tripped, jumped, tripped, jumped.

"Maybe we should do some push-ups," Edie said.

We did some push-ups. The grass was wet and freezing. Edie did girl ones, and I struggled with regular.

I was embarrassed. But not as embarrassed as I'd be if I did girl push-ups.

Gid and Nicholas had just finished running and were bent over their feet, catching their breath. Gid looked up, his eyes narrowing with focused attention. He was watching Pilar run. He finished his stretch and muttered something to Nicholas. Nicholas made a sort of whatever-floats-your-boat gesture, and

Gid went to stretch over next to the bleachers, far away from us. But Nicholas was watching us, and then, strangely, he came over, looking uncharacteristically curious.

"OK," Edie said. "Good. Here he comes. Don't stop jumping. We need to look authentic."

"I am authentically about to pass out," I said. I don't know when I had ever had my attention pulled in so many directions. I wanted our plan with Nicholas to work out and I really, really didn't want Gideon to go talk to Pilar again. She thought about her plan: no stupid flirting just for attention. She wasn't going to give him anything. At least she wasn't placing too many demands on my consciousness at present. The more you hear *First my stomach, then my mind,* the easier it gets to tune it out.

Nicholas was a few feet away from us, surveying the ground. Finding a suitable place, he plopped down and stretched out his legs. He bent his head into his knee. He stayed that way for a long time. He finally looked up. He squinted at me, sizing me up. "You guys are in the worst shape," he said.

"Whoa," Edie said. "You said Cullen and Nicholas were dicks, but I didn't imagine they'd be this much of dicks."

This was a smart tactic on Edie's part. She was good at reading people, and Nicholas tended to enjoy girls who told him off, mostly, I guess, because they reminded him of boys.

Nicholas nodded. "You do know your muscles can atrophy, even when you're young? From lack of use?"

"Interesting," Edie said.

Then Nicholas's attention was on his hamstring for a long time. It seemed like he was done with us. I gave Edie a look: this isn't going to work, I'm sorry. She looked back at me: Do something.

Miraculously, Nicholas returned his attention to us. "It's kind of weird that you just randomly, like, decided to start working out this morning. I mean, you used to always complain about Gideon leaving your room to work out in the morning. And now you're working out."

This was such bullshit. I never ever used to complain about Gid getting up. He used to complain about it and sometimes sleep in. But I never said a thing. It made me furious that Gid would blame his being lazy on me, but I guess that's what guys do. Put all their own weaknesses onto their girlfriends.

"Oh well," I said. I was determined to be breezy. "I guess you won't have to worry about that anymore."

"Seriously," Nicholas said, "why are you guys working out?"

I couldn't even say it. It just sounded so stupid. But this was Edie's part of the plan.

"Well, we're working out because it's, like, supposed to make your brain quicker."

"So what are you guys doing? I mean, why do you want to be smarter?"

"Because we're doing ATAT," I said. "Mrs. Gwynne-Vaughan's making us be on it. It's just such a drag."

Nicholas suddenly jumped up and was frantically raking his hands through his hair. "Who did she pick to be on it?"

We'd hooked him.

We listed everyone who'd been picked for the team except him.

"I am smarter than all those guys," he said, his blue eyes blazing with indignation. "I mean, I can't even believe she didn't ask me. I wouldn't do it. I mean, just because I am not a total dork. I mean, come on. Devon?"

"He does know all about sports," Edie said. "There are all those sports questions."

We all walked up the hill together. I was muddy and exhausted, but also relieved.

Nicolas jabbed his thumb toward his chest emphatically. "I know about sports. I know about sports and I'm not stupid. Or fat. And I'm not going to be high at all the matches. You know that Devon's going to be high at all the matches, don't you? I know about sports and I am a person who knows when and when not to smoke pot." When Nicholas left us at our dorm, he was still mad. "See you guys later," he said. He shook his head. "Man. Just because I'm not a dork, I don't get any credit for being smart." He walked off.

Edie looked at me and shrugged.

"Is that it?" she said.

"For now," I replied. "That went very well."

She nodded and left me on the second-floor landing in our dorm, where a circular window looked out on the playing fields and the track. The sun was breaking through the mist. Pilar was on one end of the track, doing sit-ups, special, fancy, spa-friendly sit-ups, with her arms stretched behind her head and her legs hovering over the ground. And Gid was coming up the hill. Good. At least for today, it was over.

But then he turned around. He walked back to her, and she watched him coming toward her. *I wish he would leave me alone, but I also kind of like how he ees coming toward me, so serious. I feel like I am on TV.*

"Pilar," Gid said. "Look. I'm sorry I didn't really speak up for you yesterday. I should have said something to Mads."

"Forget it," she said, playing it cool.

Then her phone rang. It was her mother. Pilar's mother

was blond, and, as the Jones part of her last name suggested, very American. "Mother!" Pilar cried. "This call is so clear! I can't believe it!"

"Yes, well, that's because we're in Boston, darling. We're taking a boat to London tomorrow."

"Tomorrow? But we . . . we start classes today."

Pilar's mother had a wry, hurried way of speaking. "We'd love to have dinner tonight, but if you're busy, we will be back on the fourteenth of December, though we're coming into New York, and I'm not sure—"

"No no no no," Pilar said. "I can make that. Wait . . . you're going to be gone for six months?"

"Well, yes, I mean, first of all, there are so many different styles of cuisine in Italy, I mean, in Umbria alone . . . and with your father, of course, every time we get to a new place he has to wheeze and rant for a time before he can manage to get himself going. Oh, darling! I have to run! I am getting a private tour of the tapestry collection at the Isabella Stewart Gardner museum. They have this particular red thread on a tapestry, and I am trying to get dye matched for a piece in the house in Tigre. I want to see if the tapestry curator will give me a strand from the restoration spools. Fingers crossed! See you at 7:30, at the Fairmont. In the Oak Room. Oh . . . and please don't be late. They have an absolutely exquisite sorrel soup, but it does run out."

Then she was gone.

"Shit," Pilar said, snapping her phone closed. She looked at Gideon, a sudden desperation in her eyes. "Can you come with me to Boston tonight? Please?"

chapter
fourteen

The good news was that Nicholas had gone home, showered, and marched straight over to Mrs. Gwynne-Vaughan's office, where he had demanded to be on ATAT.

The other good news was that I wasn't really worried about Pilar and Gid's "date," if it even was one. I wasn't afraid that Gid was going to get some. It was obvious Pilar was just doing her suede mousie thing with him.

Gid would probably fuck it up himself.

But just in case he didn't, there had to be something I could do.

Meanwhile, we had our first ATAT practice. It was in a little room off the dining hall, a depressing, forgotten corner with vinyl paneling and old travel posters from the Italian Alps.

I had not planned on being in this room ever, for anything,

but I was going to be here every night for almost the rest of this year now.

ATAT practice worked like this: Everyone was assigned a partner and had a subject, like Kings, or Cooking Terms, or Inventors. You quizzed each other for twenty minutes, and then switched partners and subjects.

Nicholas and I had Classic Rock Quotes.

"Two lost souls . . . ," Nicholas began.

"Pink Floyd, duh," I said.

Nicholas pursed his lips and tapped his black Earth shoe against the floor. "Christ on the cross," he said.

We looked around the room. Devon and Edie were doing the Civil War. Dan Dooras and Mickey were next to us, quizzing each other on African capitals. They were taking a break and Dan approached us, his gaping fish mouth open. "Uh . . . I might as well explain this to both of you," he said, "while you're taking a break . . ."

"Ah, yes, but we're not taking a break." I could tell Nicholas was totally irritated at some guy who was a complete social pariah suggesting that he knew what Nicholas was or wasn't doing.

"Dust in the wind. Everything is dust in the wind."

Nicholas gave me a *duh* look.

"I have no idea," I said.

"Kansas!" he said. "I mean, did your parents not just play that album all the time? Shit. Mine did. It was how I knew they were getting divorced."

Dan opened his mouth, then closed it, then opened it again and said, "My parents only listened to Fleetwood Mac and the Eagles. We didn't have any conception that there was another band in the world besides the Eagles though, so we just called Fleetwood Mac the Lady Eagles."

"Weren't you supposed to tell us something?" Nicholas said.

"Oh, yeah." Dan patted his flat brown hair. "I used to be Dan D," he said. "But Dan Renton, Dan R, graduated. So now I am just Dan."

Nicholas gave me an elaborate eye roll to show me how much he was being tortured. Dan blinked. "OK," Nicholas said. "Thanks."

By the end of the practice it was pretty clear who was good at what: Nicholas knew history, I knew books, Edie knew both those things too but not as well as we did but she was a lot better at math, which was good because there was a three-person math challenge in every match. Dan knew a lot of obscure stuff, especially about sports and inventions. For example, he knew who Robert Fulton was, and afterward, during a break, I overheard him telling Mickey more about Robert Fulton, until Mickey finally said, "OK, Robert Fulton, American Treasure. I get it, dude."

Edie and I were together for the last round, and we had Fashion Terms.

"A framework to expand the fullness or support the drapery of a woman's dress," I said.

"Bustle," Edie answered quickly.

"A narrow neckband with wide, pointed wings," I said.

"Shit. Fuck. I don't know whether it's an ascot or a cravat."

I smiled enigmatically.

"Shit. Cravat."

"An excellent guess," I said, "but the cravat has a bow. All right. When folded in a decorative way and used to ornament a suit, a brightly patterned handkerchief may be called a . . . ?"

Edie wrinkled up her face in scorn. "Duh, pocket square," she said. "Those are so gay."

I gasped. I had my solution.

"Molly?" Edie said.

But I was already up and gunning for Mrs. Gwynne-Vaughan, who was sitting in a threadbare chintz chair in the corner of the room, correcting papers. "I have to leave early," I said. She didn't look up at first. She was writing a comment in caps, with her red pen: YES, BUT WHY?

She gave me a withering smile. "Molly," she said quietly, "you're the captain. It's a bad example if you leave early."

I nodded. "I know that. And I want you to know I wouldn't be leaving unless it were really important."

"Did someone die?" she asked, adjusting her glasses impatiently in a way that suggested she knew no one had died.

"No," I said. I looked up at the clock. It was ten of five. I didn't have a lot of time. "No one died."

She looked back at her papers. "I hope whatever you're doing is worthy of my letting you go," she said. "If it contributes to your peace of mind, perhaps it is a worthy intrusion on our practice."

"Thanks," I said. "Really, seriously, thanks."

She didn't look up and her expression didn't change at all. She wrote again in the margin: SHALLOW ARGUMENT.

Midvale wasn't exactly a bustling metropolis, but it did have a tiny old-fashioned department store called Maury's, right next to the train station. It was wood-paneled and smelled of dry cleaning, the rubber soles on cheap sneakers and, inexplicably, candy. Maury was a wiry old man in a bow tie, reading the

Arts and Culture section of *The Globe,* and he looked absolutely astonished to find me standing there.

"Young lady," he said. "How can I help you?"

I told him I needed pocket squares.

He got a faraway look in his rheumy eyes. "Pocket squares. Very popular with young men in the eighties. Meant, I think, to evoke a sort of aristocratic British club atmosphere, but screamingly middle-class."

I nodded and said, "Exactly."

He stood there and looked at me. "All right," he said.

"All right what?" I replied.

"I'm going to go in the back and look for them." He didn't move. Then he inhaled deeply through his nose, came out from behind the counter, and exhaled. He walked to the back, his black shoes heavy on the brown linoleum floor.

He came out a few minutes later with one draped over each hand. "Red or paisley?"

The paisley had a lavender background with yellow, red, and white accents.

"Oh, paisley," I said.

"Yes," he said. "It is the more distasteful." He shook his head and smiled. "It is amazing, isn't it, how a person can just ruin their appearance with just one unsightly accessory!"

I nodded. "Amazing, and fortunate."

He briefly explained how to sew the pocket square into a jacket. He then wrapped it in a layer of yellow tissue. I tucked it into my coat and smiled at him. "I'm going to do something sneaky with this," I said.

He had twinkling, co-conspirator's eyes. "Something so hideous can only be used for revenge."

I asked him if he was Maury, and he gave a wry little laugh. "Certainly not. Maury has no idea about these things."

The boys had always kept a spare key in the well of the fire extinguisher in the hallway, and it was still there when I went looking for it. I just walked into Gideon's dorm in broad daylight, like I belonged there.

Being in his room made me feel sick. Made my heart beat and my stomach fill with acid. But I didn't have time to think about how I felt. I had a job to do. Gid was going to look like a serious loser, and he wasn't even going to know it.

There were two closets, a big one and a little one, and the little one was Gid's.

You would think—I thought to myself, as, per the instructions of my friendly clerk from Maury's, I sewed the pocket square into the lining of Gideon's jacket—that a guy would notice if he suddenly had a pocket square on his jacket where there had before been none. But if I knew Gideon like I thought he did, he was going to throw this thing on at the last minute and not even look in the mirror.

I hung Gid's jacket back exactly as I had found it, with the hanger going the wrong way. I was about to leave when I thought I might take one other precaution. I hid Nicholas's and Cullen's jackets so Gideon wouldn't be tempted to wear them. I flipped through their clothes, moving some to the back of the closet. My foot hit something, and I looked down.

The whole back of the closet was lined with seedling trays.

They were growing pot again. Even though they'd gotten busted with it before. What a bunch of stupid assholes.

I wanted to throw the plants out. I was worried for Gid. But then I reminded myself he just wasn't my problem.

Well, as long as he didn't hook up with Pilar he wasn't.

chapter
fifteen

Pilar stood near the black iron Midvale gates. A quick thunderstorm had come and gone in twenty minutes, leaving the pavement dark, the grass and leaves greener, and the air cool and fresh. She'd made her way around the track again several times and done three different Pilates DVDs. She'd selected her dress carefully—a lavender bias-cut silk dress with red polka dots, and the cream-colored T-straps she got at Neiman Marcus last year. She'd watched her Mala Rodríguez video and felt thin.

As Gid approached she tried to sell herself on his cuteness. He had just shaved, and he was getting more and more to shave. His hair was the right amount of neat and tousled. He broke into a smile, and Pilar noticed the charming, extremely slight protrusion of his left incisor.

Then she saw the pocket square. She didn't even really know what it was. She just knew that Gid looked really fucking gay. As he got closer, she could see tiny stiff black threads along the visible seams. It was cheap. It was *polyester.*

Gid's face clouded. "Are you all right?"

A Town Car slowly circled one end of the quad, and Pilar flagged it. "I'm fine." *If I mention it, it will just be worse.*

They got into the car and she sat far away from him. "So, the Fairmont," Gid said, slapping his knees in happy anticipation. "It sounds pretty cool."

Pilar opened her window. The limo driver, who also had a pocket square, was wearing the worst cologne. She sniffed in fresh air. "It is badly in need of a renovation," she said.

She didn't say anything else for the rest of the trip. She just stared out the window, thinking, please don't let my mother ask if we are dating. Every once in a while, her eyes drifted over to the pocket square, and she thought about what a mistake she'd made inviting Gid.

The Town Car pulled up to the hotel in such a way that Pilar was closest to the entrance, and she hopped out and made for the door without much regard to Gideon.

"Hello?" he said. "Remember me?" He caught up to her and put a friendly hand on her shoulder. She didn't shake it off, but she wished he would take it away. A few seconds passed, and he did.

The inside of the hotel was red and gold and ornate, pink and green with gold accents. The drapes were gold. Old women with thin lips walked in pairs, clutching jeweled purses and, in some cases, each other. The staff wore black. They moved briskly and alone, and so smoothly that it seemed they were on wheels.

"Whoa," Gid said. He checked out the menu for the Oak

Room. "This place is pretty rad, right? I mean, I can see why you think it's a little gay, but I mean, a sandwich for twenty-five bucks? That's gotta be a hell of a sandwich."

Pilar was very nervous. More nervous than she'd ever been the whole time I'd been in her head. She turned and checked herself out in a circular mirror edged with carved gold sparrows. She sucked her stomach against her back and enjoyed the fact that she was sharing her reflection with a throng of people transfixed by the sudden and arresting arrival of such beauty, pointing bellboys, jealously glaring women at the reception desk, a concierge pretending to read a map for some guests but instead staring longingly at Pilar over the top of it.

Don't let her bother you, Pilar thought. *Don't let her, don't let her, don't let her. Remember. You're OK. If you weren't, all these people wouldn't be staring at you.*

Pilar's mother was coming toward them, taking tiny steps in a pair of high-heeled blue shoes with rhinestone buckles. Her suit was white. Blond hair, obviously but carefully dyed, framed a still young, very beautiful face, heart-shaped like Pilar's but paler, and with a smaller mouth. Her eyes were light and alert, and her stick-thin body seemed to vibrate with the anticipation of people saying and doing the wrong thing.

Pilar took in her thinness, staring at her mother's hips, which were so narrow that, looking at them head-on, you got the feeling you could just pinch her with your thumb and forefinger and lift her off the ground.

She saw her mother's eyes light on Gideon, then shift slowly downward.

If she asks him where he's from, she's noticed the pocket square.

"Darling." Mrs. Benitez-Jones leaned in toward Pilar and gave her a stiff embrace. Then she backed away and took in

Gideon. "You go to Midvale as well, yes?" She smoothed her skirt as she spoke, unconsciously, repetitively, as if trying to soothe herself.

"Yes," Gideon said. He stood up straight, as he always did when talking to adults. "I met you and your husband last fall at parents' weekend. We were over near the front of my dorm, and—"

Her eyes quivered in their sockets. "And where are you from, Gideon?"

I knew it.

"I'm from Fairfax, Virginia."

"Oh," said Mrs. Benitez-Jones. "Is that horse country?"

Gideon looked at Pilar.

"It's kind of prehorse country," Pilar said encouragingly.

"I'm sure I've seen a horse or two," Gid said. "Here or there."

There was an awkward silence.

"You always see a horse somewhere," Gid went on. "That's what my dad always says anyway, 'Hey son, let's drive around until we see a horse,' and I say, 'OK, Dad, let's!' "

Mrs. Benitez-Jones, after turning away from Gideon in annoyed confusion, surveyed Pilar intently. She began at her feet, making a little hum of approval at her shoes. "Those T-straps are very slimming to your ankles." Her eyes moved up. "The perfect length on that skirt. Things are coming out a little longer this year, and of course, that's good for you, with your thighs."

Gideon giggled.

Pilar braced herself as her mother continued up her body all the way up to her neck.

Hold still. It will be over soon.

"Well, Pilar," Mrs. Benitez-Jones said, "I would advise a salad."

With Mrs. Benitez-Jones leading the way, they moved past the gold mirrors into the Oak Room.

Whew. That could have been a lot worse.

Like how? Like if her mother brought in a scale and calipers and weighed and measured her in the lobby?

Gid tried to touch Pilar's elbow. "Are you all right?" he said.

"Yes," she said, "I'm fine."

But I knew how Pilar got a tight, achy feeling in the bottom of her chest when she was upset. And she was not fine. But as they approached the table and Pilar saw her father, she put on a big smile.

Pilar's dad was like eight hundred years old, and he looked like a turtle. He barely stood up when Pilar came over to the table in the middle of the dining room. He made a noise in his throat, which I guess was sort of in Spanish. "Bleeenn," he said, and pressed his cheek against Pilar's. He squeezed his eyes. "*Amor*," he said, visibly exerted.

"How are you, Daddy?" Pilar said in Spanish.

Mr. Benitez-Jones just pointed at Gideon. It was actually less like he pointed and more like his hand just drifted up in the air, as if he were a ghost.

"Alejandro!" Mrs. Benitez-Jones shouted. "This is Grayman."

"It's Gideon," Pilar corrected her.

They sat down. "Well! This place has a certain passé charm, *n'est-ce pas?*" Mrs. Benitez-Jones said. "Where do your parents stay when they come up to visit?"

Gid laughed. "Uh, sometimes my dad stays at the Super 8. But not the one in Natick. That's a shithole. The one in Weymouth is gorgeous!"

Pilar pressed her flattering T-strap against Gid's foot, and he leaned toward her. "My mother doesn't understand the sarcasm," she muttered.

"I can see that," Gid said. "I was just trying to give her a little crash course. I think she's enjoying it, don't you?"

Mrs. Benitez-Jones did not seem to be enjoying herself at all. She tapped a pink nail on the table, and her paper-thin nostrils flared.

I don't know why boys don't know how stupeed they are when they do the exact thing you're complaining about.

I agreed with Pilar on this. I was also pleased to notice that, although my pocket square had had its desired effect, Gid's own cluelessness wasn't exactly working in his favor either.

At least he ees a distraction. That's all I expected.

Preceded by the overpowering scent of cologne, a waiter materialized between Mr. and Mrs. Benitez-Jones. He was short with gelled spikes in his hair and looked like a gay porcupine. "Have you dined with us before?" he asked.

"What kind of a ridiculous question is that?" Mrs. Benitez-Jones asked.

The waiter turned pale. "All right then. May I get you a drink?"

Mr. Benitez-Jones raised his ghost arm and groaned.

"One for me as well," Mrs. Benitez-Jones said. "See that it's here before I return from the women's lounge." She put three syllables into the word *lounge*. Then she gave them all a dark look before she spun around and stalked off.

The waiter stepped around the table toward Gid and Pilar. "I didn't get that," he said apologetically.

"They want gin on the rocks," Pilar said. "Make them doubles, but use the small glasses."

The waiter left. Gid watched him. Then he stood up and ran after him.

I shouldn't have brought Gideon. He ees out of his element. I can't really blame him. I mean, eef I went to a pancake breakfast in Fairfax, I would hardly know what to do, other than to not eat pancakes. Pilar turned to her father, forcing a smile. "How are you, Daddy?" she said.

With a gnarled hand, he shifted his cane from one side of his chair to the other. "Pilar," he said. *"Al final, estoy feliz!"*

I wonder eef he means he is happy to finally see me or to finally have pretty much checked out of life.

Gid came back, rubbing his hands together. "I just got us drinks," he whispered to Pilar.

Pilar's mother was coming back from the bathroom. She eased herself into her chair and spread her napkin on her lap.

The waiter came, bearing four drinks. He set down Mrs. Benitez-Jones's drink first, and, with her first indelicate act of the day, she set it to her lips and slurped. Mr. Benitez-Jones took some time getting his drink to his mouth, and when it did arrive, it seemed he was unclear as to whether he should tip his head back or tilt his hand up. He did both, and in an instant, drained the glass. "Keep 'em coming," Mrs. Benitez-Jones said. "I'll order for us. My daughter and I will have the endive salad, dressing on the side. Her friend and my husband will have the steak."

"Very well," said the waiter. In front of Pilar and Gideon he set down two large glasses that looked like Coke. Pilar took a sip and was relieved to find it tasted strongly of liquor.

"Delicious," she whispered.

"I hope that's Diet," her mother said.

"Oh, it is," Gid said. He smiled at her. Pilar tasted it again.

Gid wasn't kidding. She was touched that Gid had known to
get her Diet. Most guys wouldn't have remembered.

"Thank you," she said. "You're really sweet." *I shouldn't be so
hard on heem about the pocket square. He's sweet. What would eet
be like to be with someone so sweet?*

I hated, hated, hated that Gid had remembered to get her
Diet. It was such a boyfriendy gesture.

Mrs. Benitez-Jones didn't seem any more thrilled with the
idea of Gid's being her daughter's boyfriend than I was. She drank
her gin like she was Lance Armstrong and it was steroids. Then
sat back in her chair and with her straw poked angrily at the ice
cubes. She took a sip and cocked her head to one side.

"So, when do you start your job with the movie studio?"

Pilar shook her head. "I don't," she said. *Here we go.*

Mrs. Benitez-Jones shuddered. "What? I don't understand."

"It's just that . . ." Pilar gave Gideon a pleading look. "Madison got it."

Mrs. Benitez-Jones held onto the table and inhaled for
about forty seconds.

"It's all right," Pilar said quickly. "I mean, I . . ."

Her mother finally exhaled and folded her hands in front
of her. "Madison? That doesn't make any sense. She is not anywhere near as attractive as you are. How could she possibly
have . . . have taken such a thing away from you?"

"Well," Pilar said carefully. She looked at Gid, who had put
his Coke to his mouth and was drinking as fast as he could.
"I . . . I think actually I tried a leetle too hard."

Gid burst out laughing and spit a little of his Coke onto the
tablecloth.

"Whoo," he said. "Sorry!"

The waiter appeared with a sponge. He dabbed at the

spot. "How is your Coca-Cola, sir?" he said, giving Gid a sly look.

"Absolutely amazing," Gid said.

"Why were you just laughing?" Pilar demanded. *Madison probably told him all about that night. How embarrassing.*

"I don't know," Gid said. "I guess it's just cute, the idea of you trying too hard. I just got an image of that, and it seemed funny."

That's cute. Oh. Wow. I think that's really cute.

Oh, great.

But Mrs. Benitez-Jones didn't think it was funny at all. "What ever does that mean, Pilar? Trying too hard . . . I just can't believe that Madison, of all people—"

"Excuse me," Gideon said. "I feel I have to interject. Madison can be horrible, but she's not entirely without . . . well . . . It's not like Pilar did anything wrong."

Mrs. Benitez-Jones held up her glass and tapped on it with one finger. "Well, yes," she said. "You may well think that, but I think it's up to me to say whether she did something wrong or not."

"But you weren't there," Gid countered.

All I could think about was how he'd used the word *interject* in front of Mrs. Benitez-Jones, and he'd never even met my parents.

"Gideon," Pilar said, "please just let's talk about something else."

"I'm just saying that these things are competitive," Gid said. He finished his drink, and as the waiter brought over another for Mrs. Benitez-Jones, he gestured that he too would like another, and the waiter nodded.

Mrs. Benitez-Jones once again went at her drink with gusto. No one said anything for a moment.

*Good. That's over. It was sort of cute for Gid to stand up for me.
But that better be eet. He doesn't know how my mother can get.*

What? It could get worse?

"Gideon," Mrs. Benitez-Jones said, "what do your parents
do?"

"Well," Gid said, "my mother manages a candle store."

Mrs. Benitez-Jones's eyebrows arched with barely restrained
revulsion.

"And my father is the chief financial officer for Summer's
Eve."

"Ay dios mio," Pilar said.

Gid was laughing so hard he had to put his napkin over his
face. "I'm sorry," he said to Pilar quietly. "I'm just so stoned."

"That is a very juvenile joke," Mrs. Benitez-Jones said.

"That's exactly why it's funny," Gid said. He was choking
laughing, taking in big gulps of air.

Mrs. Benitez-Jones didn't even hear him, and she continued, "Particularly since I was trying to make a point, that perhaps your family doesn't have the same expectations for you
that we have for Pilar."

Gid stopped laughing. He looked Mrs. Benitez-Jones square
in the eye. "Look, Mrs. Benitez-Jones," he began.

"Oh, no, Geedon," Pilar pleaded. *Oh no, the people at the
next table are looking at us.* Pilar tucked her hair behind her ears
and gave them a big smile. "Let's talk about something—"

"Pilar," Gideon said, puzzled, "who are you smiling at?"

"The people next to us," she answered.

"Why?"

"Because . . . because they're watching us."

"Who cares?" Gid asked.

"I do. I am embarrassed."

Gid gave Pilar a really sweet smile, and she actually blushed. I felt her face get warm. Then he squeezed her arm. I felt that too.

Gideon looks cute right now. Like, really cute.

"Pilar," Gid said softly to her, "you don't have to worry about what those people think. You don't have to worry about what anyone thinks."

Gid had no idea he was doing this, but he hit some deep place in Pilar. An image of Elias Ganz came into her head, and of Madison scolding her in the car. Then she looked up and saw her mother, her hard eyes, her stiff haircut.

Pilar stood up. *I'm so hungry, and I think that salad probably has some cheese in it, but I just want to get out of here.* "I want to go," she said.

Gid jumped up. "All right," he said. "I would love to go."

Mrs. Benitez-Jones waved her drink in an arc above her head. Mr. Benitez-Jones sat up in his chair an inch. "Oh, Pilar," Mrs. Benitez-Jones said. "Don't be so dramatic."

"If you want to know, I didn't get the job because I think about my looks too much." Pilar's voice wavered. "And I think we know whose fault that ees."

"Well," Mrs. Benitez-Jones said crossly, "I'm certainly not going to sit here and be taken to task for encouraging basic grooming."

Pilar gave her mother a very stiff hug. "Good-bye," she said.

Mrs. Benitez-Jones was pretty drunk by now. Her eyes were hostile, and she turned whatever focus was left in them on Gideon. "So," she said, "you were saying something to me."

"Oh yes," Gid said. "I was saying that you don't know shit about me or my parents, and, if you'll excuse me for saying so, you probably don't know shit about Pilar." The waiter appeared with his drink. "Thanks, Buddy." Gid said. He drank it in one gulp. "Ready?" he said to Pilar.

"Ready," she said. They walked through the dining room, and several times their arms grazed. Pilar's fingers brushed his, then his hers. He grabbed her hand. She squeezed, and he squeezed back.

I know that when a boy and a girl get into the back of a car together, and it is night, and they have had a little bit to drink, what happens next is pretty obvious.

I kept hoping the obvious wouldn't happen. They sat close. I thought, maybe they're just cold. Pilar let her knee rest against his. I thought, maybe her knee is tired from running. Then Gid said, you can lie down and put your head on my lap if you want. She did that, and I thought, Well, OK, not many people do that without making out, but some of them do. When she started to cry I knew it was over.

In situations like this, chicks start crying only because they don't want to be the one who makes the pass.

"What's wrong?" Gid asked, not just falling for the bait but swimming after it.

"My mother ees so fucked up," she said.

"Well," he said, "just because she is doesn't mean you are. You don't have to be like her."

"I am like her," Pilar said, bringing on a fresh round of sobbing.

"You're nothing like her," Gid said. "I mean, your mother isn't fun. You're fun. Remember the night we talked at Fiona's in the chair?"

I remember that you had a boner the whole time.

I was in Gid's head that night, but I didn't know that. I was sorry to know now.

"Yes," she said. "We were on Vicodin. Even my mom would be fun on Vicodin."

"I don't know about that," Gid said. "Seriously. There's something so . . . exciting . . . about being around you."

"You actually really like me."

Pilar stared to cry.

"I have to tell you what happened in Los Angeles," she said.

She told him everything about Elias. "I was really slutty. It's so embarrassing. But the thing ees that I thought he liked me, like I thought I was charming and cute and stuff. But he just thought I was . . . like, slutty. And then Madison—"

"I know, the dumb hottie comment," Gid said. He tugged at his pocket square and then ripped it out of his jacket. He presented it to Pilar with a scrap of his jacket attached. She didn't take it. *I like it in the movies where the boy dries the girl's tears.*

If I just blink at him and look sad, he'll do it.

Gid took the hint.

If I keep looking into his eyes, he will try to kiss me.

Gid took that hint too.

I always wondered what would happen if I saw Gid fall for someone else through his eyes. That was my greatest fear. This was a hundred times worse. I could feel him touching her skin, feel his hand caress her face, her neck. I felt the softness of his hair through her fingertips. Worst of all were her thoughts: *Why didn't I do this sooner? Gideon Rayburn ees amazing. I want him to be my boyfriend. I wonder eef he would be? Madison will make fun of me. Oh, who cares? I am not friends with her anymore anyway. It's funny I thought the pocket square was so gay, because when he offered it to me, that was the best part of the whole night.*

chapter
sixteen

Edie came back from the library just before lights-out. I was sitting up in bed, staring into space. I was so pissed at the world.
I was pissed at Pilar for taking my boyfriend. I was pissed at her
for being so pretty. I was pissed at myself that I had tried to ruin
the date and had probably just made it better. I was pissed at
Gideon for his annoying gesture with the Diet Coke, and at Dr.
Whitmeyer for knowing just enough about this being-inside-
people's-minds shit to fuck me up even more.

Edie didn't ask what was going on, but I decided I couldn't
go through this alone anymore.

"I have to tell you something, and you're going to think I'm
crazy."

"I already think you're crazy," Edie said, sitting down on
her bed. "At least this is exciting."

"No, like, really crazy."

"Try me," Edie said.

"I'm inside Pilar Benitez-Jones's head," I said. "I'm inside her head, and I hear all her thoughts. I know everything she does. And before that."

Edie stood up. "Molly, I think you need help."

I shook my head. "I need your help. I can't just ask anyone for help. This is totally real, but I don't want to go to a mental institution," I said. "Look, let me prove it to you, OK?"

"You're going to prove to me that you're inside the mind of Pilar Benitez-Jones? And this is why you've been so weird for the last couple months?"

I still wanted to keep the Gid thing to myself. Maybe it was stupid, but I didn't want anyone to know I'd gone out with someone whose mind I was inside. It was just the worst form of desperation. So I just said, "More or less."

I don't know why I expected, after everything we'd been through in the last couple months, that Edie would just all of a sudden drop everything and be my best friend again. She got ready for bed, waiting, I guess, for me to say something else.

"We'll do this Pilar thing tomorrow after the match. I'll show you then."

Edie said, "We can do it whenever you want."

I was offended that she didn't just believe me. I was beginning to see that, with this much shit going on, I had to really take it one thing at a time. I'd show her when we got back from ATAT. Correction, after we demolished Gates Academy in ATAT.

Gates Academy sat up on a bluff above a rocky beach north of Boston. It was just a next stop on that prep school train—people went to Midvale because they got kicked out of schools like Exeter, and then, if they got kicked out of Midvale, which was kind of hard, they went to a school like Gates. The typical Gates guy had bleached blond hair and a dazed expression; even if not wearing a puka shell necklace, he looked like he was dying put one on. The typical Gates girl had wavy, wind-swept hair down to her tiny butt, and small braless breasts visible through a gauzy shirt. Everyone went barefoot, and in the winter, they wore moccasins, as if in homage to the Indian tribes who had been decimated in order to make way for a suck-ass prep school.

Before the match we had to stand around talking to the Gates losers. Mrs. Gwynne-Vaughan and the Gates faculty ad-viser knew each other and were talking some New Englandy bullshit like clambakes or Dutch elm disease or something. I was stuck talking to a girl with braids approximately the width and length of a baby anaconda. Her name was Isis, and I was pretty sure she'd been brought up on a commune and that her parents smoked a lot of pot. "History is my favorite subject," she confided with poignant sincerity. "Because I am the reincar-nation of Guinevere . . . you know, from Arthur and the Knights of the Round Table?"

"Wow," I said. "Do you get déjà vu when you go to Round Table Pizza?"

The bell rang before she could respond.

The way Academic Tête-à-Tête works is that each team fields five players. There are four quarters, and you can sub out at the quarter. Each player goes tête-à-tête (head-to-head) with the same player on the other team, three times, three questions, per quarter. That is a round. Whatever team has won the most rounds at the end of the game wins. Any player can get any question in any category, which is why it is so important to have a well-rounded team.

At the end of three quarters, we were already ahead by an embarrassing amount. Nicholas kicked the ass of some guy with puffy blond hair, Edie beat another guy with the same hair, but not as puffy, Mickey trounced a girl with a pierced tongue, and Devon surprised us all by knowing the order of the first three geological periods. "Precambrian, Paleozoic, Mesozoic," he said. As he sat down, he whispered to Edie, "Of course my favorite era is the Stone Age," and she laughed out loud.

It was at this moment I knew exactly what was going on with Edie. She had a crush on Devon. Devon. Fat, farting, but strangely attractive Devon.

Little Edie.

We won.

When we got back to school, Edie and I went back to our room and lay down on our beds for a while. Outside it was humid and all the outdoor-loving people were running around shouting and throwing Frisbees to one another. I looked out the window. Gid and Cullen were underneath a tree, lying down, staring up at the branches. I could tell they were totally fucking high just from looking at them, even this far away. Nicholas joined them, peeling off his ATAT tie, settling down cross-legged. Cullen sat up, went in his knapsack, and took something out of a Ziploc bag, and he handed it to Nicholas. Nicholas ate the thing quickly and without enjoyment, and then he lay down too. "Oh my God," I said. "Nicholas and Gid and Cullen are, like, fully hanging out on the lawn eating pot brownies. Or pot something."

Edie stacked one foot on top of the other one. "Hmm, that's fascinating. I'm kind of more interested in what Pilar's doing."

Pilar was asleep. She slept a lot. I guess she probably exhausted herself with all the math and crunches that she did all day. "Look, I can't make her wake up!" I said.

"If you're inside her head, couldn't you just make a big cymbal clap inside your head?" Edie asked.

"That just doesn't make any sense," I said. "I'm inside her head, but she's not inside my head."

"How do you know?" Edie asked.

"Well, I guess if I were inside her head, I would hear myself."

Edie nodded. "That makes sense." She paused. "If you broke up with Gid, why are you watching him out the window?"

I collapsed back down onto the bed. "Because they're there."

We lay there for a while, listening to the shouts coming up from the quad and the sounds of lawn mowers and hedge clippers and various ringtones.

Finally Pilar was stirring. She rolled over and blinked at the ceiling and realized that she only had an hour until the gym closed. She jumped out of bed and dressed herself very quickly.

Edie let out a long sigh to indicate her patience was at an end. "I think I'm going to go take a shower," she said.

I smiled at her smugly. "That's a great idea," I said. "But if you want to just wait one second, I think you should look out the window."

Edie came to the window. I went in the closet and shut the

door. Pilar was just walking through the front door of the dorm. "All right," I said, from behind the closet door. "She's going to run across the quad, wearing a pair of black workout tights and a tight pink tank top with an om symbol stitched out of baby blue sequins in the center, in three . . . two . . . one."

I expected to hear Edie gasp, but I heard nothing. Pilar was doing exactly what I said she would. "Whatever," Edie said. "You could know she was going to wear that, and it is exactly five. Maybe that's when she goes to—"

"Let me continue!" I called out from behind the closet door. "She sees a friend up ahead. It's . . . oh my, it's Madison! She doesn't know whether to stop. She doesn't. She waves quickly, with her right hand."

"Oh my God," Edie said. "You're not kidding."

I stayed in the closet, continuing to talk. "She runs to the left. Whoops. She's got to tie her shoe. She's up again. Oh shit. I think she may have forgotten something! She's got a little pocket in the side of her pants! She's checking it. There it is. You can't see what it is. But I can. It's the advanced stomach workout from *Muscle and Fitness for Women* magazine."

Edie opened the closet door. "Holy motherfucking shit!" she said. "I . . . OK. I have to get a hold of myself." She turned around in circles and watched Pilar continue across the quad. "This is fucked!"

Pilar scratched her head, and though I wasn't looking out the window, I said, "Pilar just scratched her head. It's so weird when she does normal things like that. It's really terrible when she goes to the bathroom. Not just because she's going to the bathroom, but because, well, she is Pilar."

I was trying to make Edie laugh so she wouldn't be quite so freaked out.

She fanned herself. "I keep feeling like this can't be real, but it is. I'm sorry. I swear, mostly I just want you to be OK, but I am kind of like . . . Uh, I feel scared."

"Don't worry about me," I said. "I'm fine. I'm just glad you know now."

She looked like Edie again. Of course she was wearing mascara and lip gloss and had her hair combed. But she didn't have that wall around her. Her smile was unguarded and warm, even if she did look freaked out.

I guess this was a moment where some friends might have hugged each other, but we had a joke: "Please hug me by not hugging me." Direct affection made us nervous. Especially since prep schools are full of girls kissing and hugging each other and then immediately turning around and calling each other bitches.

It was enough just to have her look at me with an expression of real sympathy. "God," she said, sitting down, seeming to make a decision to act normal even if she didn't feel it. "That must suck. Being in Pilar's head. I mean, it would suck in general. But now it must suck even worse."

"What do you mean?" I said innocently.

"Uh, because of Gid," she said.

I hoped I did a good job of trying to look unaffected by this. "It's kind of weird, I guess. But mostly it's just annoying. She does this thing where she, like, rates girls on how pretty they are," I explained.

Edie was appropriately horrified. "It's kind of impressive," she said. "Ha. We should get her on ATAT."

"Actually," I said, "I forgot to tell you this, but the other day she actually gave you a high rating . . . on your clothes. . . . She spent, like, a full ten minutes noticing that you were dressing better." I wasn't lying, but I will admit that I had ulterior motives. I wanted Edie to tell me what the hell was up with her sudden attention to her womanly presentation.

She must have known it was bait, because she just said, "Well, maybe Pilar's not that bad if she has noticed my overpowering hotness. Anyway. What have you tried to get out of her head?"

I didn't want to tell her about Dr. Whitmeyer, because that might lead to questions that would lead to Gid. "I think I ended up in her head because I wanted to know what it was like to be her, maybe," I said. "And now I know. She's not that horrible, but I mean, I get it. She's pretty and she has problems like the rest of us. Duh. I get it. So I mean, now that I get it, why am I still in her head?"

"Well, we have to try something," Edie said. "I have some ideas."

"You do?" I said. "You're the best."

Edie shrugged modestly. "I'm just glad we're having fun again." Then she looked serious. "I don't mean to imply this is fun. . . . That was really selfish of me."

"What, you mean being entertained at my expense? I'm just so glad you don't find me boring anymore."

Edie looked like she wanted to shrink away. "I think I just said that to be mean. My feelings were hurt. Do you know what I mean?"

Of course I did. I think half of what I say sometimes is just to see what people will do or say. It's not the thing I'm proudest of.

"Do you know what I mean?" she repeated.

"It's OK," I said. "We're young. I think we have a right to be emotionally immature."

She laughed, and I felt pretty good.

• • •

Edie's first theory for getting out of Pilar's head involved the theory that I needed to do what Pilar was doing and actually think her thoughts. "It's like basic physics," she said. "You get your minds on exactly the same groove," Edie said, "and maybe they will get so similar that they will repel."

Pilar was still in the gym. Edie instructed me to lie down and close my eyes. "Imagine wearing what she's wearing, thinking what she's thinking. I'm going to set a timer for thirty minutes. I'll leave. I don't want my brain waves to interfere."

I tried so hard. I felt her Lycra pants hugging my thighs and her hair on the back of my neck, and even tried to imagine having her neck, swanlike, silky. When she went down a long rabbit hole about her mother coming back from her trip and still finding fault with her weight, even though she was incredibly thin, I went with her, into every cranny of shame and self-doubt. I kept up count for count with a grueling series of leg lifts and crunches and some terrible thing where she got in a push-up position and then touched her opposite knee to opposite elbow for, like, eleven solid minutes.

Edie came back a half hour later. "Well?" she said.

I lay on my back panting. "I have much better abs, but unfortunately, I am still in her head."

"OK," Edie said. "Go down to Pilar's room. Sneak in through the fire escape. Then walk out of the door backwards."

"What?" I said. "That is so incredibly stupid."

Edie gave me a look like, do you have a better idea? "Maybe her mind will be, like, attracted to her space and will fall out of your head."

It was worth a try. And I knew Pilar wasn't there. We ran

down the hall and out to the fire escape. I leaned out over it, and pushed the window open. "Stand on my hands," Edie said. "I won't let you fall."

I dangled three stories above Midvale and hoisted myself in the window.

Pilar's room, obviously, was not a new experience for me. But it was one thing to see it through her eyes and another to see it through mine. She took it for granted, I guess, so even though the details were the same—the wallpaper, the sconces, the rich scent of expensive creams—through my eyes it had a more magical sheen. It was like a nice hotel room to her, but to me, it was miraculous. If I had seen this room before I was in her head, I would have been so jealous of her. But now, knowing Pilar as I did, hearing her fight that conversation with her mother out of her head while she did sit-up after sit-up, I understood that Pilar surrounded herself with perfection because she didn't feel right inside.

I walked backward out of the door, but I all I could hear, still, was Pilar's mantra. *First my stomach, then my mind.*

"It didn't work," I said.

"Hmm," Edie said. "I didn't really expect it to." Her eyes lit up again. "I have an idea. How about . . . OK. This is stupid too."

"Whatever," I said. I figured at least if I did one more thing, Edie was going to be moved to confide in me about Devon.

"Go back into her room." She smiled to let me know she knew this was annoying. "And get some of her shit. Shit she won't miss, but like, shit that evokes her."

From Pilar's room, I gathered a discarded Q-tip caked with blue eye shadow, a 2009 *Vogue* with Jennifer Aniston on the cover, a label from an empty container of fat-free dulce de leche yogurt and an English paper from last year, marked C plus.

"Check it out," Edie said, as it all went up in flames in our trash can. The fire had blown back a piece of the English paper, and Edie read from the teacher's comments: "You have so much potential, Pilar. It's disappointing that you don't try harder." I recognized Mrs. Gwynne-Vaughan's handwriting, and then the blue flame traveled across it, turning it to black and then ash.

"Did that work?"

I listened to my head. Pilar was getting a text message. "Not only did it *not* work," I reported. "Gid's coming to Pilar's room tonight. At least they're not going to sleep together," I said. "I mean, not that I really care. It's just weird, you know."

"You know, you wouldn't have to be in love with Gideon to not want him to have sex with Pilar," Edie said. "It's OK."

"I know," I said. "I mean. Right. Yeah, I mean, it's just . . ."

"Annoying," Edie said. Then she frowned. "I don't want to burst your bubble, but how do you know they're not going to have sex?"

I explained Pilar's policy on sex and the flat stomach.

"Wow," Edie said. "I always thought Pilar thought she was so perfect."

"Don't feel too sorry for her," I said. "She's just tortured because she thinks she's so close to being perfect."

Edie laughed. "Right. But still. She's tortured. That's really what's important. Isn't it?"

I shrugged. I wanted to say, what's important is that she never, ever sleeps with Gid. But I just said, "I guess so."

And then Edie said, "I like Devon. Love him. Ever since I was little."

Her hands were shaking.

We sat down on our beds, facing each other.

"When Mrs. Gwynne-Vaughan told me we were going to

be on ATAT, or probably, I decided that I wanted to . . . to see if I could get him. But now . . . well. He's always hitting on me, and he . . . I think he just wants to have sex with me, and I'm not up for that." Edie buried her face in her hands. "He's such a pig," she said. "I mean, I know he is! But I . . . just have such a crush on him. It's awful. It's all I think about." She dropped her hands. "There's not much more to say. I am sure I could have sex with him, but then I would just feel bad."

I didn't know what to say. Edie was right. Devon was amusing, but he was gross.

We got ready for bed. We brushed our teeth side by side in the bathroom. We peed in adjoining stalls. We went back to the room and took off our jeans and slipped our bras out from under our shirts and slept in our underwear and the tank tops we were wearing under our sweaters.

"I'm sorry I couldn't get you out of Pilar's head."

"That's OK," I said. "It was fun trying."

"We can keep them from having sex, though," Edie said. "We can do like in *Mean Girls*. We'll just send her some delicious food that she likes. I bet she thinks about food a lot."

"She does."

"I thought so. Find out what her favorite food is."

It was quiet for a while, and then Edie said, "Are boys just disappointing?"

I pretended to be asleep. Soon, I actually was.

I woke up to the sound of belt buckle on belt buckle.

Gid had Pilar pressed up against her door. She felt his belt buckle—it really was his belt buckle—against her stomach. She didn't like the feeling of the fat hanging over her pants.

She thought about how it would be impossible to take off all her clothes until it was gone. "I can't go to the dining hall anymore because I always can't help eating los cookies," she said.

"The cookies?" Gid said.

She shrugged in a cutesy way. "When I like something a lot, I sometimes say that first part in Spanish. Like . . . things I like are los sunglasses, los high heels, los cookies . . ."

"OK," Gid said. "I get it." He gestured toward the bed. "Can we lie down?"

They got on the bed. It was quiet. Pilar smiled at Gid. "Los cookies are my *enemigos*. Los cookies are my enemies."

Gid nodded, understanding. "I got that. I have taken four years of Spanish. Of course . . . that's about all I can say other than . . ."

And then he just pounced on her.

They kissed for a long time. Gid was the one in control, his hands pinning her shoulders to the mattress, then just one hand while the other went up her shirt. Pilar oohed and said yes over and over again and kissed him back. *Gid ees a good kisser. He isn't too fast and he wasn't too slow. He doesn't use too much tongue and he didn't use too little. I wonder eef I should tell him about my stomach, because otherwise . . . but I can't tell him that. I think it will be flat soon. I have to download that Mala Rodríguez video so I . . . oh no . . . he is trying to go further. . . . I will just put my hand on his hand and let him know. . . . Oh my God, is this really over? I got tits, easy. I got tits without even asking. I go for pants and I get hand block. Maybe she's just scratching her stomach. Let me go in with the other hand. Blocked again. Amazing. Well, amazing in the suck sense of amazing.*

What was amazing—amazing also in the suck sense of amazing—was that I was back inside the mind of Gideon Rayburn.

I looked over at Edie, sleeping peacefully. She's been so nice about the Pilar stuff. But I just couldn't tell her about Gid.

He continued to think about Pilar.

I continued to enjoy listening to him despite the fact that he was thinking about her, because I just liked being back with him.

I knew that was probably fucked up. I knew I should probably call Dr. Whitmeyer to seek further advice.

Maybe after I'd had a little time in Gid's mind.

The next night, after Gid had once again snuck into Pilar's room and once again made out with her and was denied the ultimate prize, I watched Gideon Rayburn march from Emerson back to Proctor, freshly annoyed at having to explain, again, his presence to his roommates.

What is Pilar's problem? She acts like she wants me, but then she gives me the hand block. What is that about? I mean, is she just playing hard to get? Or is she genuinely not interested? And then she says, "I wish that I could explain this to you, but I cannot. I am sorry." Jesus. How long has she been in this fucking country? When the fuck is she going to start using fucking contractions?

I couldn't believe Gid was actually making me laugh at the same time that I was this bummed out.

He opened the door to 307 Proctor as quietly as he could. He didn't want to face Cullen and Nicholas and their obnoxious questions about what he was doing back here and how he had fucked it all up and . . .

"What are you doing back here? How did you fuck that up *again*?"

This was Cullen talking. Both he and Nicholas were not

only wide awake, they were covered in manure and standing in the middle of a circle of blooming pot plants. The closets had been emptied of their contents, which were distributed on the various surfaces in the room, though nowhere as enthusiastically as on Gideon's bed.

"You guys seriously suck," Gid said.

Cullen was wearing overalls. He hitched them up and said, "Howdy there, pardner."

Nicholas dropped to his knees, annoyed and weary. "We're almost done. And it isn't as bad as it seems."

"What's not as bad as it seems? The mess? The flagrant lawbreaking? Or just the smell of animal feces?" Gid sank down and lay on his back in front of the door, the only available space in the room.

"Now that these doggies are good and covered up with some of this quality fertilizer," Cullen said, "I reckon they're gettin' good and ready to go."

Nicholas was spooning fertilizer over the plants as well. "Cullen thinks that if he acts like a farmer, the plants will grow better."

"It's creative visualization," Cullen said.

"Well, you're mixing your metaphors," Gid said. "You're talking like a cowboy, not a farmer."

Cullen pointed his spade accusingly at Gideon. "And what are you doing here anyway? You should be balls deep in some spicy empanada by now," Cullen said.

"OK, seriously," Gid said. "I'm not in the mood for you today. You think the world is a giant vagina, and you don't even know the difference between a cowboy and a farmer. And I don't think they have empanadas in Argentina. Latin America is divided into different countries, you know."

"Latin America," Cullen said. "That's a big word."

Nicholas said, "Why aren't you nailing Pilar right now?"

"OK," Cullen said, "Why is 'nail' better than the empanada thing?"

Gid just lay there.

"We're waiting," Nicholas said.

"OK, the truth is, I am trying to figure it out myself," Gid said, his voice surprisingly sincere. "I go over there. *She* asks *me* to come over. We start making out. And I get tit right away. And then, when I am GFB, I get the hand block."

GFB? I wanted to know. I didn't want to know.

Cullen shook his head sympathetically as he tied up a bag of manure. "The irony of getting tit right away is that the beave sometimes eludes you."

GFB was Going For Beave.

Nicholas was putting the plants back into the closet. He had a thoughtful expression. "We're going to get to the bottom of this. Let's see. She asks you over?"

"Correct."

"The fooling around starts pretty much right away?" Nicholas asked. "She's, like, into making out?"

"Yes and yes."

Nicholas put his fingers to his mouth thoughtfully. "How many seconds do you wait before going up the shirt?"

Gideon considered this. "I would say I made out with her for a good four minutes," he said.

That's pretty accurate.

"That's extremely generous of you," Cullen said from the back of the closet. "I generally combine going in for the kiss with the boob thing, because I think if a girl wants . . ."

But his voice was drowned out when Nicholas shut the closet

door and threw himself against it. "Let's finish this conversation just us adults, shall we? All right. I get it. All is well until you are GFB. What I see here is a clear example of a girl who has some issue—she didn't shave."

"She's lasered," Cullen yelled.

"Quiet," Nicholas hissed. "You idiot. We're in prep school, remember?"

There was a dull thud as Cullen collapsed against the closet floor.

"OK. Well. All right. I am thinking. Hmm. Oh. How long with the boobs before you were GFB?"

"Just a few seconds," said Gid defensively. But he was thinking, this is where I went wrong. Definitely.

Nicholas shook his head. "A girl like Pilar, a set of knockers like that. She wants you to be, like, 'Oh your tits are amazing.' Did you tell her her tits—"

Gid shook his head miserably. He couldn't believe he'd neglected this step. "No, I didn't," he said. "Shit. God, I am such an idiot!"

Nicholas nodded sadly. "You'll have another shot," he said. "Don't worry. And you know what . . . think of it this way. The more time you wait before you do it with her, well, you put off being bored by fucking her."

It was such a lovely way to view the world.

It was quiet for a minute while Gid thought about this, and then Cullen shouted, "Maybe she has penis phobia!"

"Jesus, Cullen. You stupid fuck," Nicholas whispered. "That was so loud. How stupid are you!"

Gideon scrambled up off the floor and sprang into action. "Get the fucking plants in the closet, now! Cockweed is definitely going to wake up. Cullen, I would do anything, anything, to be able to just fucking strangle you right now."

Cullen blinked at the light as he stumbled out of the closet. "Really? Anything? Would you be willing to have your rectum removed?"

Gideon just shook his head. "I know you got that joke from Mickey," he said.

Cullen shoved the plants into the closet, muttering, "It's the only explanation. Penis fucking phobia. And Mickey got that joke from *me*."

Through the keyhole Gid saw Cockweed, imposing, advancing, in an ugly tartan bathrobe. "Shit. Here he comes!"

"Oh, really?" Nicholas said. "What a surprise, considering someone just screamed 'penis phobia' in the dead of night." Nicholas shoved the last of the plants into the closet and Cullen hustled into bed. Gid hit the light and dove under his own covers, pulling his blanket on top of the pile of clothes.

Heavy, purposeful footsteps pounded down the hallway. The door opened. The light flashed on, and the three boys lay there, making a big show of adjusting their eyes to the light.

"What's going on?" Nicholas said.

Gid pulled the pillow over his head.

"Mother?" said Cullen. "Is that you?"

Cockweed filled up the doorway. "You can quit the acting," he growled. "Oscars for everyone."

Cullen rubbed his eyes. "Oscar who?" he said.

Cockweed stepped inside and shut the door. He pressed his lips to one side in an attempt to look menacing. "Is that supposed to be funny?" he said.

"No," Cullen said, "I honestly don't know anyone named Oscar."

"Look, dickhead." Cockweed pointed his finger in Cullen's face. "Someone in this room just yelled out the word *penis*. It sounded like you."

Cullen assumed a look of utter confusion. "I have no idea what you're talking about," he said. "Wait. Let me say penis—I won't yell it—and see if it jogs any recent memories. OK. Penis! No. Nothing!"

For a few seconds Cockweed was so incapacitated with rage that he could do nothing but stand there and turn various shades of pink and white and red. Finally he cleared his throat and began to patrol the room in circles, his hands clasped behind his back. He paused at the dresser, opened some drawers and peered in. He shut them and stood there for a second, taking in the room, his nose quivering like a bloodhound. He strode toward the closet. He put his hand on the closet door. He walked into the closet.

I had been in that closet. It smelled like pot. Not just a little, either.

Gideon's balls climbed up inside his stomach and then back down.

"OK, I shouted penis," Cullen said. "I did."

Cockweed didn't move.

"I shouted out penis, just to be . . . just to be funny, I guess."

Cockweed stepped out of the closet, shut the door, and turned on Cullen. "You woke up my daughter. She's four years old."

There was a long pause. Gid was still sitting up in bed, his head bowed to his knees. He looked at Nicholas, who mouthed the words *Jesus Christ*.

"I know," Gid mouthed back. How, he wondered, had Cockweed not smelled that pot?

Cockweed bore down on Cullen. "You woke up a four-year-old with the word *penis*."

"Well," Cullen said, "you have to admit it's better than waking her up with an actual penis."

Despite my belief that it would be hard for a student like Cullen, with family money, to get kicked out of Midvale, he very nearly achieved this feat. "You are on a short leash," Cockweed told him as he led him out of Dean Paley's office early the following morning. "The shortest leash in the history of leashes."

"I wanted to say, Wow, Cockweed, that's a really good analogy," Cullen said later on to Gid and Nicholas as they sat under their tree in the quad. Gid was thinking how strange it felt to sit on the quad not stoned. Everything felt smaller and less like a dream.

"Yeah, well, it's a fucking good thing you didn't," Nicholas said. "I think we need to get rid of the plants."

I couldn't believe Cockweed hadn't noticed them. It didn't make any sense.

"I think you're overreacting," Cullen said. "Let's just lie low for a week."

Nicholas stood up and brushed grass and leaves off his pants. "God, I hate sitting on the quad and not being stoned."

"I was just thinking that," Gid said.

"And I blame you," Nicholas said to Cullen. "All right. Let's give it a week."

"But what am I supposed to do about Pilar?" Gid said. "I have to sneak out to see her."

Nicholas shook his head. "You're not ready yet anyway, not after you told me about how you fucked up last night."

Cullen nodded. "Agreed. I think we need to see a list of ten . . . ten?"

"Ten sounds good," Nicholas said.

"A list of ten good compliments about her tits before you're ready to go back in," Cullen said. "It's perfect timing, actually. You should be thanking me."

Nicholas and Gid both glared at Cullen. "Don't push your luck," Nicholas said.

"What are you talking about?" Cullen said. "*I* got him out of the closet. If you think about it, I'm the one who saved us!"

Gid pictured himself back in Virginia, eating Doritos in the basement, watching *Friends* reruns, waiting for his dad to get home, or, twice a week, his mother to come pick him up and take him to Wild Thyme or Whole Foods café. He did not want to go back to that life. "If this gets fucked up," he said to Cullen, "that is on you."

chapter
seven-
teen

On Saturday morning sunlight streamed in the window of our little room. The hills were lush and soft-looking. The bad news is that we had an all-day ATAT practice. The good news was that we had won our first three ATAT matches, which meant that we were one of six teams invited to a round-robin the following Friday night. If we won that, we'd go to the finals.

More bad news: I hadn't told Edie I was inside the mind of Gideon Rayburn again, which wouldn't have been a problem except for the fact that she thought I was still in Pilar's head.

"I really want you to tell me Pilar's favorite food," she said as we were on our way across campus to practice. Flocks of squawking geese were flying north, and I pretended they'd droned her out.

"Favorite food," Edie repeated. "It's not hard. You're inside her head. You know she had her bikini area lasered, just because you know. But you don't know what her favorite food is?"

"I think it's just a question of where her focus is." I said. "I . . ." Cullen was raking leaves in front of his dorm—part of his punishment—and he waved cheerfully to us and we waved back.

"I can't believe what he said to Cockweed," Edie said. "Or what people say he said to Cockweed. I bet he didn't really say that."

"Oh, he said it all right. I know he did."

Edie looked at me funny.

"I mean, he is totally capable of doing something like that," I corrected myself.

"So," Edie continued, "at least you can figure Gid's not going to go to Pilar's room this week, what with the boys seriously on Cockweed's radar." She tried to look encouraging. "It's seems like kind of good news, right?"

"Well, I guess they won't be having sex this week, but who knows about next week. Pilar's got this stomach exercise where she gets into plank position and then touches knee to opposite elbow and so on. Well, every day her stomach is getting smaller, tighter, and flatter." That was true as of the last time I was in her head, anyway. I didn't mention the fact that Gid, meanwhile, was working on his list of breast compliments for Cullen and Nicholas, and they were pretty good. They'd given him back the first draft with some suggestions. "I think you need more nipple stuff in there," Cullen had said.

Again, I had laughed in spite of how awful it was. And then I tried to think about the fact that although Cullen's stupidity had bought me a couple days, the longer Gid and Pilar didn't mess around, the hotter they would get for each other.

I tried not to think about them having sex that was as good as the sex Gid and I had when we weren't able to be alone for a couple days.

"Pilar's favorite food," Edie reminded me. "I know she's hungry. I can see it in her eyes."

At practice I was paired up with Devon. He was looking particularly fat today, wearing skintight vintage bell-bottom jeans and a yellow T-shirt that clung to every heaving slab of flesh. Poor Pilar, totally obsessed with a light fold of skin over the top of her jeans, while Devon wore his obesity like a badge of honor.

The whole time we ran our drills—we were doing constitutional amendments, the years states were admitted to the Union, and various crap about Teddy Roosevelt—Devon had one eye on me and one on Edie. He had buggy eyes, and this divided attention made him look retarded, but, amazingly, very cute.

Anyway, this is how our practice went.

Me: "What amendment gave women the right to vote?"

Devon: "The nineteenth. Duh. Was Edie always this hot?"

Me: "I can't answer that. What state used to be part of Massachusetts?"

Devon: "New Hampshire. Did she, like, all of a sudden grow boobs?"

Me: "It's actually Maine. You can remember this because they both begin with M. And no, she didn't all of a sudden just grow boobs. I'm not sure if you're familiar with a little thing called adolescence, but—"

Devon: "No, no, no, no. Adolescence happens earlier. I think she got a boob job."

Me: "Does it turn you on to think she got a boob job? Like, that means she is somehow, I don't know, sending you a message? That as she lay there going under, she thought, I can't wait for Devon to see these?"

(Devon nods.)

Me: "Devon, why don't you just ask her on a date?"

Devon (looking at his shoe): "I forget what we were talking about."

Poor Edie. Yes, boys were always a disappointment.

At noon, pizzas arrived. "You know," Devon said. "They delivered pizzas to the Marines the night before they invaded Baghdad."

Indeed, Mrs. Gwynne-Vaughan stood up and announced we were going to be watching a video.

"I hope it's porn," Mickey said.

"Mickey, I generally enjoy your sense of humor, but today it's a little tiresome," Mrs. Gwynne-Vaughan said. "Moving along. I have every confidence we are going to do extremely well at this round-robin. And I am fairly sure we're going to win."

We all cheered.

Mrs. Gwynne-Vaughan made a grim face. "Now the bad news," she said. "The very likely opponent in the finals is going to be Xavier Academy. Now, I took the liberty of driving over to Xavier Academy one evening and videotaping their team . . ."

Edie looked at me and mouthed the words *What the fuck?*

"You're the man!" Mickey said.

"We're the New England Patriots of ATAT," Devon said. Edie giggled. He winked at her and then whispered to me, "Uh, do you think that Mrs. Gwynne-Vaughan is maybe, like, kind of fucking nuts?"

It definitely was kind of strange how much she wanted us

to win. She was like one of those weird mothers in Texas who kills her daughter's rival so her child can make the cheerleading squad.

"Say something," Devon whispered. "I want to know what's up her ass."

I raised my hand. "Mrs. Gwynne-Vaughan? Did they let you videotape them?"

Mrs. Gwynne-Vaughan snorted. "Certainly not. I climbed a fire escape, went in a window, and hid in a crawl space."

We were flabbergasted. "Wow," Devon said. "That is super hard-core, Mrs. Gwynne-Vaughan."

"You're not the only people in the history of civilization to attend prep school," she said. "Nor the only ones to break rules. Well. Moving along!" She went to the TV/DVD player in the corner of the room and slipped in a DVD. "Watch carefully, because we have our work cut out for us."

The video started out as a rumble of voices, and light coming through slats. Then it focused in on a slightly grainy image of one boy and panned out to reveal eight other boys who all looked almost exactly like he did. They were all skinny and pale, and each had a very prominent Adam's apple and an expression of total humorlessness. A slim man in a black suit who looked to be no more than a few years older than all his students paced, firing off questions.

"That's Mr. Raines," Mrs. Gwynne-Vaughan said. "He's their adviser. He's written a couple of books on the War of 1812."

Of course he had.

"OK," Mr. Raines said, "who is A. Philip Randolph? ID, historical period, significance. Jones!"

A short, towheaded boy stepped forward and announced, as if he were giving name, rank, and serial number, "A. Philip

Randolph, 1889 to 1979. Head of the Brotherhood of the Sleeping Car Porters' Union. African-American who, protesting unfair wages and treatment of his union in 1941, threatened to
have African-Americans march on Washington. Considered to
be the beginning of the Civil Rights Movement."

"Good," Mr. Raines said. He pushed his glasses back on his
head and all the boys who wore glasses, which was exactly
eight out of ten of them, did the same.

"The Crimean War. Historical period, significance. McCaskill."

McCaskill was one of the two not wearing glasses. He had
a long nose and a querulous purse to his lips. He delivered
his information as if he were angry. "Crimean War, 1853 to
1856, a conflict between Imperial Russia on one side and the
Ottoman Empire, France, and England on the other. Principal
conflict: control of the Holy Land. Florence Nightingale was a
British nurse whose exemplary service—"

"I thought Florence Nightingale was American," I said to
Nicholas, who was standing next to me.

"Yeah," he said. "I think even Florence Nightingale thinks
Florence Nightingale is American. And the Crimean War, I've
heard of it, but like . . ."

"Right," I said. "Me too."

Raines stalked across the floor and spun around. "Who is
Herb Stempel? Tate."

"Henry or Alistair?" said two voices, presumably Henry
and Alistair.

"Henry," Raines said crossly, as if this should be obvious.

"The man who faked his loss on the quiz show *Twenty One*
so that Charles Van Doren could become its new champion."

They moved on to math. They found volumes in their

heads. They did quadratic equations on their fingers. They were asked how quickly a baseball, thrown at an arc of 30 degrees, might land in a catcher's mitt 18 inches off the ground and 100 feet away when thrown with a velocity of 79 mph. Someone yelled out, "Point eight seconds."

"Very good, Tate," Raines said.

After this the tape went off.

"Was that the end of practice?" Sergei asked.

"No," said Mrs. Gwynne-Vaughan darkly. "That's just when I had seen enough."

The day of the round-robin match, Edie and I were eating on the chilly marble steps of the Administration Building. The silverware clatter and yeasty smell of the cafeteria had made my stomach churn, and frankly, so had Gid, sitting alone in the far corner, thinking to himself, watermelon, tuna, gross cheese, yellow squash. He mentally piled them all up in a bowl and poured goat's milk on them. I knew what he was doing. When he didn't want to think about sex, he did a sort of food-aversion thing.

His presence in my head and on this earth was a terrible weight. But I couldn't not eat, because hopefully one day I would be over him and I didn't want to be over him at a second-rate university, and I needed my strength for ATAT. All I could eat lately was tapioca pudding with almonds in it. The bland sweetness of the tapioca soothed me, and the crunch of the almonds kind of woke me up.

"I don't want to sit through that entire round-robin match today just to get demolished in the finals," I said to Edie. "There's got to be a way to beat Xavier."

"Of course there is." Edie nodded with confidence. "We don't know what it is yet. But it will come to us."

Just then, Gid clomped down the steps of the cafeteria and Pilar emerged from the library, and they started moving toward each other. What a vision she was, long hair flowing behind her, a short skirt baring the sheen of her legs, her butt perky on the pedestal of a pair of high-heeled boots. She waved, and as she lifted her arm, her shirt lifted up to reveal a patch of her stomach, concave, lightly muscled, golden, Mala Rodríguez perfect. They embraced but didn't kiss. I couldn't tell if Pilar turned away from him or if he turned away from her, or if they just happened to not kiss.

Then Gid thought, Why didn't she kiss me? Is she avoiding me? I'll kiss her. I might as well.

They kissed. It was a hungry kiss, and when it looked like it was over, it started up again.

Every single notion I'd had that I was OK, possibly even over Gideon, that I didn't want to be with him anyway, etc., disappeared when I watched him kissing Pilar. I tore my glance away to look at her stomach, to double-check if it was indeed approaching satisfactory proportions for her to have sex with Gid. Then I heard:

I theenk it's flat enough. I really theenk it is.

No. Please, I thought, let me be hearing this through Gid somehow.

Maybe we can have el sex tonight.

No. It was unmistakably loud and clear. I was back in Pilar's head.

"Shit," I said. "Shit, shit shit."

"What's wrong?" Edie said.

"Pilar's thinking her stomach is flat enough to have sex," I said.

Of course, Edie didn't know I had ever left her head and was confused. "She just all of a sudden thinks this? I don't get it."

I threw up my hands. "I don't know. I guess so. It's not my fault. Blame her abs, not me!"

Edie nodded understandingly. "OK, OK. Anything else going on? Anything at all?"

"And now she's . . . telling Gideon she has to go to the post office to pick up a package."

Edie smiled like she knew something I didn't. "Keep going," she said.

We sat down on the steps and waited a few minutes for Pilar to pick up her package. Gid kissed her and went off to his class.

How had I just gone out of his head into hers again?

"Molly!" Edie interrupted my thoughts. "What's going on?"

"She has the package. It's pretty big . . . like two large shoe boxes placed next to each other. She brings to it a little table outside the post office. She's opening it with her keys. There's an envelope on top. 'Pilar—you're beautiful just the way you are. Love, your dad. Enjoy.' Now she's taking out a couple layers of tissue paper. She's reading: San Telmo Bakery, Boston. She . . . I'm reading something. *Alfajores?*"

Edie smiled proudly.

"What is an *alfajor?*"

"It's a cookie with dulce de leche and chocolate," Edie said. "Pilar's favorite."

"And how did you know Pilar liked them?"

"I asked her," Edie said. I'd never seen her look so pleased with herself.

"You asked her? How?"

"We were sitting around in the lounge in the dorm, chatting, and I said, 'Oh, I love cream puffs,' and she said, 'Oh, *alfajores* are way better.' And I said, 'Really?' and she described them to me and there was actually drool forming at the corner of her mouth."

I shook my head. "You're crazy."

"Is she eating them?"

Not just eating but wolfing. I hadn't seen her eat a full meal in a while. She did kind of have to be starving. "Yeah," I said.

"Well," Edie said, "then I guess I'm not crazy. We just bought ourselves a little more time. Until we can get you out of her head."

Then she frowned. "But wait a minute," Edie said. "If you're in her head, didn't you see me talking to her? Or hear me, or whatever?"

I knew Edie was just curious, but I had that feeling of angry defensiveness, as if I were being interrogated. I tried to sound offhand, "Hmm. I don't know. Maybe I was asleep?"

Edie nodded. "Hmm. Well, it was around three o'clock in the afternoon."

I didn't say anything.

But we both knew I wasn't usually asleep at that time.

chapter
eigh-
teen

We took one of those campus vans to the round-robin. Mrs. Gwynne-Vaughan drove. On the highway a giant splatter of bird shit hit the window. "Jesus," Mickey said. "That's not a normal amount of bird crap. It's like the bird had, like, ten Oreo Mc-Flurries and then crapped."

I laughed, and I think it might have been the first time I laughed out loud since Gid and I had broken up.

"Oh my God," I said to Edie, "those *alfajores* totally saved my life." Pilar had been so full the night before she hadn't even wanted Gideon to come over. And she'd gone online and ordered more *alfajores*.

"Sometimes the stupidest ideas are the best ones," Edie said.

Devon was on Edie's right, and he leaned into her. "Did you just say I was stupid?" he said.

"No, I said stupid ideas are good," Edie said.

Devon tucked a stray piece of his hair under his barrette and looked at her approvingly. "Does that mean you want to smoke pot before the match?" he said.

Edie rolled her eyes. "I won't get high before the match, but I will some other time."

"Will you?" Devon said. "My, my, my."

"Have any of you ever had a McFlurry?" Nicholas said.

All of us except Nicholas—all of us including Mrs. Gwynne-Vaughan—had had a McFlurry.

"You're all disgusting," Nicholas said.

"Dude," Mickey said to Nicholas. "If I can do a math word problem in my head at this match, you have to have a Mc-Flurry."

"You have to get it right," Nicholas said.

"Of course I mean only if I get it right," Mickey said. "Only the son of a very rich man could think of such a thing."

"Fine," Nicholas said. "Ridiculous."

The round-robin ATAT match was at the Yarmouth School, which was a carbon copy of Midvale. Its student body was similarly made up of students too stupid to go to the best places and too in touch with reality and habits like wearing shoes to go to a place like Gates. It had a giant ugly modern library just like ours, a new theater designed by someone foreign and famous and pretentious, and the dorms were the same mix of turn-of-nineteenth-century charming and 1970s depressing. The round-robin was held in the chapel basement, a low-ceilinged place that was painted pistachio green with turquoise trim.

"It smells like sheet cake in here," Nicholas said as we settled into our chairs. There were eight different schools here. We were going up against three of them in five-round mini matches.

"What's wrong with sheet cake?" Devon said. His eyes were large and unfocused and bloodshot.

Mrs. Gwynne-Vaughan toyed nervously with the blue enamel beads at her neck and studied his face. "Devon, are you all right?" she said.

"Of course, Mrs. G-dash-V," he said, turning a lazy smile on her. "I'm just stoned out of my mind."

Mrs. Gwynne-Vaughan shook her head. "Very funny. Are we all set here? Who is sitting out the first round?"

Devon and Mickey both volunteered. As Mickey put his hand up I noticed him studying his fingers with undue fascination, and I realized he was stoned too. He winked at me and I smiled wearily, with affection. I didn't care. Those guys played fine when they were stoned.

Mrs. Gwynne-Vaughan frowned. "Dan, you sit out this round. Next round, when we're up against Waterford, you come back in and, Sergei, you come out. After that we'll see where we are."

She smiled politely and walked away to join the other faculty advisers.

"You know they really are stoned," Dan called after her. "It's not just a joke."

Mrs. Gwynne-Vaughan didn't turn around.

Dan knew he was only going in for Sergei because Waterford sucked. She never took Sergei out unless she absolutely knew there was no chance of losing. And it wasn't that Dan sucked. He was good. But everyone else was better than he was.

We took our seats, Edie, Nicholas, Sergei, Mickey, and me. Devon went and sat on the bench and started to play some video game on his phone. Dan stood there complaining. "This is lame," he said. "It's not fair."

We beat Yarmouth, Tisdale Academy, and Thomas Paine Regional High—the one public school that was, for reasons unknown to me, in our conference. We had one team left, some Catholic girls' school from Fall River called Holy Virgin. Mrs. Gwynne-Vaughan checked her watch. "I just heard from Sister Martha, their adviser, and they're just pulling in right now." She lowered her voice. "So, I don't anticipate any real problems here. . . . I don't think these girls are all that brilliant, honestly. Now, you know if we win this, we're in the finals, so if everyone can just keep their wits about them and—"

At that moment, the door at the end of the hall creaked open, and the girls from Holy Virgin started to file in.

All conversation and rustling of paper and scratching of pencils came to an abrupt halt as six of the most stacked teenage girls I had ever seen in my life came through the door. They were wearing long-sleeved white blouses, but they were tight and buttoned low, and their breasts burst out of them. Their plaid skirts rested high up on their butts. They were wearing stockings, but they were sheer and sort of shiny in this way that made the effect even dirtier, in a way, than bare skin. All of them wore black boots. Two of them wore glasses, like smart porn stars.

"Holy Virgin," Mickey said.

Dan's and Sergei's mouths fell open. Dan's eyes were big and fishlike. Sergei just looked like he was going to cry.

"Just picture them in their underwear," said Devon, smiling evilly and giving a proud pat to his giant gut. He and Nicholas were unfazed. They'd had sex with pretty girls before. Mickey was certainly overstimulated, but he had a sense of humor, and he had experienced his dick being touched by something other than his own hand. But this was kind of a nerd nightmare.

Dan's and Sergei's sexual frustration was literally seeping out of them. Sergei's brow sprouted beads of sweat, and when Dan ran his hands over his Dockers, they left wet spots.

Mrs. Gwynne-Vaughan gathered us into a huddle. "All right," she said. "Is everyone OK?" She's already told Dan he could go in this round, and considering his being upset before, she couldn't very well change the roster now. But that was too bad, because he was a mess. So was Sergei, who was also in for this round.

"I don't think they should be allowed to wear those clothes," Sergei said. Dan's livery tongue kept clearing gross white stuff from the corners of his mouth. Mrs. Gwynne-Vaughan took a small bottle of water out of her bag and handed it to him.

Nicholas opened it for Dan, who seemed quite devoid of motor skills. "Drink this," Nicholas said. "Then pour the rest of it on your penis."

A nun—one of those sort of modern-looking nuns, in a habit, but wearing pants—approached a lectern a few feet away. "Are we ready?"

Dan looked fearfully at Nicholas.

"Just drink the rest of the water," Nicholas said. "Let's just get this over with." He looked at Sergei.

"Are you all right?" he said.

Sergei made a sound kind of like a humpback whale.

Dan drank the water and handed the bottle to Nicholas.

"What the hell?" Nicholas said. "I'm not your mother."

Dan made whimpering noises to indicate that the trash can was behind where the girls were sitting, five pairs of perfect round breasts and silky hair in a row. One of them crossed and uncrossed her legs. Another leaned over to whisper to another, and a strand of her hair swung between another girl's ample cleavage.

"Wow," Sergei said. "It almost looks like she was going to make out with her."

"Don't make me go over there," Dan pleaded.

"Oh for Christ's sake," Nicholas said. "Give me that."

He went to throw away the bottle. As he walked by, the girls all swiveled toward him. Dan and Sergei both caught it, and their faces went red with jealousy and rage.

"Life sucks," Sergei said.

Thank god Edie was going first, up against one of the girls with the glasses.

"The Chicago Museum of Art is home to the great master-work in the painting style pointillism . . ." the nun read.

"*La Grande Jatte*," Edie said.

Glasses and Breasts pouted. Pants and Habit frowned. "Correct."

Edie was similarly aggressive with the rest of the questions and won the round. I went up against a blond girl named Daphne. "Hi," she gurgled at me. Her body looked like it was made out of tan Tupperware. "I love your earrings." I thanked her and won the round handily.

Now Sergei went up. Sergei's opponent pitched slightly forward on her toes as she shook his hand so that her cleavage found its way to just under his face. He didn't really sit down so much as fall into his chair, casting a helpless look at Nicholas and Devon, who gave him a thumbs-up.

"Physics," the nun announced.

"Physics," Sergei repeated. It was the last word he uttered for the round. He just sat there with a sort of dumb, apologetic smile on his face until the other girl came up with the answers. When it was over he said, "Good job," and went to shake her hand, but she pretended she didn't see, and flounced back to her seat.

Dan was next. His mouth was still open in that weird gaping-fish-mouth expression. His opponent's name was Ursula, and she was appropriately Bond girl–esque, tall and bodacious, with long coppery hair.

"Who missed a crucial ground ball in the 1986 World Series?"

Dan's mouth widened and narrowed, as if he had encountered some plankton.

"Bill Buckner," the Bond girl answered briskly.

"In what city was basketball invented?"

Even I knew this.

"Springfield," said the Bond girl.

"You have a pretty voice," Dan said.

She gave him a sweetly insincere smile.

The last question was so fucking easy: who was the first American to win five medals in the winter Olympics?

"Uuuhhhhh," Dan said.

"Eric Heiden," the girl said, and her butt twitched triumphantly as she went back to her seat.

The match was in Mickey's hands. I had confidence.

Until I looked at him and saw his glassy-eyed stare.

I leaned over Edie's lap to get to him. "Get it together," I hissed.

"Shit, guys," Mickey whispered. "The one I am up against is the only one I think is really hot. I just see such pathos in her eyes, you know? And she keeps looking at me."

"Oh Jesus," Edie said, disgusted. "She's looking at you because you're her opponent."

"Mickey," I said. "Those two are freaks. But I know you can do this. I know you can."

Mickey gave me a hopeful, sad smile, and then his eyes drifted up. I looked and saw his opponent lacing up her boot, bent gracefully over it like a deer rubbing its nose against its paw. "These girls look vulnerable, but they're not. And even if Dan and Sergei probably will never get their hands on a piece of ass like that, you very well might."

"Really?" Mickey said. "Even if I don't grow a lot?"

"Yes," I said. "You're funny. Girls like this. We care about this thing that you have called personalities."

Mickey nodded, mystified. Edie widened her eyes, encouraging me to give him more.

"Mickey, someday a girl like this—maybe even one of these girls—is going to drive you insane. You'll be wondering how you can get rid of her. Or you'll be in a custody battle with one of them. Or if you do marry one and stay married, she's going to redecorate your house every time she gets her period. You think you want to take care of a beautiful girl, but you really don't. They're more trouble than they're worth. Trust me. I know."

Mickey nodded. I think he had drawn some strength from what I said.

The nun cleared her throat. "Are we quite ready?"

I can't believe my college education hinged on whether Mickey Eisenberg was going to be able to resist getting a boner in the next five minutes.

He gave me a confident look as he took his seat across from one of the girls. She was blond with brown eyes, and her lower lip quivered with a vulnerable sensuality. "Hello," Mickey said to her evenly. "How are you?"

"Fine," she said. Her voice was bitchy and irritated. It was exactly what Mickey needed.

The nun cleared her throat. "Twenty-seven to the one-third power times sixteen to the . . . one-half power."

About three seconds passed and Mickey said, "Three-quarters."

The nun pressed her lips together. "You are correct."

The next question involved finding the volume of a sphere. Mickey got it.

The last question was another math problem, harder, and Mickey got that one too.

We had won the match.

"Nothing says 'You managed to keep your dick out of your brain' like whipped fake ice cream and crushed cookies full of trans fats," Mickey said. "I think I'm having a McFlurgency!"

It was ten on a Wednesday night, but the McDonald's off 128 was packed. Tables were full of guys just off work, hunched over their burgers, their jaws working in unison. At other tables, little kids sat up on their knees and used their skinny little bodies like shields against their brothers' and sisters' attempts to eat their french fries. When we walked in they all stared at us—a bunch of overdressed prep school kids and a lady in a skirt with tiny pink ducks, each swimming in its own tiny blue lake. After we'd gotten our McFlurries and Nicholas had paid for all of them, Mrs. Gwynne-Vaughan touched her pearls, her nostrils flaring in instinctive reaction to the attention. "Let's go outside," she said. "And have a little chat about how the hell we're going to beat Xavier."

We sat in the McDonaldland playground, around tiny

tables, our knees up in the air. My McFlurry was amazing, and made even sweeter by the fact that Pilar was back in her room at Midvale trying, and failing, to ignore her *alfajores*. She ate half of one and then sat on her bed, chewing it with tightly closed eyes, willing herself not to go back for the other half. She counted to ten. But she couldn't stop herself. She ran over and ate the other half, and started in on another one.

"Oh my God," I whispered to Edie. "It's working! Pilar is totally chowing those *alfajores*."

"Of course she is," Edie said. "Because they're *alfajores,* and she is Pilar Benitez-Jones."

Mrs. Gwynne-Vaughan was toying with her straw. "My, these are delicious," she said. "Mickey, thank you so much for encouraging me to experiment with the Oreo. Now. As we saw demonstrated on the videotape earlier, Xavier Academy is really quite an astounding team."

Nicholas shook his head. "They're going to kill us," he said.

"Yeah," Dan said, and went to give him a high five.

Nicholas gave him a perfunctory high five back, then said, "I didn't want to leave you hanging, but you should know that you high-five people when you agree with them about something, sort of, well, positive. You don't do it to say, 'Hey yeah, that's exciting, I think we're fucked too.'"

Dan nodded seriously. "OK, thanks," he said. "I appreciate your help."

"I refuse to believe we're fucked," Mickey said.

"Me too," said Edie.

"I'm going to get another McFlurry," said Devon.

"You're not going anywhere," Mrs. Gwynne Vaughan said. "We absolutely have to figure this out."

"Besides," Edie said, "you hardly need it."

Devon looked at her, surprised. "What did you say?"

Edie waited until he sat down, and then she whispered, "You shouldn't eat another one of those. I mean, you're kind of fat."

I couldn't tell if Devon was mad or what. But he didn't get another McFlurry.

I turned my attention back to the real problem.

"Look, Mrs. Gwynne-Vaughan," Nicholas said. "Facts are stubborn things. And we can't deny—"

"We can't deny that we have to win," I said. Pilar was eating another *alfajor*. Edie was the best. She wasn't even inside Pilar's head, and still she came up with a better plan than I did.

"Those guys are such unbelievable geeks," Nicholas said. "They study all the time. They know everything."

Devon looked forlornly into the bottom of his empty McFlurry cup. "Well," he said. "The good news about that is that we can just forget about actually trying to beat them."

"What the hell do you mean?" Nicholas said. "Just because you're lazy doesn't mean the rest of us are."

"Don't put your negativity on me," Devon said. "I am not a negative guy, OK? Negative guys do not wear barrettes, OK? I was just saying we can't beat them on skill. So we need to think about secret weapons."

"It's kind of a drag that none of the girls on our team are hot," Sergei said.

There was a silence as everyone waited to see how Edie and I would react. We looked at each other and burst out laughing. Then everyone else started to laugh. I laughed so hard my side ached. Sergei was such an idiot. Didn't he know that was the worst thing you could say to a girl? Girls were all insecure about how they looked, and to actually tell them to their faces, as if they didn't already know it, that they weren't the kind of girls who made boys stop in their tracks and rendered them absolutely unable to . . .

Suddenly I had an idea. Edie nudged me. "What's up?"

"Edie, do you remember when you said before sometimes the stupidest ideas are the best ones?"

She nodded. I whispered in her ear. Her eyes lit up. "Oh my God," she said. "Those girls are like . . . are like toy versions of her. But . . . is she smart?"

I didn't want to admit this. "She's not entirely stupid. She's eager to learn."

Edie nodded thoughtfully.

"It's not such a dumb idea, right?" I asked.

She laughed. "It's totally a dumb idea. But it seems like it might just work!"

chapter
nine-
teen

As Pilar slept, her beautiful face glowed with well-sugared contentment. Her hand rested on her stomach, curled tenderly around it as if the cookies that Edie had sent to make her chubby and averse to sex were her friends. I slept well too, but at 3 A.M. I woke up and couldn't go back to sleep.

"Are you awake?" Edie said.

I was touched that we were back to a state where she could sense this, and care. "Yeah. I was just thinking how weird it is that Pilar is both the source of all my problems and possibly the answer to one of them."

I think I could feel her smiling in the dark.

"Am I doing the talking tomorrow, or are you?" she asked.

"Hmm." This was a good question. "I don't know," I said. "I mean, if I talk, I'll be able to adjust myself to what she's thinking, and that's pretty helpful. I mean, I guess it could be pretty helpful."

I was glad Edie couldn't see my face. I felt like I had just practically admitted to her that I had been in Gideon's head.

But she just said, "We'll just see how she reacts."

How she reacted in the morning is that she woke up and let out a loud shriek. I heard it in my head, but Edie heard it all the way down the hall.

"What the hell?"

I leaped out of bed and did a little dance on the cold floor. "Pilar is fat! I mean, for her, she's fat. She is freaking out about her stomach!"

I jumped on Edie.

"Help! Physical affection alert. Help." But she was laughing.

I pushed myself up off my hands and landed on the floor. "Let's go talk to her now. She's feeling vulnerable. She's going to want an ego boost."

Edie was stepping into her jeans and socks and then, modestly, putting a bra on under her T-shirt.

I took a little care getting ready to talk to Pilar. I combed my hair. I wore boots instead of just boring clogs, and jeans that actually fit instead of the loose ones that felt comfortable. Edie took notice of my unusual attention to detail and put a little makeup on me—a smudge of dark shadow at the edge of my lashes and some lipstick.

The moment Pilar opened her door and saw Edie and me standing there, she commenced compiling a mental list of what we should change about our appearance.

Apparently, I needed lowlights. I think I kind of knew what lowlights were. Edie needed contacts. (Pilar, genetically perfect, had apparently never heard of LASIK.) I needed to work on my shoulder muscles because I slouched, and finally, Edie could be pretty if she would get her upper lip enhanced, but it would have to be done by someone really good.

Pilar opened her mouth to ask Edie if her mother knew a good plastic surgeon, and I figured this was as good a time as any to interrupt.

"We want you to be on Academic Tête-à-Tête," I said.

Edie nodded enthusiastically. "We do. We all really do."

Thees is a joke. They're making fun of me.

With the fat freak-out this morning I should have anticipated this kind of insecurity.

But before I could say anything, Pilar jumped to her own defense. "I'm actually really smart, you know. I mean, Mrs. Gwynne-Vaughan told me once even I was smart. I theenk I have one of her papers right here saying so."

I decided to totally ignore Pilar's bout of insecurity and make myself look like the one who was insecure.

"So, Pilar," I said. "You're probably thinking, Wow, ATAT is for losers."

Wow. Are they not making fun of me? Do they really want me to be on ATAT? Does Mrs. Gwynne-Vaughan really remember that she said I had the potential?

"We have a lot of gaps in knowledge," Edie said. "Like, you have traveled a lot and . . . you're from another country. So you know different things about history . . ."

"And other kinds of wildlife," I said. "Like . . . penguins! They have penguins in Argentina, right?"

Do they have penguins in Argentina? I can't remember eef we actually have them there now or eef they just wash up on shore now because of the global warming.

Pilar's eyelashes—which were long, lush and embellished

with an amazing new mascara that was not paint, but in fact tiny black latex tubes—fluttered as she modestly bowed her head. "Well, I mean, do you think I could, like, try it out?"

"Sure," Edie said. "Why don't you come to a practice, and we'll see how you like it. We wouldn't want you to do anything you're not comfortable with."

I really want to do it. I know I was supposed to do my stomach first and then my mind, but as long as I screwed up my stomach, I might as well get going on my mind, right?

I couldn't resist saying, "I think this will be really good for you, Pilar."

To my surprise, she looked at me like I was her long-lost friend. Like I understood her as no one else could.

"Molly," she began.

She was about to say that she really admired me.

"Excuse me," Edie said, sensing we should be alone. She left.

"So," said Pilar Benitez-Jones.

"So," I said.

She slipped one foot out of a rhinestone flip-flop and scratched the top of her other foot with her toes. It was the sort of sexy-casual thing that she was very good at and I was very bad at. "Is this . . . weird for you?" she said. "I mean, you must know I am going out with . . ."

I didn't feel very professional about this, but I wanted to keep my dealings with her as clean as possible. It was already a little creepy that the whole reason we were having her on ATAT was that she was hot, but hey, I wouldn't have minded being used for my body rather than my brains. For once.

"It's a small school. We really want ATAT to win. I mean, it's . . . important. To a lot of people. And I think if you join the team, we have a really good chance of winning the finals. I . . . Gid and I broke up. I mean, I did break up with him, so, I mean, technically, why would I be the one who is upset?"

My voice wavered as I said this, because I knew I wasn't telling the whole truth. But I managed to get it out, and she had no idea. It made me feel good to say it, even though it wasn't true. I hoped she wouldn't figure out the real reason we wanted her on ATAT. Then again, I don't know why I cared. I mean, she was the one who thought that I should get lowlights and that Edie needed bigger lips.

Pilar showed up at practice in a green miniskirt, white boots, a button-down lace camisole, and a motorcycle jacket. A subtle shadow hinted at vast stores of cleavage. Her beauty was electrifying—she was like a human disco ball. Everyone stared. Dan was the guy in the room who had probably spent the least time in any proximity to Pilar, and also, not coincidentally, the least likely to ever sleep with her or, for that matter, probably anyone vaguely attractive. He looked as if he were going to burst into tears. Sergei looked mad. Mickey winked at me and made an obscene show of adjusting himself in his chair. Even Devon and Nicholas, though too jaded and sexually experienced to be transfixed by Pilar (and also because they knew her, let's face it), nodded admiringly.

Pilar was like ten Holy Virgin girls. Those girls turned heads because there were so many of them together, but taken individually, they weren't heart-stopping beauties, monuments to physical perfection, like Pilar. Plus, the Xavier guys would be seeing her for the first time. I thought about everything you had to process when looking at a girl like Pilar—her face, her body, the amazement that they went together, the fact that she was in front of you. Then, if you were a guy, you had to factor in the incredible thrill of seeing such perfection while simultaneously trying to process the horrifying fact that there was no way you were going to get to do anything but look.

I took it upon myself to greet her. "Thanks so much for coming," I said. "I think you know everyone."

"I've seen you," Dan blurted out, "but never, like, right in front of my face."

Oh my God, Pilar thought, *He's so ugly. I don't think he should talk about hees face! It makes people look at it.*

Pilar shook his limp hand and came away with her own moist and gluey. The only sound in the room was Nicholas and Devon, quizzing each other.

"Gunpowder was invented in . . . China?" said Devon hesitantly.

Nicholas frowned and went through his papers for a second. He looked up with a bright, fake smile. He wasn't Pilar's biggest fan, but he was competitive and he understood her importance as well as anyone. "Right you are. But do you know when Chang and Eng were born?"

"Chang and Eng?" Pilar said. "Are they Siamese twins?"

We were all surprised and impressed but tried not to show it.

Pilar was very pleased when Nicholas said they were.

She gave a modest shrug. "There's a boutique in Shanghai called that. And their logo ees that. So . . . I figured."

"Pilar, keen instincts are very important. You should always go with your gut," Mrs. Gwynne-Vaughan said.

"My gut?" Pilar had never heard this expression, and she wondered if Mrs. Gywnne-Vaughan was suggesting she was fat.

"We are so pleased to have you," Mrs. Gwynne-Vaughan said. "Shall we begin with some recent history?"

I assumed Mrs. Gwynne-Vaughan was going to play to Pilar's strengths.

Pilar, why don't you go up against . . . Dan?"

Dan and Pilar sat in front of the room. Dan kept shifting in his seat, and I smiled to myself, thinking I should teach him Gid's trick about the pile of gross food and the goat's milk.

Pilar closed her eyes in concentration.

"Who shot Gianni Versace?"

"Andrew Cunanan," Pilar said. She smiled and added, "He was a gay drifter."

"Correct."

Dan snorted. Pilar clapped her hands together. "Yay!" she said.

"Number two. How many ex-husbands does Elizabeth Taylor have?"

"Eight," Dan said, sure he was right.

"No," Pilar said. "Eight marriages. She married Richard Burton twice. Eight weddings, seven husbands."

"Correct," said Mrs. Gwynne-Vaughan. "Number three. Who took over the House of Chanel in 1983?"

"Karl Lagerfeld," shouted Pilar, leaping clear out of her seat. "Wow!" she said. "This is, like, so amazingly fun!" She'd never cared about knowing the answer in class before, but this was different. It was like, everyone was watching her, and she had won. It felt like something else, she thought, knowing the right answer.

"Pilar, you're free to go," Mrs. Gwynne-Vaughan said. "We've seen enough. We're happy to have you if you're happy to have us."

"Oh, I am!" Pilar said. Being this happy made her look more beautiful than I had ever seen her. "Oh," she said, before she left. "What should I wear to the match?" Mrs. Gwynne-Vaughan's eyes took in Pilar's outfit from her spike heels up to her cleavage, and I saw a quiver of distaste across her lip before she said, "What you're wearing is perfect."

After she left, we all stayed quiet for a minute. Seeing Pilar in action had made me feel very calm. I saw that Nicholas was looking at me with an admiring smile. So were Mickey, Devon, Sergei, and Mrs. Gwynne-Vaughan, even Dan. It was Dan who started to clap, a slow, steady clap. Everyone joined in, filling the room with applause.

"Brilliant," Nicholas said. "I mean, I thought I was used to her, but that girl knows how to walk into a room."

"I'll say," Mrs. Gwynne-Vaughan said. She wiped her glasses on the cuff of her sweater. "I'm a sixty-year-old woman, but I can see it. She's an atom bomb."

chapter
twenty

After the practice, Pilar went back to her room and flopped on her bed and screamed with joy. She pressed her hands into her mouth and felt herself tingling all over. She rolled over onto her stomach and laughed into the mattress out of pure glee. She was smart! What did her mother know? She was smart and she was going to help carry the Midvale Academic—what was it called again? Well, whatever it was, they were going to win, and she was going to help.

It's amazing I decided to cultivate my mind and now I am actually going to get a real chance to prove, beyond a shadow of a doubt, that I am not just hot.

She sat on the edge of the bed. She wondered if she should study, maybe? Math? No. She needed help to study math. But maybe she could get out a history book or something and just look it over. She knelt down by her bookshelf. There was her pile of Italian *Vogue*s, her pile of British *Vogue*s, her *Elle*s. Her textbooks looked lonely. She picked up her history text from last year. She opened it to a page of someone being tarred and feathered. *Oh my God, I always thought that was just an expression, like it just meant to yell at someone. People actually did that?*

She ended up reading the entire chapter on the Revolutionary War. When she finished that, she saw that the next chapter was called "Trouble with Europe."

She wanted to know what this trouble with Europe was, and she started to read when she saw that she was late to meet Gideon in the dining hall for dinner.

When she got there he had an empty plate in front of him and was holding the newspaper up in front of his face. She recognized him by his shoes, and she kicked one of them as she approached.

"Hey," she said. "Sorry I'm late." Gid didn't look right. He was distracted.

"What's wrong?" she said.

"Nothing terrible," he said. "It's just that we had a bag of pot in our room, and it's missing now. I don't know. I mean, I think Cullen probably got really high and left it somewhere. But then I just worry."

Pilar nodded, but she didn't care about Gideon and his pot. *Boys just smoke pot to be cool. Pot's not even that fun. It just makes me paranoid I'm as fat as a whale. But eef Geedeon didn't smoke pot, he might not be so cute. He might seem like he was too good. Anyway. We might as well talk about me.*

"I was studying," Pilar said.

"You?" Gid said. "Studying?"

"Yes! I learned about the Stamp Tax! And the . . . uh . . . Old Eeronsee-days."

"I think you mean Old Ironsides," Gid said.

"I am on Academic. Shit. I can't remember what it's called."

Gid looked at her incredulously. "You're on Academic Tête-à-Tête?"

"Yes," Pilar said. "Isn't that just, like, the greatest thing! It is so fun. I knew who killed Gianni Versace. And I knew who Karl Lagerfeld was."

Through her eyes I saw suspicion cloud his face.

"What is it, Geedeon? Aren't you happy for me?"

Gideon put his hand on his leg and smiled into her eyes, and I had the unpleasant sensation of feeling his loving gaze upon me without being its actual focus. "Of course I am happy for you," Gid said gently. "I'm sure you're a great addition to the team."

He stood up abruptly. Head down, he started to charge out of the cafeteria.

"Where are you going?" Pilar called after him.

"I have to go take care of something," he said. He lowered his voice to a whisper. "Some bullshit with the missing pot."

"Oh, OK. Well, I'm going to be in the library later, so you might want to come find me." She wanted to talk more about ATAT.

Gid leaned over to kiss her good-bye, and from the light brush of his lips on her cheek I knew that he wasn't really paying attention. I didn't need to be inside his head to know he was coming to find me.

I positioned myself at the bottom of my dorm stairs with a giant pile of ATAT materials. Gid walked in muttering to himself, "Look Molly, the thing is," clearly practicing for our confrontation.

As usual, when we were in the same room, I would feel like the air had suddenly been set on fire. Gid looked hot. It was clear, especially seeing him this close-up, that going out with Pilar—despite the obvious setbacks—had given him a great deal of confidence. Just being seen with her had set his shoulders back an inch or two, had lifted his head, and had brought a sort of lampish glow to his cheek, so that his extremely short whiskers were tipped with gold. He had that amazing hollow about two inches southwest of his ear. I swallowed as I felt my heart shudder up into my throat. The unfinished, frayed edges of ourselves were touching each other.

He finally said, "What are you doing sitting there?"

To which I responded, "I live here."

"No." Gid scowled impatiently. "What are you doing sitting on the stairs?"

"Nothing," I said, my tone defensive. "I sit here a lot."

"You never sit there," Gid said.

"Gid," I said, testing my luck, "did you come over here to argue about where I habitually sit?"

He looked at me. "No. I came over here to talk about why the hell you put Pilar on ATAT."

"I didn't put her anywhere," I said. "Mrs. Gwynne-Vaughan did. She thought she'd be good for the team."

Gid snorted. "That is just so much bullshit," he said.

It was both annoying and hot that he knew I was lying. "It is not," I said. "You can go ask her."

This was just a ridiculous thing to say because we both knew it would be a cold day in hell before Gid stormed into Mrs. Gwynne-Vaughan's office and demanded to know why she'd put his hot girlfriend on ATAT, because let's face it, she wasn't a genius.

"I just don't know why you'd want to humiliate her like that," he said. He shook his head. "I just don't . . . I mean, I always knew you were jealous of Pilar."

I thought I was so good at hiding things. Being inside Gid's head, and then Pilar's, I forgot that other people had normal capabilities of perception, and that they could look inside my head as well.

Gid continued. "But I never thought you'd go so far as to purposely humiliate her."

A lot of things could have come out of my mouth, but what did come out was "Don't flatter yourself."

I didn't know what this would do to Gid. I didn't think it would be good, but I didn't expect it to have the effect it did. "Flatter myself?" he said, and his face reddened and I saw his hands start to shake. "I am hardly capable of flattering myself. I mean, Molly, for Christ's sake, you broke up with me without any explanation, when I was . . . when we were . . . Do you have any idea how humiliating that was?"

"Humiliating?" I said. "That's the worst thing you can say about it is that it was humiliating?"

"What's worse than being humiliated?" Gid said.

I wanted to say, seeing your boyfriend get himself into a state of arousal by picturing another girl in a white bikini. But I just shook my head.

"Look," Gid said, and the sudden lowness of his voice, not quite intimate but around the edges, made my stomach turn over on itself. "Can we at least talk about what happened?"

Gideon still had feelings for me. There was no way he really wanted to talk about my putting Pilar on ATAT. He wanted to know if I still cared.

"Molly, talk to me."

I shook my head. "I can't explain it right now. I have . . . I have a lot of studying to do."

He looked at the wall, about to punch it, but drew his fist back. "Fuck," he said. "That wall looks pretty hard."

I wanted to say, this is what you get for not wanting me enough, but I couldn't. So I just watched him stare at the wall until he walked away.

Gid wanted to know if I still cared, and I wasn't sure whether I wanted to be honest about the fact that I still did, or just keep it to myself. Now that Pilar was studying more, she was also eating more *alfajores,* and since they definitely weren't going to sleep together today, well, as far as letting Gid know I still cared, I wasn't about to decide today either.

chapter
twenty-one

That night, Pilar and I were both in our respective rooms, both studying for ATAT.

She had decided that tonight she was going to memorize facts about the Habsburgs, the Windsors, all the Louis and their wives, and I decided I would do the same. Whatever she read, I would read at the same time. "This is awesome," I told Edie. "She reads slower than I do, so I take in the information and then take it in again just a few seconds later. It makes memorizing this stuff so easy."

Pilar was very excited by the fact that Queen Victoria, whom she had thought was somehow related to Posh Spice and still alive, had invented the concept of wearing white at weddings.

White. Milk. Pilar wanted some milk to go with her delicious *alfajores*.

Walking across the quad to the campus store, Pilar thought

about how she had always imagined that white was her color and that she looked so good in it that no one else should wear it. With some shame she recalled the night that Madison had worn that nice white dress and gotten the job from that sleazy producer. It didn't have anything to do with her dress, Pilar knew that now. Madison had just presented herself as a serious person. But maybe in a way she was lucky she had fucked that thing up, because Elias was a dick anyway. Maybe, she thought, now that I'm on ATAT, I could get a more serious job. Like not just for some gross person.

Pilar was so busy having all these things in her head that she just forgot to think about whether anyone was looking at her. She thought about how she wasn't thinking about how anyone was looking at her because she was thinking. She laughed and clapped her hand over her mouth. This was all surprising.

Pilar had always held it in her head that it would have been better if she were more glamorous, but when you were glamorous, did there ever come a point where you stopped worrying about being glamorous and enjoyed it? I don't think so, she thought. It seemed like maybe all the time you were thinking about being pretty you couldn't enjoy it. Like her stomach, she hadn't thought about it all day, which was good because it was of course still fat and if she had thought about it she probably would have had trouble concentrating. But maybe first her mind and then her stomach was a good idea. Her stomach. Gideon. Sex.

Why did her mind have to move that fast?

I had been making that association, but I didn't want her to make it too.

She got her milk and went to her room and drank it and

studied some more. She fell onto her bed, exhausted. She felt herself starting to fall asleep when there was a knock on her window. She sat up.

It was Gideon. She let him in.

"Pilar," he said. He sat down on the bed. He looked uncomfortable. Scared. He looked like he had something to say. The second he swallowed and looked at her with pained eyes, she knew.

Oh my God, she thought, *he is going to break up with me.*

I think she was right.

"Pilar," he said again.

No, no, no. He can't break up weeth me. I thought I felt better because I was studying and stuff, but now I feel really bad. I feel better because I have a boyfriend who won't break up with me, and now, he ees someone who would break up with me, and that can't happen. Plus, I know that he still thinks he likes Molly. And even though she is thinner than me, my number is 9.87 and she is only a 7.2.

A 7.2! That fucking bitch. I would have sworn I was at least an 8.

She was thinking, *It's Molly.* But she couldn't admit that. It would make her look too insecure. "I know it's been hard for you, me saying no," she said. In the split second that it took him to even begin to respond to what she was saying, Pilar had whipped off her shirt and stood there naked to the waist. I had seen them—her breasts—before. But I had never seen a guy see them. I saw a glaze come over Gid's eyes, and his hands left his side involuntarily and he reached out and felt them. "Oh," he said.

"Let's just have sex," Pilar said.

Gideon said one word: "But . . ."

He had been there to break up with her.

She took her pants off.

Please, Gideon, I begged silently. Say no and leave. If you leave now, and you try to get me back, I will forgive you. I will believe you.

I saw resolve in his eyes. He did want to go.

But then Pilar took her underwear off. His eyes closed a little. I saw his body give in. He was a guy. She was a girl who had taken her clothes off. It was going to be harder to resist what his body wanted than to just take what it was offered. I saw him forget what he'd come here to do as instinct took over.

As I took off down the hall, I felt Gid's hand, I felt it like it was on my own neck, the soft pads of his fingers and that tip of his right finger that was callused from holding a pen. I felt his soft lips on her neck and his hands on her slim flanks. I felt her lift her knee to help him.

I started to tear through the bathroom trash. I found the Design New England section of *The Boston Globe*. I lit the page on fire and watched the flame climb up, burning away a headline about the appeal of Roman blinds over Venetian ones.

The alarm sounded with a force so hard it was more than sound. It felt like actual metal tubes were pushed in my ear. I ran the burning paper under the faucet for a few seconds and flushed it.

I opened the door, and a few seconds later—crucial, no one had seen me—girls were already starting to stream out of their rooms, giggling, self-consciously braless, holding their arms over their chests in skimpy nightshirts.

"Girls." It was Captain Cockweed's wife, wearing a long flannel nightgown with hearts on it, clogs, and a gold down vest. Our dorm head had to be out for the night, and she was filling in. "Everyone out. Let's go." She had her frizzy brown hair in one of those plastic clips, a giant one, the size of a potato masher.

The quad lights came on and it felt a little like an outdoor concert. The stars were bright. It was a warm night, and some girls spread out bathrobes in the grass. Giggles echoed off the brick and floated up into the piney air.

I was pacing.

In my mind, I thought, OK, this will just interrupt them. Pilar will come outside, Gid will hide.

Pilar and Gideon were still inside.

The noise had so shocked Pilar that she had jumped off Gid like he was a hot stove, as if touching him had set off the alarm. *"Dios,"* she said. "That is fucking loud. I can't stand it. I think I'm going crazy. Geedeon. Isn't it driving you crazy?"

She dressed herself as quickly as she could in a pair of black yoga pants and a white tank top and a red pashmina. *Maybe I should just wear a black tank top, because it's just better for night.* She crouched down and shoved a pile of shoes against the wall to make space for him to sit. Gid got in the closet. She kissed him. "I'll be back," she said. She started to walk out the door when she looked down at her feet. She was wearing sneakers. Sneakers and pants made her feel fat.

If only she had walked right out the door.

Instead, she came back to the closet. She smiled at Gideon. "Hey," she said.

"You better hurry," he said. "They're going to check the rooms to see who's not there."

"I'm just grabbing a pair of flip-flops," she said, and as she headed out the door, Gid called, "Good luck."

The hallway was dark, and the instant she opened the door, Cockweed was standing there with a flashlight. Gideon still hadn't quite shut the closet door. "Rayburn," he said. "Fancy meeting you here."

chapter twenty-two

I felt terrible. It had been just an impulse.

I couldn't help myself. I just hadn't wanted to see them have sex, and I just went crazy and lit that fire.

Cockweed. Ugh. I mean, what the fuck was I thinking! I mean, it's prep school. Someone is always lurking, waiting to get you into trouble, right? All you have to do is just ask for it a little and you get it. And they had gotten it. Being in opposite dorm rooms was absolutely forbidden. Especially naked.

Gid was going to have to go back to Virginia.

Life with Jim Rayburn. The Sears couch and the matching recliner. The dinners with his mother, driving his mother's new PT Cruiser instead of the timeless white Beamer. Nicholas and Cullen, his best friends, he'd basically never see them again.

With Pilar gone, there was no way we were going to beat Xavier.

I wasn't going to get my scholarship.

Worse . . . I would never see Gideon again.

I wanted to hate him because he was going to have sex with Pilar even though he was planning to break up with her. But I just didn't hate him. Some people you can try to hate, and they might even deserve it. But if you think someone's hot, you're probably just not going to keep hating him for very long. It's just kind of impossible.

Pilar packed and cried. She was stunned that her time at Midvale was coming to an end. *I had just started to like it here. I didn't have to really hang out with that bitch Madison anymore, and Geedeon is so nice. And I had a purpose, and I was managing to get maybe kind of smart and not totally just be the pretty girl, not just be that stupid girl that Elias Ganz felt up but to be smart too. OK, so most of my dreams about the ATAT match didn't get beyond what I was going to wear, but I was psyched to go.*

Edie was doing her best to make me feel better.

"It's really not all that bad," she said. We were in our room, lying on our beds and staring at the ceiling like we always did when we were bummed, or thinking, or both. "Now you won't have to deal with them anymore. Well. I mean, who knows how long you could be in Pilar's head. But at least they won't be here."

The idea of Midvale without Gid seemed terrible to me, like a death. Even though we had broken up, I still had opportunities to see him, and be mad at him, and that was better than his not being here at all.

"So," Edie said. "You did still like Gid. I kind of didn't believe that you were so over him."

I didn't say anything and she went on.

"Yeah. You know what? When you're attracted to someone, everything just flies out the window. Like Devon, for example. He's a fat fuck and he smokes too much pot. I am, like, a hundred times smarter than he is. And yet, I still spend just about every waking moment thinking about him. And it's torture, because, you know, I don't really have any way of knowing whether he actually really likes me or if he is just going to, like, have sex with me and break up with me."

"Oh, Edie," I said. "I'm pretty sure—"

"Pretty sure doesn't cut it," she said. "I want to know."

"But even if you knew, you wouldn't know," I said. "Girls' minds are pretty complicated, but I mean, boys' minds are even worse because they're not. I mean, seriously, I think we just happen to have holes that they want to stick things in. We're interchangeable to them. They're not interchangeable to us. Which means we just have to find them and figure out how to get them to avoid another girl's holes. But even if he said, 'Oh, I am so into you,' all it means, well, all it could mean is, I am so into having sex with you until someone prettier than you wants to have sex with me."

My voice reached a dangerously high pitch.

Edie looked at me. Her face was very serene, very pretty, and serious. She spoke in a gentle voice. "You've been in someone else's head," she said. "A guy's. I mean, I've guessed that what you're saying is true, obviously, or I wouldn't be all weird about this Devon thing. But you're talking like you know."

"Pilar's is the only mind I've ever been in," I said.

Edie shook her head, and she even looked like she might laugh. "You are such a bad liar! Come on, Molly! I've seen you for the last year. You've been out of it. Your head has been somewhere else. Besides, why didn't you tell me you were in Pilar's head earlier? What would you have had to lose?"

I hadn't told her I was in Pilar's head basically because she would have thought I was insane. And also, more important, because I was so embarrassed to have gone out with Gideon when I was in his head. How insecure Edie was about guys, well, I think I was maybe even worse. I felt like if anyone knew I was in Gid's head, they'd think, Oh, that's the only way she could get him to go out with her.

But at this point, everything was such a mess it didn't seem important to keep in a secret anymore. "OK," I said. "I was in Gideon's head."

The birds chirping outside suddenly seemed very loud.

"Wow," she said. "I . . . why didn't . . . wait. Since when?"

"Since that very first day," I said. "When his dad honked at us. Well, actually right before that. It started when he was just at the end of his drive up here. I was in this guy's head, and he was so sweet and scared, but funny. And it was the strangest feeling, because I felt like I understood him . . . because I was thinking about how afraid I had been to come to school here, and then I heard someone else thinking that." I shook my head to try to explain better. "I heard a voice in my head having the thought, but since it was the same as mine I didn't notice it, and then, well. He started thinking about his balls, and . . ."

Edie smiled. "And you were like, hmm, I don't have balls."

I nodded. "Exactly," I said. "And then, well, it turned out he was coming toward me. I couldn't help feeling he was for me, you know. We were both thinking about how scared we were of Midvale." I laughed, this time without humor. "He changed so much here. He grew up so much. He used to be so afraid of Cullen and Nicholas."

Edie nodded. "Well. They are dicks." Then she twisted up her face.

"What?" I asked.

"Why didn't you tell me?" She looked so hurt.

"I felt stupid," I said. "I thought you would think that the only reason that Gideon went out with me was because I was inside his head."

"What?" Edie was shocked. "Molly, Gid was so lucky to have you. He's great, but you're . . . greater."

Now I laughed for real. "I guess part of why I started to really like him was watching him have the nerve to become friends with Cullen and Nicholas. I always really respected that. Imagine if you came here for your first year, and Madison Sprague was your roommate."

"No, thank you," Edie said. "She'd probably have had me skinned and turned into a pair of boots. I would probably have suggested it too, just to make her happy."

"I love him," I said. "I think he's amazing. I don't want him to go. I want to get back together with him. But it's just that . . . Shit."

I told her the white bikini story.

"What a dick," she said.

I nodded. "That's kind of how I felt."

"Of course, it's not really his fault," she said.

"No," I agreed.

"But that doesn't make him not a dick," she countered.

"No?" I asked. "Why?"

"I don't know," she said. "Are people dicks for their feelings?"

"I don't know either. But I couldn't keep going out with him. I felt like an idiot. Like he was having his cake and eating it too."

"Well, you can't really blame him for going out with her," Edie said. "Based on your holes theory. You took your holes away. Doesn't he have a right to get new holes? Especially if he was sad about losing access to yours?"

I snorted. "How could you possibly think that Gideon was going out with Pilar to get over me?" Even though this is sort of what I had been hoping since Gid got pissed about Pilar's being on ATAT.

"Because it's totally obvious. And I think it would be pretty much obvious to anyone who wasn't you."

"Not to Cullen and Nicholas. They think Gid unconsciously got me to break up with him so he could be with Pilar. Which is, in a way, kind of what happened."

Edie waved me off. "Molly, what do we know about those guys? They're dicks. Forget about what they think! Wait. OK. You were in Gideon's head."

"Correct."

"And then . . . you were in Pilar's . . ."

"Yes," I said. "Then his again and then hers."

"And . . . OK. Wow. You are a freak. I thought I was a freak, but you are a serious freak!"

"Thanks," I said.

"But that's not what I was going to say," Edie said. "You have to be able to figure out why."

"You'd think so," I said. "But we haven't."

"We?" Edie said.

I told her about Dr. Stanley Whitmeyer.

"Dr. Stanley Whitmeyer! That is, like, the most fake name I ever heard!" Edie laughed.

"No . . . he writes me. And I can tell he understands."

"OK, OK," Edie said, but she still looked skeptical. "What does this Dr. Whitmeyer say?"

"He keeps telling me to think about why I want to get out of their heads and why I want to stay," I said. "And I'm like, I don't want to stay, and he says if I didn't want to stay I wouldn't be there. I hate that shit!"

"So. You got into Gid's head without even knowing him, and the old guy thinks it's because he was, like, coming toward you, and you were so psychically aligned? Like, meant to understand each other?"

I nodded. "I guess that's pretty much it."

Edie started to take notes. "And then you got into Pilar's head, trying to get out of Gideon's?"

"Correct." I said. "And he was like, you have to tell your head you couldn't take being in Gid's head. That it was too sad. And it worked. Well, except . . ."

Edie kept writing this down. "You went into Pilar's head, Molly. What were you thinking when Gid came into your head for the first time? Do you remember?"

"Of course I do," I said. "I was thinking I didn't want to go to school here, that I didn't know if I belonged."

She nodded. "And what were you thinking about, exactly, when you went into Pilar's head for the first time?"

This was harder, but I remembered. "This is embarrassing. I was in Buffalo, and I was asking myself if Pilar was in fact the hottest girl in the world, because Gid, while he was kissing her, had whispered that to her."

Edie smiled sympathetically. "OK, that sucks. But as far as I'm concerned, this isn't that complicated."

"That's what Dr. Whitmeyer says," I said.

"OK, listen," Edie said. "You found your way into Gid's head because you thought the same thing as him. It's like your brain was on some current and so was his, and they melded."

I desperately wanted this to be something I could understand, but I was wary. "So then why didn't he go into my brain?"

Edie surprised me by laughing. "Well, I'm guessing the dominant brain current takes over. And I'm just guessing that would be yours," she said.

That was probably true.

"So," Edie continued. "You understood what it would be like to be new here, to feel weird, and then, like, he was hot, so you stayed in his head, and then, after you start going out, you just stay because all you can think about is his thoughts. It's like the current of his brain is holding yours prisoner."

I followed.

"OK. Then you're really ready to get out, but then Pilar, well, she up and thinks the same thing at the same time as you—you think she's the most beautiful girl in the world, and she thinks, I am the most beautiful girl—and you end up in her head."

"But then I ended back in Gid's head, and back in Pilar's, and those times I wasn't thinking the same . . ." I felt my insides go to ash. Edie was right: I got back into Gid's head when we'd both been wondering whether Pilar's hand block meant she was done fooling around with him. Mine was wishful thinking that she was, his was panic that she was. And then, I'd gone back into Pilar's head when we'd both thought about whether her stomach was finally flat enough for her to have sex with Gideon. Obviously, we were all on different sides as to whatever we'd wished for, but we were both obsessed with, and basing all future happiness on, the same thing.

We were getting there. "But what about the kissing?"

Edie shrugged. "Well, I'm sure that just helped you get into her head. Expedited it."

"Shit," I said to Edie.

"Yeah," she said. "I know. Shit."

We had to go to ATAT now.

"I guess we'll talk about this later?" I said.

Edie laughed. "What else are we going to talk about?"

As we walked there, I thought back to the two times I'd gone into Pilar's head: the first time, and the second time, when Gid was walking across the quad toward her the other day.

"I think I ended up in Pilar's head because I wanted to feel what it felt like to have Gid look at me the way he looked at her," I said to Edie.

Edie shook her head sympathetically. "Oh, Molly," she said. "I think the way Gid looks at you is pretty good."

I wasn't sure. And with his leaving, I wasn't going to find out.

"I think there's something wrong with you," Edie said.

"Duh," I said. "I'm inside Pilar's mind."

Edie shook her head. "No," she said. "Besides that."

The feeling at ATAT was very glum. We all got our partners and went to our various corners of the room to work our drills, but no one bothered to actually engage with the material. Everyone was talking about what happened, and how fucked we were.

I partnered with Nicholas. He looked more bummed out than I had ever seen him.

Then I saw that Nicholas was . . . well, not exactly trying not to cry, but as upset as someone like him gets.

"I just can't imagine life without Gid here," he said. "I just wish there was something I could do. Cockweed's had it in for us for a long time. He's always wanted to take Gid down. Oh my God. A few weeks ago, Cullen was making a lot of noise—long story—and Cockweed came in and looked around our room, and he went in the closet, and we have shitloads of pot in there, and he didn't even see it or smell it or anything. And I thought, Wow, we're home free." He managed to pull off a thoughtful smile. "It's so weird this is what happened. It totally came out of left field."

"How's Gid?" I asked.

Nicholas shook his head. "He's upset."

I had expected as much, but I still didn't like hearing it. "When is he going home?"

"Well," he said, "apparently, the damning part of this whole thing is that Gid . . ."

He didn't want to tell me, but I already knew, and plus, it was gossip anyone who knew anyone could have had access to.

"I know," I said. "Gideon didn't have any clothes on."

We couldn't help smiling at each other. I guess we were both picturing Gideon in Pilar's closet, naked and helpless with Cockweed's flashlight on him. The only difference was that, through Pilar's eyes, I had actually seen it.

Nicholas smiled—and this was an expression I had never, ever seen on his face—affectionately. "You kind of got to hand it to Gid," he said. "He comes here a virgin, and he ends up getting kicked out for being naked in the closet of the hottest girl on campus."

Nicholas went on, completely oblivious to the idea that I might not have loved hearing Pilar referred to that way. "Apparently there's going to be some sort of a hearing. You know.

The various parties give their sides of the story. It's in two days. But at this point . . ." Nicholas looked down at his feet and shook his head. "It's pretty much just a formality."

I looked around the ATAT practice room, at this depressing little place with its peeling-edged Klimt prints and a wall of boring, useless books. Edie and Devon were sitting very close and whispering, and Devon was so bummed out he wasn't even bothering to look down her shirt. Sergei thumbed through *The Lancet,* a British medical journal, but I could tell he wasn't reading. Mickey Eisenberg was rolling a joint, and Mrs. Gwynne-Vaughan, sitting at a metal desk in the corner, grading papers, her mouth straight and stiff, didn't even notice. Poor Dan's hair looked even flatter than usual today.

I could smell Mickey's joint from here. It made me wonder how Cockweed could have avoided smelling the pot in the boys' room.

Then I thought about how some of that pot had gone missing.

Finally, I remembered overhearing Cockweed talking to his friend on his cell phone that morning we were hiding out in the chapel. He'd said, "I'm not in the right frame of mind for thinking."

Because I thought Cockweed was so stupid, I hadn't really thought about it. But Cockweed didn't think he was stupid. And he clearly wasn't going to brag about his own stupidity.

Cockweed smoked pot.

It was just a hunch.

Bu considering my ability to know what people were doing and thinking, there had to be a chance it was a good one.

chapter
twenty-three

Pilar was sitting on her fancy sofa with her eyes closed, trying to pretend this was all just a dream. She opened them and saw around her the proof that it wasn't—neatly stacked T-shirts, jeans, her stable of hotel-quality sheets and towels zipped inside their protective plastic sheaths. The white-hot fear she'd felt when she saw Cockweed standing outside her door, that stupid flashlight on his head, had lasted overnight. The next morning, when the drama was over and it was clear that she and Gid were just going home, it had turned into a dull, empty ache.

Her life at Midvale was over. She would never walk up the stairs of Emerson, wrinkling her nose at the common smells of Pantene and White Linen, and make a mad dash for her room, where she would be so very relieved to find herself enveloped in the delicious scents of her far superior products, her Kérastase, her Jo Malone orange blossom cologne, the delicate rose scent of her Chanel lipstick. She would never go to the dining hall and make her special low-fat dressing out of vinegar, cottage cheese, and the chopped cilantro she brought in herself, or run around the track as the sun came up, cheering her, reminding her that her ass was growing smaller while the other girls of Midvale merely slumbered and thickened.

Back in our room, I told Edie about my Cockweed pot theory. She jumped up in the air. "No way," she said.

"Why are you so excited?" I said. "I mean, we don't know where he keeps it. We don't know if it's true. We'd have to follow him around and bust him, and we only have a few days before Gid and Pilar leave."

Edie looked at me and shook her head. "Are you dense?"

How was I supposed to respond to that?

"You have a superpower," she said.

"Yeah," I said. "But I'm not in Cockweed's head."

Edie sat down with her pen and paper. She frowned over it for a while, scribbling down ideas. She wrote the word *superpower*. Then she circled it.

"Pilar," she said. "Of course."

I sniffed impatiently. "I'm not following."

"Pilar has a superpower, too," she said. "Being hot."

I still didn't follow.

"Let's just tell Pilar that we think Cockweed may have pot, and that we want her to stay."

"OK, but that means that we have to get Pilar to kiss Cockweed?" I said. "There's no way that's going to happen."

"Ordinarily, I would say that's right. But you do have special powers," Edie said. "That changes everything."

"Edie, just because I'm in someone's mind doesn't mean I can get them to kiss a gross pig like Cockweed."

Edie shook her head, like I was a child who had refused to learn to tie her shoes.

"Molly," she said, "if you're in someone's head, I think you can get them to do just about anything. OK. Pilar kisses Cockweed, and you get into his mind. That way, you can find out where he keeps his pot."

She clapped her hands as if it were all so simple.

"Edie," I said, "I hate to burst your bubble, but how do you propose we explain to Pilar that she needs to kiss him?"

Edie thought about this. "That's a good point. We don't tell Pilar anything. We just tell her Cockweed has pot. We came to her because we want her to stay, and we thought maybe she would help us." She raised her eyebrows suggestively.

I thought about Pilar's eagerness to be on ATAT. She felt like a useless ornament. She wanted to be useful. But the more we let her think things were her own idea, the better chance we had of getting her to do what needed to get done. "If we don't tell her we need her to kiss Cockweed, she might kiss him."

Edie looked unsure about this. But she smiled confidently. "If Cockweed has pot, and Pilar gets any kind of significant time alone with him, I'm pretty fucking sure she can figure out how to find it."

Pilar was surprised to see us. The first thing she said was "I bet you're glad."

She turned away from me and went and sat in a red velvet chair in the corner of her room.

I guessed we were supposed to follow her in there.

"Why would I be glad?" I said. "I thought you—respected me. I thought you . . . Oh, I don't know."

"I do." Pilar took a handful of her amazing hair and then looked at my hair. "Have you ever heard of lowlights?" she asked.

"I have heard of them," I admitted. "But I can't say I know what they are."

"They're . . ." Pilar shook her head. "They're nothing. They're not important. You can sit down, you know."

I moved a pile of cashmere sweaters and sat. "You're a very neat folder," I complimented her. "You know, you would have been very good at ATAT. Part of it is just keeping the question in your mind. Knowing what part of your brain the answer is in."

Pilar blinked a few times. "So like, eef you can keep your sweaters neat, you can do well on ATAT?"

I nodded. "Something like that," I said.

"I am going to my aunt and uncle's," she said. "I am going to day school. Do you know what it is like, thees day school?"

I shrugged. "It's like when you went to school when you were really little, except you're older now. You know, you go to school and you have your friends, and then your sleep at home."

Pilar pondered this with visible distaste. "I don't want to sleep at home. Or near my aunt and uncle. I hate sleeping in the same house as adults. You wake up, they are there, telling you must eat two eggs instead of one, asking you los questions."

I realized that Pilar was drunk. Well, not drunk. Drinking. How had I missed that?

It was quiet for a moment, and then she said, "What are you doing here?"

I said, "What if I told you I came up with a way you could stay here?"

She looked unimpressed and drank her wine again. "What do you care? I mean, you want Gid to stay here. Why do you care about me?"

I decided to tell her a reasonable version of the truth. "I want you on ATAT. We need you."

I had told Edie that we should try to act calm and casual, but I think we were both too tense about the stakes of the game and what Pilar would have to do to help us win.

"You guys are scaring me," she said. "What do you want me to do?"

I would have to just dive right in.

"Cockweed has pot," I said, "or we think he does. And we want to be able to blackmail him with that, to tell him that unless he backs off on his charges against you guys, we'll tell Dr. Frye. And we don't really know what to do."

But Pilar just snorted. "I do," she said. "We have to find the pot."

I was annoyed that I thought she didn't get that. "Right," I said. "Finding the pot is crucial. It's the how part that—"

But Pilar cut me off, snorting again. "How? Ha. Cockweed loves me. I just have to make him think I want to sleep weeth him. He'll tell me where it is. If I showed him my underwear, he'd tell me where was Hope Diamond."

Pilar crossed the room and lit a white gardenia candle. In her tragedy she was arresting. Dressed in a white sundress and a woven shawl and tan cowboy boots, she moved with a gentle grace, her soft hair floating down a back held straight and dignified against her recent and public humiliation. When she turned back to look at me, her dark eyes were both mysterious and vulnerable. *I shouldn't act like I am so sure of myself. Cock-weed ees a deesgusting moron, but what if he attacks me?* "I don't know," she said. "I am feeling that I am just going to take my punishment and go."

Edie looked at me and mouthed the word *superpower.*

I decided not to focus on Pilar's saying no, but on her feelings. "Why are you nervous?" I said.

She immediately got an image of Cockweed bearing down on her with his tongue out. So she was nervous about the one thing that had to happen for this to even possibly work. And not without reason: Cockweed by himself was gross. Kissing Cockweed was unthinkable.

"Look, I know the grossest thing when I think about Cockweed would be kissing him. I mean, when I think about having to even pretend to flirt with him, I just get this image of him, like"—I looked down modestly—"coming toward me with his tongue out."

Pilar grabbed my wrist. "Me too," she said. "That is so weird, I was just thinking that exact thing. I swear!"

"Really?" I said. "The other thing that would freak me out a lot . . ."

I had nothing in mind. I was just waiting until she thought of something. I pretended to think as I watched her mind working. Now she was imagining Cockweed on the phone, telling his friends about her, how hot she was, how much she wanted him.

"I just imagine him telling his friends I was hot for him. Like calling up his old buddies from here and being like, oh, I just bagged this chick."

Pilar looked as if she'd seen a ghost. "That is exactly what I was just thinking of." She seemed to soften. "So you do understand—like, really understand—how hard it would be to even go near Cockweed. I mean, you really get it."

I put my hand over my heart. "Of course I get it," I said. "I mean, I would do it myself. But I don't have the same kind of feminine powers you have."

Pilar's beautiful eyes sprang open. I had hit a nerve.

"You really are so beautiful," I said. "And there is so much power in that. Unfortunately, with power sometimes comes responsibility."

I kept my tone of voice as grave as possible, and I saw that I was really having an effect on her. She was getting tears in her eyes.

"Molly," she said, "people don't get how hard it . . ." she faltered, embarrassed.

"People don't get how hard it is to be beautiful?" I said.

Once again Pilar lit up with the spark of someone really getting her. "Yes," she said. "You can't stop comparing yourself to other people. And it's not that you want to be better than they are. . . . Well, yes, you do, and maybe you even are, but that's not the reason. The reason ees that you're afraid every second that you don't prove to yourself that you're prettier than everyone, you're going to get everything you have and everyone you know taken away from you."

I nodded understandingly. "And meanwhile," I said, "people think, oh, she thinks she's so great, and you don't feel that way at all."

She was brimming with gratefulness. "I just don't know how you get this."

"Pilar," I said with as much earnestness as I could muster, "I am beautiful enough on the inside to understand people who are beautiful on the outside."

Pilar smiled, but she thought, *Molly is really gay.* "So," she said, "you don't know that he has pot, but you think eet?"

I nodded and shrugged. I still needed to know one thing. "What if he won't show you the pot? Like, you've flirted with him and told him you want to get high . . . but . . . he's resisting you?"

"I am not going to sleep with him," she said. "But I guess I could go through the motions of pretending I did. I could . . . I could kiss him." She made a horrible face. "Once I kiss him, just once even, I know he will tell me anything." She thought about her beauty. About Cockweed ravishing it. She took a deep breath and swallowed the fear as the bad taste of the Elias Ganz incident crept into the back of her throat. *My beauty is a sword, and it is also a wall. I will stand in it, and fight with it, and I will win.* "If he has pot, I will find eet." Pilar nodded confidently, and I believed her.

chapter
twenty-
four

Luckily, Mrs. Cockweed had study hall supervision on Tuesday and Thursday nights. The disciplinary hearing was Wednesday.

We only had one chance to get it right.

I instant-messaged Dr. Whitmeyer. I thought it would take a long time to figure out how to get myself into Cockweed's head, but he wrote back:

> *Wanting to know where he keeps his pot will probably be enough.*
>
> How do you know that?
>
> *Molly, I have read many people's minds looking for no other information beyond this. This girl will really kiss him?*
>
> She is prepared to go the distance. She is a seduction master.

This is the same girl? The girl who stole your boy-
friend? You are unlikely allies.

I didn't know what to say.

I just want to take down this Cockweed. And between the two of us, I think we can do it. Shit. What happens if I get into Cockweed's head. Forever?
Let's cross that bridge when we get there.

Pilar came to my room at 7:30. ETA at Cockweed's was
8:00 P.M, and she had two hours to get him where we needed
him. Which meant that she'd either get him to bust out the pot,
or if her charms weren't working, she'd have to go the distance
and start making out with him. That was unfortunate for her,
very unfortunate, but at least we'd get the desired result.

She really nailed her Cockweed outfit. She wore tight jeans
that were kind of high-waisted, a white tank top, and a pink
sweater, unbuttoned to show off just a little cleavage, a pair of pearl
earrings and high-heeled light blue espadrilles. Her hair was pulled
back in a ponytail, and she wasn't wearing a stitch of makeup.

"Wow," I said. "Seriously. You look like the girl Cockweed
couldn't get at Midvale back in 1985."

She smiled shyly, glad she had impressed me. "I theenk I
overheard Cockweed saying once that girls who wore makeup
were whores," she said.

"That definitely sounds like him," Edie said. She was sitting on my
bed, and she peeked around me. "You're gonna do great, Pilar."

"Thanks," Pilar said. She shook out her hands, and I saw
she had polished her nails a demure shell pink.

We both shook hands with Pilar and she left.

I started to straighten some books on the shelf, but Edie put her hand over mine. "Stop," she said. "There's nothing else to do."

For the last twenty-four hours I had been incessantly cleaning and straightening the room in a desperate attempt to feel some control. But at this point, it was all in Pilar's hands, and there was nothing left to do except sit and wait to see how she did.

I sat with my back against the door.

Edie lay down on her bed. Then she sat up and looked at me. "You know you could go sit under the fire escape behind Proctor. That way at least if something happens you can run in there and—"

"What?" I said. "Both of us can get sexually assaulted by Cockweed?"

"I don't think he's the sexual assault type," Edie said. "I think our biggest fear is that, as stupid as he is, he's actually not going to be stupid enough to believe Pilar wants him."

I decided to stay. If things got fucked up—not that they weren't already fucked up—I was going to need Edie's advice.

Pilar smoothed her hair. She made herself a solemn promise that if this worked, she was going to stop just relying on her looks to get what she wanted.

She wasn't going to ignore them, of course, or let them go to waste, but the full-scale exploitation thing, that was over.

She knocked on Cockweed's door. When she saw his shadow move across the peephole she inhaled, thrusting out her cleavage a little, and let her lips part slightly into an inviting, appealingly nervous smile.

He opened the door. He had a sixteen-ounce Coors Light in his hand. He just looked at Pilar and didn't say anything. She felt her knees start to knock together and her breath waver.

"Hi," she said. "How are you?"

He still said nothing.

"I probably shouldn't be here . . ."

Damn, this ees hard. If I could just get a sense that he ees at all happy to see me, I would know where to take thees.

She was going to have to take it up a level.

"I probably shouldn't be here, but I just found that I couldn't . . . stay away."

The wolfish glint she was waiting for came up in his eyes. He didn't open the door any wider, but his stance relaxed a little and behind him, on the coffee table in the living room, Pilar saw a stack of Coors Lights. "Stay away . . . from what?"

The back of her neck started to sweat as she considered what she should say next. *Thank God he ees drunk. Men always have to have sex, which he is not going to have but he is going to theenk he have, when they are drunk.*

"She's almost in," I told Edie. "She's trying to decide whether to keep it cool or come right out and say it."

"Come right out and say what?" Edie asked.

"That she wants his johnson. Duh."

Pilar looked at Cockweed's face. He still looked suspicious. It wasn't the right expression for a come-on. She didn't know what the right expression was. But that wasn't it.

"It's just that . . . I really want to talk about what happened. How you caught us. I want to know something. And I don't know why, but I feel like you're the only one who can tell me."

I watched Cockweed through her eyes, very carefully.

I hoped she saw what I saw. His face softened, but his eyes

stayed hard. He thought she was the fool. He thought she was the one who didn't understand the rules of this game, and that he was in control. He was just trying to look sympathetic.

Pilar thought, *So far so good.*

"I hope you're not here to try to change my mind about what happened," he said. "Because what's done is done. I don't ask you kids to break the rules, but I can't help but enforce them when you do."

Pilar put her hand over her heart, consciously letting her wrist press against her breast a little so Cockweed could get a sense of how soft it was. "Oh no," she said. "If there's one thing about me people know, it's that when I have been bad, I can take being punished."

Cockweed made an involuntary squeaking noise in the back of his throat, like he wanted to speak but couldn't.

He opened the door, and Pilar stepped inside. And walked past his arm, extended in invitation. As she got a few feet past him, she looked over her shoulder, ostensibly to smile at him, but he had to look up quickly to meet her eyes—he was, as she had suspected he might be, fixated on her ass. His eyes moved up quickly, his face doglike with unconcealed shame. Cockweed wasn't smooth. He tried to look stern, and Pilar gave him a frightened, appeasing smile to make him think he'd gotten away with it, but she was thinking, Oh, I think I have him where I need him.

"Poor Pilar," Edie said.

"What do you mean?" I said. "She's kicking fucking ass."

"Yes," Edie said. "But what if she actually gets to the point where she has to kiss him? Can you imagine?"

But I had to put that out of my mind or I would feel guilty. I told myself that if I were in her place, I would make out with

Cockweed, and decided to remember this moment as the very last time I wished I were stunning and traffic-stopping instead of just kinda cute.

Cockweed's apartment was cavernous and old, and like the boys' room, which was on the same floor, sloped down at the edges. Furniture was functional, a futon sofa, a couple of old chairs covered with canvas slipcovers, a big, old television. The walls were covered with Midvale memorabilia.

"The baby's asleep," Cockweed said as he indicated that Pilar should sit on the sofa, and he sat in a recliner at the end of it. "And the kids are at their friends' until ten—watching that *American Idol* nonsense. You don't watch that, do you?"

Pilar loved *American Idol,* but she said that she didn't watch it. "It's a leettle childish for me," she said. "I . . . know I'm only sixteen, but I feel that I have . . . well, we have an expression in Argentina. I have *el alma de mujer* . . . the soul of woman."

She looked right at Cockweed with her giant brown eyes. He adjusted himself in his chair. Then a sour expression came over his face, and he said, "Look, Pilar, I don't have all night."

Pilar tilted her head girlishly. "Of course you don't. Well. I guess I felt kind of weird about the other night. And I just . . . wanted to talk to you about sex."

Cockweed made a fussy adjustment of the slipcover and then tugged at his pants again. He was definitely tugging at his pants a lot—nothing wrong with that. He coughed formally. "OK," he said.

"I . . . oh, this ees so embarrassing," she said.

She had him now. Naturally, I wasn't in his mind, but it was clear that he was extremely eager to know what this absolutely gorgeous girl about a third of his age who wanted to talk about sex was so terribly embarrassed about.

"I want you to know that I am a virgin," Pilar said. Her heart stopped beating when she said this. Could she hear his pounding? His cheeks looked as if they'd been injected with red pen ink.

"And why did you want me to know that?" he asked.

"Oh," Pilar said. "I just didn't want you to think anything bad about me. Because I always thought you were one of the cool teachers here. I mean, like, you could be a hard-ass, yes?"

"Yes," Cockweed said, looking off into the middle distance with wistful self-importance. "That I can."

"But, like, you are not full of yourself. You totally know who you are."

Now he looked at her. "Really? Is that what people think of me?"

Now Pilar did something really brilliant. She pretended not to hear him, and stood up. *He wants something from me, and eef I try to go now, it will be almost like it was his idea for me to come over.* "Thanks for listening," she said. "I just didn't want you to think just because I had a guy in my room that I was, like, you know, totally loose like all of the other girls here. So. Anyway, it was nice knowing you."

She started to walk out. A brilliant move. Cockweed stopped her with his voice. "I think it's very admirable you're a virgin," he said.

His voice wavered a little. Now he was the one taking the risk. Pilar stopped and turned, dramatic, like a heroine in a telenovela. "Thank you," she said. "Gracias."

"I have to admit I am curious about how exactly . . . you've managed to preserve . . . ?

"My maidenhood?" Pilar said.

His eyes glittered. "It's just that I rarely get to know the kids one on one," Cockweed said.

Pilar paused. "Well," she said. "I guess we are having . . . one of those conversations that doesn't really make any sense, you know."

"Yes," Cockweed said. "I don't know if you know this word, because English isn't your first language. But we Americans might call this an interlude."

She returned and sat down. She took a deep breath. This was her moment, the crucial moment, and she knew it. She felt sick and she also wanted to laugh. *Who ees the dumb ass who doesn't know what an interlude ees?*

She sat down, crossing her legs demurely. "Well," she began. "I guess I just find that young boys are just after one thing. You know? They just want to have sex, and you get the feeling that they just want to do eet so they can, like, say they did it, you know? I guess I have always been looking for more of a sensual experience."

"Hmm," Cockweed said, trying to keep his voice light and curious. "Tell me more about that."

"Well, you know, they're just dying to get your pants off. They don't like to relax and share . . . casual *relaxing* times together, *unwinding*."

It was a good hint, but Cockweed shook his head in an elaborate display of sympathetic disgust.

"Those boys," he said.

She looked at the floor. "You probably think I am being really silly," she said. "I get thees way sometimes when I am feeling uptight and need to just let my hair down."

"No, Pilar." Cockweed shook his head. "I think you're just being very real."

Pilar counted to ten, letting the silence, and the tension, build.

"It's just lonely sometimes," she said. "Feeling like a woman, but having to live in the rules of girls. I like adult things. I like to have a good time just like everyone else . . . but most of the things people do to have a good time here . . . it's not worth doing eet with those people, right?"

Cockweed said nothing. He's either onto me, Pilar thought, or he's eating out of my hand. Either way . . .

She went in for the kill.

"I mean, Gideon Rayburn is a nice boy, and he's cute, I suppose, for a kid, but he's a boy, you know, and . . ."

Cockweed started to look angry, which basically meant that his head was going from a tender pink color to a vibrant red. Pilar's eyes darted nervously around, looking for an escape if he blew up.

"Oh fuck," I said to Edie. "He's onto her."

Edie put her hand over her mouth and we sat, not moving, as Cockweed stood from his chair. "Goddamn it," he shouted. "I can't believe this shit."

Pilar looked at him imploringly and was about to open her mouth and say something, anything, when he spoke again.

"It makes me sick, sick to my stomach, that those boys get their hands on a girl like you."

Pilar bowed her head so he wouldn't see her smile. She said nothing.

"Oh my God," I said to Edie. "I think she did it."

Cockweed almost shook with indignation. He slowly lowered himself back to sit. He looked at Pilar. "I'm sorry," he said. "That was inappropriate." But his eyes got kind of puppy-doggish, like he expected her to say something.

"Oh no, Gene, but seriously, don't you think maybe we should . . . take theengs down a notch here? Mellow out?" *Jesus. I can't make thees any more fucking obvious. If he doesn't fall for this shit, I guess I am just going to have to start getting him turned on and then say I like to do it on pot. And then I am going to have to run or something.*

"Mmm," Cockweed said. "Why don't you show me what you mean by taking things down a notch?"

My beauty is a sword, and it is also a wall. I will stand in it, and fight with it, and I will win.

And then Pilar Benitez-Jones fell to her knees, placed her hands on Cockweed's thighs, and gazed upon Cockweed's meaty face with quite as much reverence as if she were Guinevere gazing for the first time at her Lancelot.

She forced herself to slide her hands up his thighs as she felt her stomach turn over.

Cockweed pulled away. "How do I know this is for real, Pilar? How do I know this isn't some kind of trick?"

Pilar swallowed. She knew she didn't have much time to think. The really obvious, cheesy stuff had totally worked with him, so she might as well just try more. "It would be your word against mine," she said, "and I'm not wearing a wire. See?" With this, she whipped her shirt open. She was wearing a bra.

Cockweed leaned toward her.

"Would you like to see how a real man kisses?" he said.

"Oh yes," Pilar breathed. She closed her eyes tight, and her whole body stiffened.

"She's kissing him," I told Edie. It was easy to guess what Cockweed was thinking right now, because he was staring at Pilar's breasts: *Pilar has awesome breasts. I can't wait to see them, Pilar has awesome breasts, I can't wait to see them.*

Her mouth was inches away from his when there was a sound of a key in the lock.

Pilar didn't even think. She ran for the bedroom closet, diving behind a pile of coats. From behind them she watched as Cockweed hurried to straighten up the couch. When his wife came in, he was just plumping up a pillow.

She lit into him right away. "What the fuck are you doing, Gene?"

Wow, Pilar thought, *Cockweed's life sucks.*

Mrs. Cockweed was wearing a raincoat and a sort of silly, floppy rain hat. She disappeared down a hall, and Cockweed, scratching his head in panic, followed her.

"All you do is sleep," Mrs. Cockweed railed from the other room.

"That's bullshit," Cockweed said. "I was just straightening up the couch because you're such a terrible housekeeper."

OK. Maybe I don't feel so bad for him. I mean, not that I really did. Just for a second.

As the Cockweeds continued to bark and snipe at each other in the living room, Pilar inched out of the closet.

I failed. I didn't get the pot. Molly and Edie are going to theenk I'm a loser. Who cares? They're not that great. But I really wanted to find the pot. Look at Cockweed's stupid shoe tree in his closet. His wife's shoes are all so ugly. You can't blame a guy for being mad when he's married to a woman with such ugly shoes. Oh my God, his slippers are so gay. I guess I'm just going to wait een here? Maybe all night? No. When she goes to the bathroom. Except the bathroom's een here, and if they're married, she probably pees with the door open. I can't stay here all night. His slippers are corduroy. They have, like, thees gross bow on them. Ew. Imagine having bows on your slip-

pers. Wait. She stepped forward and poked the bow with her finger. It made a crinkling sound. It was a bag of pot.

Cockweed appeared in the doorway. He hissed, "Get out of here! My wife's making microwave popcorn. You have two minutes."

Pilar stepped out and started to walk around him to the front door.

"No way," Cockweed hissed. "The window."

The bedroom window was open, and there was a tree outside, the tree that was the twin, symmetry wise, to the tree that grew outside Proctor 307.

OK. I gotta get out of here.

"Come on, Edie," I said. "We gotta go."

Edie ran out with me and didn't argue.

It was a good thing that even under all those layers of *alfajor* chubbiness her core muscles were still so strong, because Pilar needed them to get out of that window and onto that tree. It was easy enough to climb down, until she got to the bottom.

The lowest branch was fifteen or so feet from the ground. Pilar leaned on a branch at waist level. Her arms started to shake. *If I jump out of a tree, I'm probably going to break an ankle. Or a wrist. Or a knee.*

"Pilar!"

Pilar looked down. Edie and I were standing there, smiling up at her, each of us holding two cushions that we'd grabbed off the sofas and chairs in Emerson.

"How deed you know I was—"

"There's no time for that," Edie said. "Jump."

Pilar crossed herself and then jumped.

It wasn't a jump worthy of crossing yourself. We each got

one of Pilar's arms, and we all fell backward. The cushions went flopping off to the side of our ugly human heap, totally useless. It didn't feel good, but none of us were going to die. We all lay there for a minute, and then we heard the sound of a window closing above. We looked up. It was Cockweed. He blinked into the darkness. "Stand up," I whispered. "Wave to him."

Pilar stood up. She waved. Cockweed waved back. The window closed, and Pilar turned away from us and vomited into the grass.

chapter
twenty-five

Before the hearing the next morning, Pilar came into the bathroom while I was brushing my teeth and looked at me in the mirror. "Hi," she said.

"Hi," I said.

She couldn't not check me out—couldn't not look at my hair, my mouth, even my ears, and to wonder if maybe Gid still loved me, if he still thought about me.

She decided that he probably didn't.

"What are the chances that you're going to be able to take care of thees?" she said.

"Hundred percent," I said. "You don't even have to go to the hearing. It's not even going to happen."

Maybe, Pilar thought, *Gid liked Molly not just because of her body and stuff, but because she was cool.* This was an amazing thought for her.

"OK," Pilar said. "I am going to stop packing. I will just relax. Maybe I will just watch *The Hills* on my computer."

We just stood there. "I know you mostly did thees to get Geedeon back in school," she said. "But I really like him. I know he . . . has feelings for you. But I think he has feelings for me too and . . ."

I set my toothbrush down. Pilar was afraid of me now, just as I had been afraid of her. "I promise I won't fuck with you and Gid," I said. I meant it. Pilar had been pretty cool to go through with what I wanted her to do with Cockweed, and I just wasn't going to mess with her anymore. I had to get out of her head eventually. And Gid would pick who he wanted. There was nothing I could do about it.

She didn't believe me. *Molly will do anything to get Gid back. She still loves him, and he ees everything to her.*

"I know you don't believe me," I said, "because, yes, I do still have feelings for him. But I will be OK. I . . . what I really want more than anything right now is for us to win that match. That's really what I want right now."

Her face lit up. It was amazing how, when you knew some-one's fear and were honest about it and addressed it, they felt better. "I believe you," she said. Then she frowned. "I don't know how I am going to not be freaking out until thees is over," she said.

"Go study," I said. "Go study and just assume you're going to that match with us."

There was a rule at Midvale that, if you were going up against the judicial board, you were entitled to have any mem-ber of the community present at your hearing. So when Edie and I stepped out of Emerson that morning, dressed neatly in the same prim, preppy outfits we wore for Academic Tête-à-

Tête, we were quickly joined by Nicholas, Cullen, Devon, and Liam coming down the path from Proctor, all looking grim in sport coats.

"This is so gnar-gnar," Devon said, touching what looked like a painful stripe of razor burn on his cheek. "It's total Angnartica."

Nicholas shook his head. "That's a really bad one."

"Gideon's already there," Cullen said to me. "He just went to the room where they're having the hearing to just sit there, I guess. I guess he feels like he's getting it over with that way."

"I can't believe it's called a hearing," Nicholas said. "Like anyone is going to hear anything. But I think we prepared a very good statement about why he should stay."

"Dude," said Cullen, turning to me. "We describe being friends with Gid and how when he first came here he was a chickenshit loser with, like, Dave Matthews records. And how he's so much not that much of a fag anymore, and how Midvale made him kind of cool. I mean, we made him cool, but we say Midvale."

Nicholas shook his head at me to let me know that the statement was only like that in Cullen's mind.

Cockweed stood on the steps of the Administration Building, his chest puffed up with pride. A smile at the corner of his lips let me know that his magical evening with Pilar Benitez-Jones was dancing around somewhere in that monkey brain of his. The sun shone off the top of his head, and he was flanked on one side by the headmaster and on the other by Mrs. Gwynne-Vaughan. Cockweed's mouth was flapping, and the headmaster was nodding intently, but Mrs. Gwynne-Vaughan wasn't listening. Her eyes found mine across the quad, and she gave me a look of resigned sadness and defeat. I knew she probably didn't care that much about this except that she knew Pilar was probably our key to winning. I gave Mrs. Gwynne-Vaughan a big confident smile and kept smiling that way until I had walked right up to all of them. Then I stuck my hand out.

"Good morning, Dr. Frye," I said.

The headmaster, a bald man in his fifties with watery eyes, shook my hand.

I nodded at Mrs. Gwynne-Vaughan, and she nodded back and stepped away. I think she knew I needed my space.

"Mr. Cavanaugh," I said finally, shaking his hand and holding it a little longer, looking him right in the eye. "I would be so delighted if we could have a word."

Cockweed made a face: who is this lowly student who thinks she is going to talk to me?

"I really think not," he said. "I am very busy right now, and Dr. Frye and I—"

"I really think you're going to hear what I want to say. And actually, if you'd prefer"—I smiled sweetly at Dr. Frye—"I am more than happy to open this conversation up to Dr. Frye, because I am quite confident he too would—"

"All right, all right," Cockweed said, interrupting me this time. He looked intently into my eyes, trying to convey intimidation, but underneath it was fear, plain as day. "Let's step over here."

The moment we were out of earshot, I said, "I know about your pot."

He tried to roll his eyes, but they only made it about half-way around.

"You can forget about denying it too," I said. "I know where it is. It's in your closet. In your slippers."

He opened his mouth.

"I'm not done," I said. "I know you stole pot from the boys, too. So, while that might get them in trouble, it's also really not going to look very good for you. At all."

Cockweed swallowed once, hard.

"What do you want?" he asked.

"What do you think I want?"

Cockweed shook his head. "Absolutely not," he said. "You know I can't do that."

"Do I?" I said. "I don't think I do know that."

I noticed that everyone was looking at us, whispering in their little groups. Cullen, Nicholas, Devon, and Liam were animated, all gathered around Edie and asking her questions, but she just kept shrugging, as if she knew nothing. The headmaster had his arms crossed over his chest. Then I looked up and saw Gideon standing in the window of the Administration Building. He looked scared. I looked up at him and smiled bravely, and a look of total bafflement came over his face.

Cockweed turned around and looked at everyone. The headmaster tapped his watch.

"What do I say?" Cockweed said, all attitude gone from his voice, completely helpless.

"You say, 'I was mistaken.'"

"I can't say that," he whined.

"Try it," I said.

"I was mistaken," he said.

I nodded approvingly. I think Cockweed was so fucked up at this point that my approval actually made him feel good. "Now follow me."

We walked right up to the headmaster. Cockweed lagged a few paces behind me. "Chop-chop," I said. "OK. Now tell him what you just told me."

Cockweed cleared his throat and said, "I was kind of thinking we should cancel the disciplinary hearing."

Cockweed suddenly flushed, and I saw that Liam, Devon, Nicholas, and Cullen were coming toward us.

"Why is that?" Dr. Frye said.

"Well, the thing is, I'm not exactly sure that I saw Gideon in that room."

The headmaster frowned and set an oxblood briefcase on the railing of the Admin Building. He took a document out of it and read it out loud. "Found Gideon Rayburn crouched naked in a closet in Pilar Benitez-Jones's room."

Cockweed nodded. "Right," he said. "There are some inaccuracies in that statement."

Dr. Frye's watery eyes blinked. "In which part?"

"Uh," Cockweed said. "Uh."

Dr. Frye sighed and put the document back into his briefcase, closed it, and locked it. Glowering, he regarded the campus and the lines of students streaming out of their dorms toward the dining hall and classrooms. Then he almost smiled, and I knew what was going to happen—nothing. If Cockweed had done something stupid enough to be forced into retracting a disciplinary action, Dr. Frye figured it had to be unseemly. He would, very smartly, stick his head in the sand.

"Very well, Gene," Dr. Frye said. "I do need a statement to put in the file."

Cockweed didn't know where to look. He finally tilted his head toward the sky, as if God might help him. "I was mistaken," Cockweed said.

chapter
twenty-
six

Edie, Pilar, Dan, and I drove to Xavier in Mrs. Gwynne-Vaughan's
powder blue '70s Mercedes. Devon, Nicholas, Mickey, and Sergei were in the white BMW. They passed us on the highway
at one point. Nicholas was driving, and the rest of them were
passing a joint. Mrs. Gwynne-Vaughan saw them, but they
didn't see her. She looked at me in the rearview mirror, as if for
guidance.

"It doesn't affect their performance," I said.

"I don't even know what you're talking about," Mrs.
Gwynne-Vaughan said, and smiled.

Pilar sat up front. She was rigid with concentration. Her
head was full of dates and battles and abbreviations from the
periodic chart. I looked for Gideon in there—I thought she
might be hiding him behind some facts. But I didn't see him.
He had texted her after the meeting was over, and she had
written back, "Getting ready for match. Let's celebrate later."

What would this celebration consist of? Well, I would find out soon enough. For now, I had a match and a scholarship to win.

As we pulled off at the exit to Xavier, Pilar turned around and gave me a tiny smile and mouthed, "Thanks."

I smiled back but thought, the more she likes me now, the more she's going to hate me if this is a totally humiliating experience. Basically, Xavier made Midvale look like a toxic waste dump. Midvale would have been considered well ordered for a campus, but Xavier Academy would have been considered well ordered for a French king's garden. Buildings, paths, and rows of flowers were laid out in perfect symmetry. The brick of the buildings, all of which were old—no ragtag 1970s add-ons like we had at Midvale—was robustly red. The white trim at Midvale, which was cleaned and repainted yearly, seemed here to be removed hourly. The lawns were gleaming and velvety, and the sprinklers chugged efficiently under lush blooming trees. Discreet signs cautioned pedestrians against trampling the grass. The passing members of the all-male student body—in neat crew cuts, pressed khakis, and blue jackets with red and gold insignias and ties—were almost as indistinguishable from one another as were the red tulips lining the walkways. It wasn't a military academy, it was only a Catholic school, but they naturally walked almost in formation, not looking down, not looking around, but looking straight ahead, as if the bright futures they sought lay precisely six feet in front of them. Books clutched tightly in their hands, they walked quickly, each with slight torque in his hips that indicated the sort of sexual frustration so deep that its sufferers had no idea there was anything wrong with them.

Pilar was wearing a paisley dress made of silk jersey—it wasn't overly slutty but managed to cling in all the right places and provide a tiny, tasteful shadow of cleavage. The skirt swirled flirtatiously around her calves and over a pair of red T-strap sandals. The effect offered a nice combination of glamour, sexiness, and girlish approachability. It was a nice day, but when she stepped out of Mrs. Gwynne-Vaughan's car, it was as if the sun had risen again. Every boy on the lawn turned toward her. It was almost eerie.

The BMW pulled up and the boys got out, trailing a lightly herbal cloud. They tore across the lawn, laughing and hooting, totally oblivious to the staid atmosphere. Nicholas fell into step with me on the serpentine path to the Assembly Hall, which had a rectangular marble plaque on its side stating it had been built in 1876. We watched Pilar walk.

"She looks good," he said. "If you go for that sort of thing. I wonder why she doesn't turn me on," Nicholas said, and I was about to feel all warm and fuzzy toward him when he added, "Maybe it's because she's fucking Gid. Or, I guess, as the case may be, *not* fucking Gid."

"Nicholas," I said, "I know you don't feel sensitive, but could you at least act sensitive?"

"Hmm," he said, as if this were an idea he was hearing for the very first time. "It never occurred to me that I could pretend to be different. That I could not say my feelings. . . . Shhh. Look!"

We entered a narrow hall with a stained-glass window at one end and long, multipaned windows on either side. At the far end of the room, two long oak wood tables were set up, facing each other. The Xavier team was already assembled and sat together facing the entrance, the power position. But then Pilar entered, and just as she had had the effect of making the Xavier quad seem brighter and sunnier, she made this room seem vaster and even more elegantly austere. She led Midvale's pack down the middle aisle, like a gorgeously carved masthead plowing through surf at the front of a ship. Her eyes were luminous but sharp, thick with dark makeup. A pleasant cross breeze moved through her banner of luxuriant ebony hair.

Every single member of the Academic Tête-à-Tête team was staring at her, their eyes buggy, their cheeks flushed. Only one of them seemed to be occupied, delicately cleaning the nails of his left hand with the nails of his right.

In a tense, ominous silence, we took our seats in a row: me first, then Edie, then Nicholas, then Sergei, then Mickey, and finally Pilar, who was, as is fairly typical, oblivious but not oblivious. She had that little buzz that she got when faced with undeniable evidence of her attractiveness. She wondered, *Have people at Midvale maybe forgotten how I am pretty because they see me all the time? It would be so great to go to a new school and just have everyone talk about how hot I was for, like, weeks.*

Dan sat behind us, scowling darkly at the floor and tapping his feet. Devon, sitting next to him, growled, "Quit it," and he did.

Across from us, Xavier Academy's ATAT team was tugging at their cuffs and collars, even at their trouser fronts.

"OK," Nicholas said. "They are fucking freaking out."

Mr. Raines, the adviser, wore the same sober outfit he'd worn in the video. Frowning, looking at his feet, he went up to a lectern between the two teams and flipped through some papers. Several times he pretended to look at the clock or to inspect the far end of the room as if someone might be coming and he couldn't quite make out who it was, but the extreme paleness of his forehead and a deep, dark line of worry down its center let me know that he too was distracted by Pilar, the slope of her feet in high-heeled shoes, the length of her leg, and the shadowed cavern between her breasts. "Take your places," he said, and his voice caught a little. I went up and sat. My opponent wiped a little sweat off his lip and sat down. He too pretended to be idly looking around the room, but his eyes kept taking him back to Pilar.

I went up against the kid McCaskill I remembered from the video.

The question. "What is the surname of the family of the former Shah of Iran?"

"Pahlavi," I said.

Oh my God, Pilar thought as Raines frowned and tugged at his collar. *Molly is so incredibly smart. I know Iraq is that place with Saddam Hussein and Iran is that other place, but that is like, it.*

Raines glared at McCaskill, who reddened, looked at the floor, and, as soon as Raines turned away, looked right back at Pilar.

The next question, concerning the family name of the queen of England—duh, Windsor—I got as well. If you got the first two, you didn't need to be asked the third.

Edie was next. Her opponent got the first question—How many football teams have bird names? Five. Edie got the second. And then Pilar yawned. It was an epic, sensual yawn for which she bound her hands together and twisted them behind herself as she let her neck fall back, and her breasts sort of floated in the air.

The kid started to sweat. He wiped sheets of water from his forehead, unable to take his eyes off her breasts. The next question was a calculus question, finding the area of a cylinder with a slice out of it. The kid put his pen on the paper, but that was as far as he got with it, and then Edie shouted out the answer and the round was over.

Raines snapped his fingers. "Team meeting."

The guys on the Xavier team reluctantly followed their adviser into a corner of the room, casting wistful glances at Pilar as they went. Raines spoke in low, growling tones, and they looked at their feet as they shuffled back to their chairs.

Nicholas was next against that boy named Tate. Tate walked up with his hands over his eyes, like horse blinders, and a powerful erection pressed into the front of his pants. A math question: "What is the circumference of a circle circumscribed in a square with a diameter of x?"

"Pi X," the kid said.

"Fuck," said Nicholas. "Pi X. That is so fucking easy I couldn't even do it."

"Nicholas," scolded Mrs. Gwynne-Vaughan.

The next question—Who was the vice-presidential nominee to run alongside Adlai Stevenson in 1956?—Nicholas got. "Estes Kefauver," he said triumphantly.

I squirmed excitedly in my chair. I really wanted to win.

The next question came. "President McKinley was shot in what city?"

"Pittsburgh, Pennsylvania," Nicholas said.

"Sorry," said Raines. Not sounding sorry at all.

"Buffalo," said Tate, shifting in his chair.

That should have been mine.

We were at 2-1 now. Then Sergei won his round, and Mickey

lost, to the kid who had been cleaning his nails. As he sat down, I saw something in him that made him seem older than the other students, something mature and disinterested. He looked right at Pilar, and he even smiled at her. Then he smiled at me, like he saw me studying him. What was his deal?

It was up to Pilar to see if we would leave the half at a tie or win—a great advantage psychologically going into the next half. She was up against the kid they called Jones, that short, towheaded kid who was the first one we'd seen on Mrs. Gwynne-Vaughan's spying video. He was young and small, with pink skin just starting to sprout yellow fuzz. He got the first question—What do you get when you combine the element Sn with the element Cu? Bronze. She got the second—To whom was Mia Farrow married when she made *Rosemary's Baby?* Frank Sinatra. The third was math, and the first step of the problem—just the first step—was trying to figure out the radius of a circle. Pilar was still trying to figure out if this was all the way across or halfway when Jones shouted out, "Four."

It's OK, she soothed herself. *It's just God's way of telling you that you're steell pretty far from knowing everything.*

Or anything.

We gathered on the Xavier lawn under the statue of a famous scientist who was an alumnus of the school. "We're doing very well," Mrs. Gwynne-Vaughan said. "Better than expected."

"I messed up," Pilar said.

"No, no," Mrs. Gwynne-Vaughan said gently.

"We lost too," Mickey said, "me and Nicholas."

"That's right," said Mrs. Gwynne-Vaughan brightly, "so . . ."

Dan crouched in the shadow of the statue, glaring. "Yeah," he said. "Except she's not supposed to be here."

At first Pilar felt ashamed. *I could just run away from here*, she thought. *I don't have to be here at all. What am I trying to prove?* But Mrs. Gwynne-Vaughan was right. She wasn't the only one who had messed up. "Dan, don't you think you're, like, hurting my feelings?" she said.

Dan picked the grass with his fingers, sulking.

"And I know why I am here," she said.

Dan looked scared. "How?"

"Everyone understands who they are and what people want from them," she said. "Not just smart people."

Dan didn't dare respond to this. "Do you want me to stay in?" Pilar asked Mrs. Gwynne-Vaughan.

"Absolutely," Mrs. Gwynne-Vaughan said, and Pilar blushed at being the object of such confidence, even if the reason she had to stay in was so that she would remain in full, distracting view. "We need you front and center."

When we filed back in, Pilar looked even sexier, even more in control. She sat down and tucked her legs demurely under her chair, but even the cross of her ankles carried an erotic charge. The Xavier team was still transfixed, but before, their interest had been sort of hopeful. Now they just looked angry.

I was still first. "Good luck," Pilar said as I went up against Jones. He scowled at me with a tiny mouth as we sat down. As Pilar shifted in her chair, her bangles tinkled—a siren song. Jones put his hands over his ears and shut his eyes.

"What was the name of Thomas Jefferson's mansion?" Raines said.

"Montebello," Jones said.

I raised my hand. "Monticello," I said.

But because sports just aren't my thing, he got the second

question—Who was the first black MVP in football? Franco Harris.

The third question was so easy. "What was the first southern state to secede from the Union?"

I was just about to blurt out the answer when Pilar thought, *If we win tonight, I am totally going to sleep with Geedeon. It will be a sign that I am supposed to be with him, and I will sleep with him, and I will totally try to stay with him too.*

The answer flew right out of my head.

"South Carolina," Jones said, jumping up from his seat. "Better luck next time."

It was the first ATAT round I had ever lost. But I didn't blame Pilar, per se. If I was going to be in her head, it my responsibility to control the noise level. But the problem was, I still wanted to know what she was thinking.

I wouldn't get out of her head until I stopped caring.

Then Edie lost her round. Nicholas, up against that Tate guy who had put his hands around his eyes, got the first question, lost the second, and then, on the third, the kid coughed, covered his mouth, and, having left his vision open again, saw Pilar and completely missed the last question. Sergei won, and Mickey lost again. We were at 6-5, with Xavier leading. Now Pilar was up against the blond kid, Yates. "Hi," he said as he sat down. "Are those shoes pleather? Stella McCartney, right? They're really quite lovely."

He was gay. He gave Pilar an eat-shit grin as the first question was asked. "What's the difference between ale and beer?"

"Ale uses yeast that gathers on the top, and lager uses yeast that ferments on the bottom," said Yates.

"OK, whatever!" Pilar said.

Raines scowled at her and moved on. "Who directed *On the Waterfront,* and what is the historical significance of this film?"

I thought we were fucked, and Yates was twirling a pencil, winding up to give an answer, but Pilar shouted out in a rush, "Elia Kazan, and the film was allegorical for his involvement in HUAC."

She pronounced this *Hoo-Ac,* and you could tell she had absolutely no idea she was talking about, but she *was* right.

One more question. Raines cleared his throat and gave a dirty look to Yates. He began.

"*The Titanic—*"

"White Star Line!" Pilar shouted. "I saw that movie, like, twelve times!'

"I didn't even finish the question," Raines said. But I knew from the way his face got all puffy and sort of ugly that we'd gotten the answer. We were tied.

We were tied.

We didn't have time to gather outside. We just went in a corner. We were all quivering. The final round would be just one question, asked to the entirety of each team, and whoever got it would win.

"No matter what happens, you've done a great job," Mrs. Gwynne-Vaughan told us. "Just try to stay relaxed."

We all sat down. The Xavier guys were kind of over Pilar by now. They just looked pissed. They would have totally destroyed us if we hadn't had her at first and they knew it, and they knew we knew it.

Mrs. Gwynne-Vaughan was the one who got to ask the final question. It was in a sealed envelope. She opened it and read the subject. "Math," she said.

Sergei put his pen down at the edge of his paper, ready to write. "If object A is ten feet long, eight feet wide, three feet deep and weighs four pounds per square foot, and object B two feet long, four feet wide, three feet deep and weighs five pounds per square foot, which one is heavier?"

Before I could even start this problem, Pilar's mind went off in mine like an explosion. This was just like the formula! The formula she used to see if a girl was as hot as she was! It was so easy. I looked over at her. Her eyes were closed. She didn't even have to use a pencil. This formula was like breathing for her. In ten seconds, she shouted out, "Object B!"

"Yes," Mrs. Gwynne-Vaughan said, beaming and shocked at the same time.

We won!

We were in a massive crush of hugging. Dan was hugging Sergei, Mrs. Gwynne-Vaughan was hugging Nicholas, Edie and Devon were dancing in a circle. Mickey sprinted around the outside of our mosh pile shouting, "In your face! In your face!"

And I was hugging Pilar Benitez-Jones. Her arms, fragrant and soft with verbena lotion, were wrapped tight around me, and mine were wrapped around her, and we were jumping up and down, both of us laughing and so full of exuberant relief. *I did it, I did it, I did it,* she thought, and pulled back, looking at me, transfixing me with that glorious smile.

In a rush, I remembered what she had promised to do when she won. "Excuse me," I said. Pulling away from her and our group, I made a mad dash outside.

I gulped fresh air and tried to take in the day, the blue sky, the magnificent cultivated greenness around me. I had what I wanted now, I had what I had come to Midvale for. I just didn't have Gideon. There was a chance I could wrest him away from her, but at this point, what kind of person would that have made me? A person I couldn't stand. Not that I was doing such a great job of standing being without him.

But it was probably better to be able to live with yourself than to just become anything, any kind of person, to get what you wanted.

I walked slowly to Mrs. Gwynne-Vaughan's powder blue car, thinking of the comforting, slightly sour animal smell of its leather seats. Speaking of animals, Edie and Devon were in back, making out. I opened the door and leaned in. "Uh, guys," I said, "Mrs. Gwynne-Vaughan's coming."

Edie blushed a little as Devon extracted his hand from under her shirt.

"We decided to go out until the end of the year," Devon said, as if he could read my mind. "I've never gone out with a girl before. I'm probably going to get bored and want to have sex with someone else. But I won't know until I try it."

Mrs. Gwynne-Vaughan came back and started to get into the front seat. "OK, Devon," Edie said, "you go with the guys."

Devon pouted. "I want to go with you."

But Edie made a face. "Come on, Devon. I'll see you back at school."

He gave her a deep, long kiss.

"OK, Devon, that's enough," Mrs. Gwynne-Vaughan said.

Devon slunk off to Nicholas's car, blushing and looking over his shoulder at Edie.

I shook my head at Edie, impressed. "Wow," I said, "you seem to have him wrapped around your finger."

Pilar got into the front seat. She had a half smile on her face and was thinking about Gid. *Finally, we will have sex. And now I will have sex not just as someone worried about my stomach.*

I wonder what sex ees like when you think you're smart? I wanted, truly, to reach up and grab her around the throat. But this was Edie's moment. Mrs. Gwynne-Vaughan smiled at Edie in the rearview mirror as we backed out.

"Yes, Edie, what's your secret? I'm not sure I ever learned how to manage men."

Edie was thoughtful. "You just have to make them think you're always busy," she said. "He asked me out. And I was going to say, 'Well, I'm afraid I want more than you can give'—girl stuff—but instead I said I was kind of into this guy back in Seattle, and we were supposed to hang out this summer. And he got all sad and was like, 'Well, can we go out until summer? And see what happens?'" She shrugged. "I feel a little bad but . . . not as bad as I would feel right now if I'd listened to the big speech about how he doesn't like to be tied down, and blah blah blah!"

Edie was absolutely right. If she'd said what was in her heart, he absolutely would have said that.

I regretted showing Gid so much love. Why was Edie so smart, and I so stupid?

At the very least, I was hoping I could have a nice nap, an hour or so of the empty rhythm of the road, before being forced to live through Pilar and Gideon finally having sex.

"Well, girls, congratulations," Mrs. Gwynne-Vaughan said. "And Molly, congratulations on your scholarship."

Scholarship? What ees a scholarship? I'm too embarrassed to admit I don't know.

Ha. Yeah. You should be. The inevitable was finally about to happen, and I wasn't going to stop it. No matter how bad that moment might be, there had to be something on the other side that was better than waiting for it to happen. Mercifully, I slept my way through a little of that wait.

chapter
twenty-
seven

"So," Edie said, "what are you going to wear?"

"A black veil," I said.

We were getting dressed to go over to Mrs. Gwynne-Vaughan's. The party was mostly for winning ATAT, but of course we were also celebrating Gid and Pilar's not getting kicked out of school, and the amazing humiliation of Cockweed.

Edie looked extremely cute in a gauzy yellow sundress. She even had some glittery makeup on her eyes. She planned on sleeping with Devon tonight, which meant that I was going to be sleeping in her old hangout, the closet. I put on a brave smile. "Wow," I said, "it's awesome that I'm going to get to go to college for free."

I'd already got some weird videotaped congratulations e-mailed to me by Ross Volker.

"It is," Edie said.

She could see that, behind my big smile, my eyes were sad.

"Are you sure you don't mind sleeping in the closet tonight?"

"Of course not," I said. "In life, we can expect our nights of wild passion, but we can also expect our nights on a closet floor."

Meanwhile, Pilar was packing her stunning cleavage into a demi cup black and violet lace bra. She hooked it and stepped into a pair of matching underwear. As she let her recent application of pear blossom body butter soak into her skin she fluffed her pillows, straightened her duvet cover, and set some candles around the room.

"I really am trying to look on the bright side," I said. "I'm going to have plenty of privacy to experience Gideon and Pilar's first night together."

When we arrived at Mrs. Gwynne-Vaughan's, she was sitting in a big green-and-white-striped chair, drinking an enormous cocktail. *Foyle's War* was cued up on the television. "Everyone's in the basement," she said. "No drinking."

"We don't drink," Edie and I chorused. We didn't have a problem with it: it just made us both sick because we had nerd stomachs.

Dan and Sergei emerged from the kitchen, carrying cans of Coke and bowls of nuts and potato chips.

"What are you guys doing up here?" I asked.

They sat down on the couch next to Mrs. Gwynne-Vaughan. "I love *Foyle's War*," Dan said. "I can't believe she has season seven. She got it from a friend in England. You're cool, Mrs. Gwynne-Vaughan."

"I don't like parties with girls," Sergei said. "They always talk about gross things."

"Like their periods?" I couldn't resist. Sergei stuffed a handful of nuts into his mouth and ignored me.

We headed downstairs.

Devon was sitting alone in a big chair watching *Battlestar Galactica,* and Edie walked over to him. "Hi," she said. Very methodically she took off her shoes.

Devon pulled her into his lap. "You're fat and scary," Edie said. "But you're hot."

Devon laughed. I didn't know if he was a creep or not, but I thought it was cute that her nerdy straightforwardness appealed to him.

In another room off to the side Cullen was unpacking the bar they'd brought. Liam was at a sink, washing glasses. "I can't believe how dusty her glasses are," Liam said. "She doesn't seem like the type who has dusty glasses."

"Duh," Cullen said, dumping a fist full of ice into a very old, thick glass blender container. "She lives alone. What is she going to do, spend all her time polishing glasses she never uses?"

"That's what my mother does," Nicholas said. "Uh, douche. When you're drinking and you don't want someone to know, you don't use a fucking blender. Or glasses. Or ice. I brought soda cans. Vodka only. It doesn't have a scent."

Cullen dutifully removed the ice, cube by cube.

"What does Nicholas's mother do?" Gideon said as he walked in. God, he looked hot. He was wearing a blue faded T-shirt with a pocket, and with a terrible pain in my chest I remembered what it had smelled like, and how the cotton ribbing of it had felt against my cheek. For a brief, delighted second I thought he was alone, and I smiled at him, actually using—without meaning to—the technique that made Pilar's smile so dazzling: she held her smiles for longer than most girls. But you can never smile at a guy long enough. Or maybe you shouldn't smile at him for too long. Who knew?

Gid smiled back at me, and for about five brief seconds I felt that weird feeling of being alone with him, even though we were in a room of people—just like I had felt the morning Cockweed dragged us into the dean's.

But then Pilar came in behind him. I knew she would, since, after watching her put on her matching underwear, I'd seen her put on her tight, knee-length jeans, black platform boots, a James Perse tank, and little white cashmere hoodie. I had seen her walk over here with Gideon, touching hands, their hips bumping, feeling, as I had felt so long ago myself, the velvety softness of Gideon's ear as she whispered into it that she was psyched for the party but even more psyched about, well, the other thing.

"Hi, Molly!" she said. "Happy?"

It seemed like a trick question, but it wasn't. "Very!" I said. "I am really glad that we won."

"Me too," she said.

"I can't believe you guys care that you won at that shit," Liam said. "It's so gay."

"Liam," I said, "what are you even doing here?"

"I don't know," he said. "What else am I supposed to do?"

"Who wants a drink?" Cullen whispered, proffering soda cans filled with God knows what.

"I do!" I said. Why not?

"I do too!" Madison stomped in, skinny, hypertall in some very serious red boots, smelling of cigarettes. She licked the side of Cullen's face.

I didn't care what it was. I chugged it. As I did so, I watched Pilar take demure sips of hers, images of the Elias Ganz night floating through her head. She thought to herself, correctly, Molly's probably never had an Elias Ganz–type night.

"Whoa, check you out," Cullen said to me. "I don't usually figure you for much of a drinker."

"I'm usually not," I said. "I just think that, considering how much we have to celebrate today, I can make an exception."

I chugged the rest of it and put my soda can up on the bar for more. I tried not to look at Gid. After one drink I was already starting to anesthetize myself against the experience of seeing him, and seeing him with Pilar. A drink and a half and I figured maybe it would be possible for me to look at them as just some random people, without much connection to me. I would be able to think, What an attractive couple! No feelings of rage, animosity, jealousy, suicidal ideation . . .

Then Gid put his hand on Pilar's neck and began to caress it. I could see the tips of his fingers under a curtain of her hair, near her ear. I couldn't take my eyes off them.

"Whoa," I said.

It was only when Pilar thought, *That's weird that Molly just said whoa,* that I realized I had said it out loud. I went into the other room, sat on the couch, and smiled helplessly at Edie. She and Devon were holding hands.

"Are you OK?" Edie said.

Then Cullen burst in to the room, carrying a full blender. "All right, everyone! Drink up! We're going to be playing spin the bottle! Can't play sober." He handed out anchor glasses to everyone and filled them up.

"Spin the bottle is stupid," Madison complained.

"You're stupid," Liam and Nicholas called from the other room.

"You're fags together," Madison said, slumping next to me on the couch, hugging a pillow against her concave stomach. Cullen sat next to her, and she snuggled up against him like a cat. "Hey Pilar," she called out. "Have you and Gideon slept together yet?"

Not yet, Pilar thought, *but soon.*

I stood up. "I have to go to the bathroom," I said.

I had to get out of here. I would come back. I would maintain dignity. But I just needed a moment to pull myself together.

Cullen said, "We'll wait for you. We're supposed to be a unit."

"You're a unit," said Liam, coming into the room as I left.

The basement was carpeted and heated, so I figured there had to be a bathroom somewhere. A door at the end of a short hallway looked promising, and I opened it, just ready to splash some water on my face and breathe for a few minutes. I pulled a string hanging from the wall, and a single lightbulb lit up not a bathroom but a storeroom, filled with boxes, all the same size and shape. One of them was open.

It was filled with blue pamphlets. Embossed across the top of them in gold was the title "Shared Consciousness."

I opened up all the other boxes. They were all filled with pamphlets. One of them contained a packing slip: 1000 copies of "Shared Consciousness" sent to Mrs. Audrey Gwynne-Vaughan in 1979.

I went upstairs and stood in the living room doorway. Mrs. Gwynne-Vaughan, Sergei, and Dan were all fixated on the television. "Is that the person who stabbed the policeman in the barn?" Dan asked. And at the same time, Mrs. Gwynne-Vaughan and Sergei went, "Shhhh."

"Dr. Whitmeyer, I presume?" I said.

I thought Mrs. Gwynne-Vaughan would be more surprised, but she just looked relieved. "Dan and Sergei," she said, picking up her purse, "run down to the Cumberland Farms and get some ice cream."

"But we don't want ice cream," Sergei said.

"Yeah," Dan said. "We're not twelve. We want to—"

She thrust some money at them. "Go," she said.

They went. Both shot me jealous looks through the window. She turned to me. "I left that door ajar. I knew you'd be led to it."

"You too?" I asked.

"Yes," she said. "When I was first here. It lasted about a year." She smiled. "It's how I met my husband. Of course, we didn't have girls quite like Pilar back then. But I was very jealous. It was very hard."

I knew we'd talk more about this, but now wasn't the time. I had to get to that spin the bottle game. "I want to get out," I said. "Why won't you just tell me how to get out? I'm inside Pilar's head right now, and she's thinking about how she's going to sleep with my boyfriend. I really would rather not be around for that."

She smiled enigmatically, and I felt a surge of rage build up in me. "Look," I said. "I don't have a lot of time. I think if I can kiss Pilar I can get out of her head and back into mine. I think I just have to think what she's thinking. But I just want to stay out for good. Oh God. Please don't ask me why."

The enigmatic smile again. "Why?"

They were getting loud downstairs, and I knew they'd start without me if I didn't get down there.

"Because I don't even really care anymore. I like Gid. I love him. But if he likes Pilar, well, fine. She's actually not even that bad. I don't want to be best friends with her, and I would much, much rather be me. . . ."

"What did you just say?"

"I said I don't want to be best friends—"

"No," Mrs. Gwynne-Vaughan said. "After that."

"I said I'd rather be me."

She smiled again, but this time it was warmer, even a little sad. "Remember I was inside someone's head that I was in love with once too. And you said you wanted to be you, but how about all that time you spend just trying to do whatever you thought would make Gideon like you best? Was that wanting to be you?"

I shook my head. "No. I just wanted to make myself into whatever Gid was going to like. And I realize now I guess he's going to like what he likes. He likes Pilar, maybe he likes me better, who knows? Just because you're inside someone's head doesn't even mean you know them."

She smiled. "Did you know we can have one thousand thoughts per minute?"

I nodded. "It's in your pamphlet. When I read it, I was like, 'That's a lot.' But I didn't really get it."

Sergei and Dan appeared at the door, but she held up a finger. "Do you get it now?" she asked.

"I think so," I said. "I don't need to know what Gid wants. I don't need to know what Pilar wants. I just want to know what I want."

She nodded sagely and beckoned for the boys to come in.

"What are you guys talking about?" Dan asked.

Before I could say anything, Mrs. Gwynne-Vaughan said, "Our periods."

I arrived just as everyone was arranging themselves in a circle on the floor.

"Gotta mix it up, gotta mix it up," Cullen said, rubbing his hands together, the drinks warming him up to his role as master of ceremonies. "OK. Madison, you here. Liam, you and Devon next to each other. Pilar, you're next to Gideon so you can paw each other while you're playing. OK, Edie, you at a good angle where Devon can reach your tiny boobs, and, Nicholas, you're making drinks and not playing because you're gay."

"Thank God," Nicholas said. "I know that this is supposed to be sort of ironic that you guys play this, but it is so embarrassing."

Cullen spun first. He got Edie.

"I don't know, Edie," he said. "I think the Old Monster might be a little big for you."

"Are there *any* rules about commentary?" Edie asked.

"No, there aren't," Cullen said, and slipped a hand around her waist. "Wow. You're just a little slip of a thing." He kissed her, then winked at Devon. "Congrats. You can always spot the spinners."

Edie was next. She got Madison. Madison sighed. They stalked to the center on their knees and gave each other a peck. "I don't understand how you suddenly entered our social circle," Madison said as she went back to her place in the circle. "It's so weird."

Edie gave me a look like, I always thought these people were freaks, but I had no idea how bad it was.

Madison spun. She got Devon. "I wish we were playing a game where we could just make the person we got go on a diet," she said.

"I wish we were playing a game where we could tell the chicks we were playing with that they were annoying cunts," Devon said. "Oh, I guess I am playing that game."

He grabbed Madison and gave her a wet willy.

"You are disgusting," she said.

"I'm not disgusting," Devon said. "I am just fat and greedy and, sadly for all who come in contact with me, unbelievably sexy."

Edie giggled. Devon actually got kind of sweet and blushy. He turned around and, from the top of a table, took a plastic flower and handed it to Edie. Then he took her tiny face in his fat hands and started to kiss her. They kissed and kissed. Then Devon whispered something in her ear and they got up and left.

"Wow," Madison said. "That was almost romantic."

"Who is supposed to spin now?" Cullen shouted. "Let's keep things moving!

"How about Pilar?" Cullen said. "She is kind of the guest of honor, after all."

Nicholas poked his head in from the other room. "Hey Pilar," he said. "Could you please explain to me how exactly you got that problem today? I mean, how did you get it that fast?"

Pilar shook her head and smiled. "I don't know. It just reminded me of—a problem I used to do a lot."

"It reminded you of a problem you used to do a lot?" Nicholas said. "What the hell does that mean?"

What if Pilar got me?

If we kissed, and I thought the right stuff, I could get out of her head. But it would have to be for a long time. And people didn't kiss for that long in this game. If she got me, I would have to force the kiss to last longer, and that would be weird. But seriously . . . whatever. So I would look weird. But I would be out of Pilar's head. I could deal with people thinking I was weird.

Pilar spun the bottle. I shut my eyes and willed it to come to me, and when I opened them, there it was.

We went to the center of the circle. Everyone was looking at us. Gid put his drink to his mouth and drank furiously. Cullen put his hand on his crotch and said, "*Oh* yeah." Madison put an unlit cigarette in her mouth. Pilar and I started kissing. I made it last longer. I felt her pulling away from me, but I kept kissing her. I wouldn't stop. I wouldn't let up. I knew her well enough that I could follow the trajectory of her thoughts, and I thought right along with her: *Is Molly wasted? What ees she doing? She must be so into Gid that she is, like, trying to turn him on by making out with me, or maybe she's* . . . Silence.

Silence so complete it felt almost as if I were floating through space. I kissed her just a tiny bit longer, to make sure that this was in fact really happening, that I was really out of her head.

I was.

"Sorry," I muttered, and pulling away from her, I ran up the stairs, ran through Mrs. Gwynne-Vaughan's living room, and went to my dorm and lay down on the floor of the closet— Edie had been nice enough to leave a camping pad, a blanket, and a pillow—and fell asleep.

I did like lying there in all that absolute darkness and silence.

My brain was mine.

My thoughts were mine. I was alone. Very alone. It doesn't get much more alone, I think, than being in a dark closet while your boyfriend is having sex, for the first time, with a very beautiful girl right down the hall.

I closed my eyes, but I didn't sleep. In a little while there was a knock at the door.

"Edie?" I said.

The door opened. It was Pilar Benitez-Jones, standing in a strip of moonlight, her hair loose, her eyes tired but luminous.

"Can I come in?" she said.

She crowded into the closet with me, and we sat facing each other, hugging our knees.

"I know you would never try to make out with me like that eef you weren't totally into Geedeon," she said.

"I had lots of reasons for making out with you," I said. "I don't want to get in the way of you and Gid anymore. I swear."

"I know that you just put me on ATAT because you thought I was pretty," Pilar said.

This must have been one of the thoughts I didn't hear.

I was embarrassed. Pilar said, "Don't be embarrassed. I knew from the beginning."

"OK," I said. "So why'd you do it?"

"Because I wanted Geedeon to think I was smart," Pilar said. "Smart like you."

That was hilarious. "I always wanted him to think I was pretty like you."

I snuggled down under my blanket. I smiled. "I feel like we're at camp, trading secrets in the dark. If we met under other circumstances, do you think we'd have been friends?"

Pilar considered this. "I don't know," she said. "That depends on whether you think it's funny that Devon is such a fat fuck and thinks he's hot."

We had to put pillows over our faces.

"I know Geedeon still loves you," Pilar said when we stopped laughing.

My immediate thought was that she was inside Gid's head now. "What do you mean?" I said. "What do you mean, you know?"

"I just know," she said. "Well, and when we were about to have sex, he called me Molly."

I felt bad for her as only someone who totally understands can. "Maybe it was your name and it just sounded like Molly."

Pilar smiled, grateful for my feeble attempts to make her feel better. "English may be my second language," she said, "but Molly and Pilar don't sound the same."

It was weird that I really did want to make her feel better. "Look," I said. "When I was with Gid, he thought about you. Now he's with you and he thinks about me. It's not rocket science."

That's why I knew I was out of her head for good. Because I really knew I no longer needed to see what made her tick or to feel what it felt like to have Gid look at her. She probably wanted to know what it felt like to have Gid look at me. He was just a person, with eyes—however he looked at us, we just imagined how he was looking.

Gid poked his head in. "Here you are," he said.

"Are you talking to me, or Pilar?" I said.

Gid seemed to think about this for a second, and then he said, "I'm looking for you, Molly."

Pilar Benitez-Jones sighed and stood up. "Good enight," she said.

Now Gideon sat on the floor with me. "Pilar told me to get back together with you. She said that she thinks we're really in love."

"What do you think?" I asked.

"I never didn't love you," Gid said. "You broke up with me."

"Because I knew you were into Pilar. You thought about her all the time. Don't try to tell me that you didn't."

"So what?" Gid said. "And I didn't think about her that much."

I didn't want to argue with Gid about how much he thought about Pilar. I was lucky that Pilar had enough of a sixth sense that she knew Gid was thinking about me, so Gid wasn't wondering how I knew that he had thought about her. Was the problem not really Gid? Was the problem that when you went out with someone, you just wanted their mind all to yourself? Maybe being inside someone's mind was just a worse version of the general problem of life—we spent so much time trying to figure out what everyone is thinking, and when we find out, we just wish we hadn't.

Now it seemed like Gid was reading *my* mind. "Molly, my thinking about you, my thinking about Pilar. That's going to happen with every guy you ever know, Molly," he said. "So the question is whether you want it to be me or not."

I actually smiled. "Is that the only question?"

Gideon shrugged. "Pretty much."

It wasn't fair that girls had to live like this. For the rest of my life, whether I was inside someone's head, whether I was with Gideon or not, it was just going to be this way, whether I liked it or not. Never knowing. Being scared. Wondering if someone really loved you or not, no matter what they said, and even what love meant, if it meant anything at all. I closed my eyes and let myself be sad about this for a minute. Then I opened them and decided, for this instant, to be happy. "Yes," I said.

"Yes, what?" Gid looked cute and hopeful.

Hopeful is not nothing.

"Let's go to the chapel. I think we have some unfinished business there."